The Gift

The Return of Wonder

By
B. E. Howard

ISBN: 149437594X
ISBN-13: 978-1494375942

DEDICATION

To those who believe
Hold tight to your dreams
And embrace your imagination
Near to your heart
Know in your mind
Youth in its way
One's importance
Unity
Make your dreams come true
Yearn for the good
Settle for nothing
Honesty Only
Everyone matters
Love my family
Love my wife

Chapter I - Out of Darkness

BEEP. "Twenty-four hours of air remaining, Dr. Hunter," declared a synthesized voice resembling a Scottish Noble.

After a full day's search over the Atlantic Ocean's floor near the coast of Cadiz, Spain, for a presumably sunken city, the frustrated sixty-year-old marine archeologist had nothing to show. "What am I missing here? Signs of straight grooves would indicate some sort of city-like structure. Large circles would indicate the unique ring-like design Plato described." Having found evidence of neither, Dr. Hunter challenged his studies.

"Had Atlantis ever existed? Who lived there? Who led its people? How could anyone let such a city sink? Could they have survived under water? Could the city still exist under water?" The panicked questions poured out of the doctor as he peered through the window of his one-man, car-sized submarine for any signs to validate his fixation.

1

"Are these rhetorical questions, sir?" asked Venator, the Scottish-sounding remote intelligence program the doctor uploaded into the ship's operating system.

"They might be." Theorizing that it made no sense for any human-like creature to live under the ocean, Dr. Hunter commanded, "Venator, relate the origin of the Atlantis story."

"Aye, sir," Venator replied. "The only historical record comes from an old blind man in tattered rags who washed up on the shores of Spain. The man rambled on and on about a stone city, a great gathering of god-like humans, several earthquakes, and a flood. His story remained at the core of myth until a resurgence of Atlantis seekers sprouted up in the late nineteenth century. Scientists and scholars around the world continue to obsess over this. Present company excluded, of course."

"Obsess might be a bit strong, but I will find the truth. It will be the greatest treasure man has ever found."

Now fighting encroaching fatigue and the cramped space, the lanky doctor turned to one of his few vices and unwrapped a 'Jolt-Pop.' He counted on the candied energy-providing sucker that kept him up for days during his research to do the same while he explored.

"How about some chess?" Dr. Hunter asked, instructing Venator to display a chess game on one of the monitors. The doctor's gaze jumped from the windows to his monitors and back in a seamless cycle. He made sure not to miss a single detail as his hands expertly moved across his keyboards and guidance controls while at the same time strategizing his chess match.

"The rest of the story, if you please," the doctor requested of Venator.

"The old blind man, who ventured to Atlantis to seek a cure for his ailing wife, claimed that the entire city met in a central coliseum, but he arrived late and could not enter. He banged on the shuttered archways to be let in to no avail. As he stood outside and listened to the cheers, the ground began to shake and he could hear screams from inside. That's apparently when the ground started to disappear from beneath his feet. He said he fell onto the street over and over again until water started to rise up from his toes to his legs and eventually carried him away."

"So, what if someone sunk the city intentionally?" Dr. Hunter thought out loud. "Maybe all of those god-like humans had entered the coliseum, got into some sort of struggle, and destroyed everything around them. So, maybe the city crumbled into pieces—

"Pieces!" The revelation exploded in Dr. Hunter's mind like fireworks.

He pulled up satellite and sonar imaged maps on his computer and scanned them for any odd shapes he may have overlooked. He skimmed them for large stone blocks, smooth arcs, and any shape that could not form naturally.

BEEP. "Twenty-two hours of air remaining," Venator notified.

The doctor's bloodshot eyes remained fixed on his computer screens, but he found nothing. "I'm better off looking for a needle in a haystack than a rock in an ocean." He began postulating again. "Would it sink straight down? Where would the currents take it?"

"Valid questions sir, though the solution is near impossible. I can compute a wide range of estimates, but you'll wind up with more options than a rooster in a hen house."

"Just run the numbers. I don't want to rely on chance."

Reinvigorated by the possibility that his latest theory would finally lead him to the ever-evading evidence of the past, Dr. Hunter took Venator's projections and spent the next several hours navigating his new course, venturing a great distance from where he had spent most of his time already.

BEEP. "Fifteen hours of air remaining, doctor."

Dr. Hunter had only completed scanning half of this new area when panic started to set in. He needed ninety minutes to climb back to the surface, which left him only thirteen-and-a-half hours to conquer what seemed an almost hopeless charade.

Seven hours later, he had nearly completed his latest course when an odd reading popped up on his radar. His computers revealed an odd reading just beyond his plotted course. With the lack of activity his excursion had generated, Dr. Hunter did not hesitate to investigate. He piloted toward the object.

"Why didn't I make a left turn when I started this confounded course? I would have found this hours ago."

"Based on estimated probabilities deduced from intrinsic data, fluid dynamic efficiencies infer..." Venator began.

"It's because I listened to you," the doctor interrupted.

He approached the location and shone the lights of the submersible toward the targeted area, but only saw more sand. He checked his readings again.

"My sensors indicate a root like system, sir," Venator indicated.

"This is an odd place for plants." The doctor continued to peer through the window, but could not see what his machines had picked up. As he moved closer to the first location, more readings branched across his radar. "Maybe it's under the sand."

He reached for the controls to the dredges, two cylinders he attached to the underbelly of the vessel that protruded like arms on a toy robot. He dialed them to 'suction mode' on a low power setting, just enough to vacuum a little sand slowly off of the ocean floor, and then went to work. The dredges sipped the sand through their tubes and spit it out behind the submersible.

Gently and carefully he sifted through the glowing grains under the ship's intensified lights. It only took moments for him to see what his computers found.

"Fulgurite?" A hardened collection of sand in the form of a multi-pronged lightening bolt began to reveal itself. "Only large amounts of electricity could create such a formation. But how could that happen this deep in the ocean?" He maneuvered the ship and the dredges to clear a bit more of the area, and found more remnants to his left versus any other direction, so he followed the path. "The electricity's impact with the sand turns it into glass, but could it maintain its shape under this amount of pressure?"

"To date, no fulgurite has ever been discovered in the ocean. However, glass becomes stronger as more uniform pressure is applied to it," answered Venator.

He continued to dredge, inching the vessel along. He eyed a few similarly shaped pieces of varying sizes. "Look at these formations. Only lightning strikes could create this. Which would not make sense under the water. If it happened elsewhere, above the surface of the ocean, or inside a building… then it must have sunk! I'm a genius! King me!"

"That reminds me, sir. Queen's Knight to King's four. Check," uttered Venator. Dr. Hunter navigated along until the snaking path of rigid glass suddenly ended. "The traces of fulgurite end here, doctor. I am now detecting traces of gold, diamond, onyx, silver and various volcanic elements."

"These shouldn't be here." The doctor double-checked and confirmed the findings. "I guess if I don't find Atlantis, at least I found some buried treasure." He cranked up the dredges, putting to faster use of the sand-sucking tubes. He didn't find any more fulgurite, but he did succeed in exposing jagged rock formations. He maxed out the power of the dredges and pushed the limits of his scanners for more of the elements nearby. They pinged with every duplicate trace dotting his radar, plotting out the form of what appeared as a massive cylindrical rock made up of precious minerals.

"This has to be it; at least part of it. This is hardly the remains of a city. Could this be what's left of the arena?"

BEEP. "Eight hours of air remaining, sir."

The exposed portion of the rock formation housed barnacles and a variety of crustaceous sea life. The dredges worked, but they worked slowly. After an hour of sucking away the debris, he spotted what looked like a diamond, embedded in stone. "Finally! Something to take a picture of." He snapped a few dimensional-resolution images that would allow him to continue his work after the exploration, building 3-D replicas.

BEEP. "Seven hours of air remaining."

"I've still got time. I need to see what else I can clear off. I feel like the rest of the city is under the sand."

Energized by his discovery, Dr. Hunter cleared off as much as he could. Thoughts raced through his mind. "Will I have enough time to uncover the evidence I need? Is this really the first proof of Atlantis? What else could this be? This has to be it. I've got to get a sample. Maybe I can take that diamond. Excavating this would cost millions. I'm going to need funding. I can go to the museums. Oh, and magazines. My colleagues are going to love this. The world will finally take me seriously. This will be huge! I'm going to need more proof. More pictures."

Another BEEP interrupted his thoughts.

"What? Only three hours left? How can that be? This is taking forever!"

"Did you not hear my last four notifications, sir?"

Dr. Hunter snapped a dozen more photos and backed up all of the information he collected on his computer, while he imagined himself at the top of the archeological world with the greatest discovery of all time. His censors could not give him a clear indication of the object's thickness or how deeply embedded the giant block sat, but every precious stone he revealed fueled his eagerness even more. He repositioned the submersible, switched the dredges' airflow, and set them to blow full blast. They created quite a cloud. He could only see the tips of the dredges where the air's force blew everything away. He started moving a little faster over the areas his radar had mapped out. The slab's shape had proven relatively consistent thus far, so he showed little concern as he worked with minimal visibility.

BEEP. "Two hours of air remaining, doctor. Thirty minutes until surface departure."

The doctor continued dredging, until—crunch. Alarms sounded.

"What did you do?" Venator asked in a mocking tone.

"You tell me."

"My sensors indicate that one of the dredges is no longer functioning properly."

Dr. Hunter turned off the dredges and stopped the propellers.

"Great. I just ruined Atlantis. Idiot!" When the blown sand settled, he saw that close to five inches of the dredge had pushed through the rock. "It's hollow?" The doctor's curiosity shot up again. "I don't have time to explore this anymore. I'll have to wait until next time."

With bit of a crunch and scraping, he slowly extracted the destroyed dredging tube from the slab. He took a moment to marvel at the hole, contemplating the best way to discover its contents as he watched a rush of bubbles emerge and float into the darkness above him.

"I'll have to come back." He calibrated his settings to conclude the expedition. As he flipped his last switch, he caught something out of the corner of his eye. He initially paid it no attention and continued repositioning the lights for his trip upward, but he eventually felt the need to investigate. He shone the lights into the newly created void, but saw nothing. His computers indicated nothing unusual.

He turned off his lights and peered into the darkness. The instantaneous darkness shrunk the expansive ocean into a blacked-out closet. An instant later, he noticed faint streams of red, orange, and yellow emanating like a peacock's tail from the infinite recesses of the apparently hollow rock. Too curious to ignore this new development, Dr. Hunter switched the lights back on, grabbed the controls of the ship and drove the crumpled dredge back into the slab, expanding the cavity.

Red lights flashed inside the submersible. Alarms sounded. "Dr. Hunter! This is not a bulldozer," Venator scolded. "By the way, you have ninety minutes of air remaining. We—well, you—must resurface immediately."

"I've still got time."

"No, you don't."

Dr. Hunter flipped a switch labeled 'Mute.' After a few more aggressive slams of the dredge into the slab, he pulled back, aimed the light into the opening, and waited for a miracle. He saw nothing. He turned off the lights and took another look. Darkness. His heart sank. He felt more anxious and frustrated over the diminishing amount of air and the growing curiosity of the slab's contents, but set his course for his rushed return to the world of the walking. He flipped his switches dejectedly, ready to depart.

Then, as Venator began to rise, the colors beaconed once again from the blackness. Even with the submersible's lights on, the brilliant shades of blue and purple mixed with the reds and yellows and shone like a spectrum of light through a perfect prism. Dr. Hunter took the controls in his hands, gripped them, rocked the ship back one more time, and rammed through the slab to enlarge the hole.

He waited for the dust to settle and, only moments later, like a train bellowing through a dark, smoke filled tunnel, the radiant light emerged, beaming through the cloudy debris, and came into full view. A magnificent floating sphere of colors stood suspended in front of Dr. Hunter. Never had he seen anything so beautiful. He felt helpless and in awe.

The colors on the beach ball-sized bubble shifted and rolled over each other like a school of hungry koi.

The light reflected off of the gemstones still embedded in the slab. Oblivious to the myriad of alarms blaring inside the ship, Dr. Hunter sat mesmerized as the bubble floated slowly skyward, away from him, until its light faded completely away. Once out of sight, Dr. Hunter remembered he should have left nearly an hour ago.

He flipped the 'Mute' switch off and immediately Venator chirped, "You have twenty-eight minutes of air remaining!"

"I'll never make it," he thought. He reached over to a knob on a tank that read 'nitrous oxide' and twisted, releasing the gas to induce his sleep. He then adjusted the cabin pressure to compensate for a faster resurfacing and extended decompression once he departed the ocean depths. He struggled to keep his eyes open as the gas took effect. He strained for one last look at his computers.

"With these settings, it will take approximately sixty minutes to reach the surface. You have twenty-five minutes of breathable air remaining," indicated Venator.

With his eyes fluttering, Dr. Hunter activated his homing beacon and the ship raced skyward. It only took seconds for Dr. Hunter to catch up to the bright twisting globe and its luminous light.

"Queen to King's Bishop 2. Check mate," said Dr. Hunter and then he saw no more.

Below a tranquil sky Venator exploded through the ocean's serenity like a bullet through glass before belly flopping and bobbing on the surface of the ocean. Inside, Dr. Hunter lay motionless, incapable of hearing the homing beacon signaling for his rescue.

Less than an hour later, the mystical bubble hatched from its watery shell, rose out of the ocean and floated straight into the sky as if an angel upon a cloud fished it from the water. It exuded its magnificence in the setting sun until it disappeared behind a single cottony puff in the sky.

First, a whisper of thunder tumbled through the air. Suddenly, the single cloud that swallowed the splendid sphere rapidly multiplied. Within a matter of seconds, clouds rippled outward from the source and covered the sky in every direction, blocking out the sun and coating the ocean in darkness. Thunder echoed like a symphony of timpani drums. With a single strike of lightning and a mighty crack, extraordinary colors decorated the sky like a million finger paintings at play on the cloudy canvas across the horizon. The ocean reacted with wild ferocity, launching mountain-high waves into the air that fell back down with the power of a waterfall.

In the distance, Dr. Hunter's crew braved the catastrophic weather as they finally tracked him down. They worked quickly to haul the submersible onto the deck before extracting the doctor. The crew had to resuscitate him. They strapped him down on the ship's wooden stretcher and performed CPR. Over and over they blew into his mouth and pressed against his chest, but he showed no signs of life.

If the doctor's eyes had opened, he would have seen that he lay directly below a group of clouds whose colors had begun to swirl. The clouds followed suit and formed into a funnel as the colors mixed together until they turned black with specks of bright light flashing amidst the darkness. The funnel descended on the crew and the Atlantic, but before it touched down, a single drop of rain, blacker than onyx, fell on the bridge of Dr. Hunter's nose and rolled into his eye. If his eyes had opened, he would have seen the beginning of the end of life as he and everyone in the world had known it.

The noise intensified. The howling winds blew louder and faster, increasing until the men aboard the ship were thrown into the turbulent waters. The ship spun like a top as waves crashed into it from all directions. Dr. Hunter's stretcher, still on the deck, slid aimlessly until a wave consumed the ship and sent the stretcher crashing against a guardrail. Another wave came and lifted the stretcher overboard. Dr. Hunter, in mid-air, feet from crashing into the ocean, finally opened his eyes.

Chapter 2 - See Shell

      Shell Wayburn spent the day before her first day of high school volunteering at the Palisades Medical Center, running the same errands that had bored her all summer. Straying from the standard issue red scrubs, indicative of her candy-striping status, Shell opted for a collection of items she retrieved from the Lost and Found; a pink football jersey, white sweatpants with 'PINK' written in large block letters on her rear end, and her throw-back Adidas shell-toe shoes to go with her mandatory white apron.

      "We have a new patient for you, Shell," called her mentor, Nurse Janie, from the nurses' station.

      "I would love to make a brand-new friend on my last day of work," Shell replied with a slight gleam of subdued sarcasm in her light green eyes.

"It is, isn't it? We're going to miss you around here; especially that outfit of yours."

      "Just making sure you don't forget the little people."

"Come now, you're not little," Nurse Janie encouraged.

"I was born the runt of the world," Shell affirmed.

"Well, you have made up for it with all your hard work." Shell blushed at the compliment. "So why don't you go make friends with Ms. Betty Harmony and give her a taste of what we'll all be missing? I'll have some other things for you, as well; the usual stuff. Should I get one of the volunteers to help you?"

"Nope. Not a problem. I'll be fine."

"Independent to the end, huh?"

"Things are just easier with fewer people involved," Shell replied, making the smug comment sound as sweet as possible.

"I'll page you in a little bit when everything is set up."

And with that, Shell started down the hall, her curly golden ponytail waving side to side. She always felt a twinge of nervous curiosity about new patients. She had met so many strangers over the summer. Most of them commented how she looked like their granddaughter. The rest of them took out their grumpiness on her. She figured her tan skin and mixed features made her culturally flexible. Her small stature seemed to inspire many people to treat her like an incapable toddler, thus urging her to always prove herself.

She found Betty, an older woman, sitting in the lone chair the hospital room offered, still dressed in her traveling clothes instead of the customary hospital gown, and holding an umbrella.

"Good afternoon, Ms. Harmony. My name is Shell, and I'm here to help you get comfortable."

"Comfortable?" the middle-aged woman retorted with a southern accent. "My word, darlin.' This chair is terrible!"

Shell stared at the woman, somewhat stunned by her response. "What brings you in today?"

"I'm not sure, now that ya mention it. The bus? My daughter? A van, maybe." Betty squirmed her way into a more comfortable position. "This may be the cheapest hotel room I've eva stayed in. I expected more out of Cabo."

"Cabo?" Shell asked.

"Cabo San Lucas. Mexico? Donde estoy?" Betty's line of questioning made less sense once she opened up her umbrella.

"Umm… Ms. Harmony, you are in a hospital. We're in New Jersey," explained Shell as she closed Betty's umbrella and placed it in the closet.

"Hey. I'm gonna need that. You never know when it's gonna rain." Betty glanced around and then examined Shell with squinted eyes. "Do I know you? Ya look familiar."

Shell fought out a smile instead of rolling her eyes, sat on the bed and faced Betty. "Do you have grandchildren?"

"Possibly." A troubled look smothered Betty's face. "I think I rememba grand… My kids like to hide things from me. They think it's funny." Again, Betty fell speechless. "So, your name is Shell and I'm in a hospital. Tell me somethin' else I don't know."

This interaction had not gone like her others, and Shell stuttered before finally mentioning, "I—I start high school tomorrow."

"Ain't that wonderful! I remember my first day of high school. That was the day I fell in love." The woman's eyes wandered toward the window as if her memories played on passing clouds. A few of her stray gray hairs seemed to settle down on her disheveled auburn mane. The heavy creases at the corners of her eyes softened into pale streaks of wisdom. "He was the first boy I laid eyes on when I walked in the door. I didn't know who he was, but it didn't take long for me to find out that every girl in the school had a crush on him. He was super smart, amazin' at every sport—ya standard high school stud."

"So what happened? Did you sweep him off his feet?"

"'Course not!" she replied with a laugh. "Neva said a word to him. He always had his friends, cheerleaders, or some other girls swarming 'round him. He did pick up my pencil once. I thought I told him, 'Thank you,' but my friend said I squeaked like a little ol' church mouse."

Shell laughed. It surprised her to get such a story out of the woman that came in complaining about Mexico.

"Are ya excited 'bout your first day?"

"Kinda. I mean, I guess I'm a little nervous."

"Nervous 'bout what, dear?"

"Well," Shell began. "My mom made me go through the eighth grade twice, so I'm glad I don't have to go back to middle school again." She paused, half expecting Betty to ask her why she repeated the eighth grade and half embarrassed she admitted such a flaw, but the older woman only smiled with eyes eager for the rest of the story. "So, all the kids I used to go to school with will be there, but a year ahead of me."

"Sounds like you'll be the cool kid who knows all them upper classmen."

"I don't know. Maybe. I didn't talk to them that much when I was in their class. I doubt they'll talk to me now. They probably won't even remember me."

"Who could forget a sexy little thing like you?" Shell blushed and breathed a sigh of relief as she stared into Betty's kind brown eyes, feeling a connection she rarely felt with others. "It's just embarrassing. It's not like I'm not smart, or anything."

"Obviously. You work in a hospital! Either way, it'll be nice to see some familiar faces," Betty said with some sadness, but she brought her smile right back. "High school was the best time of my life. College was pretty fun too, but I'd totally do high school again. Any boys you lookin' forward to seein'?"

"No, not really. I guess I haven't seen my friend Topher in a while."

"Is he cute?" Betty inquired. "Them boys somehow manage to get cuter as they get olda."

"Oh, I don't like him like that. I mean… He's just a friend."

A call came over the intercom speaker built into the side of the hospital bed Shell sat on. "Paging candy-striper Shell. Please report to the nurses' station." The message repeated as Shell recognized Nurse Janie's voice.

"Duty calls?" asked Betty, giving Shell an easy exit out of the conversation.

"I'll be back a little later. You just get…" Shell paused as she patted a folded hospital gown at the foot of the bed, "a little more comfortable and I'll be by to check on you."

Betty gave her a slight wave as she watched her leave the room. "I will see ya on the beach, darlin'."

For the rest of the day Shell delivered food, made beds, changed out bed pans, and ran a host of other errands around the hospital, doing as much of it with as little help as possible. She preferred working alone and the excitement about her last day of candy-striping kept her smiling and energized, outweighing the butterflies she felt in her stomach when she thought of starting high school the next day.

After returning a few trays of mostly uneaten lunch to the cafeteria for cleaning, she made her way back to the nurses' station to await more errands. Along the way, she passed the atrium where she liked to hide for an occasional ice cream cone break when work got on her nerves. The small fishpond there offered a peaceful reprieve from her assignments. It made her smile to see Betty enjoying an escorted tour of the facilities, though she looked somewhat annoyed by the wheel chair she sat in.

On her way through the lobby to the elevators, Nurse Janie and several other nurses, along with some visitors, huddled around one of the waiting area televisions hanging from a ceiling. Shell always wondered how they could make televisions so small look so heavy. It resembled a magic box more than a television. Shell had more familiarity with the modern televisions you could fold up or stick to a wall.

"Good evening citizens of the Tri-State area," said a frazzled and distraught weatherman on the television screen. "This is an emergency weather bulletin. An unexpected storm has formed over the middle of the Atlantic Ocean and is rapidly spread out in all directions. Satellite images indicate a growing number of giant waterspouts forming over the Atlantic. We have reports that this storm has already capsized dozens of ships and destroyed several essential weather measurement instruments. Several branches of the National Oceanic and Atmospheric Administration indicate the path of this storm will strike the coastlines of New York and New Jersey within the next hour." The station used a satellite image to simulate a time lapse of the storm that looked like green paint dumped on to the planet and spreading like a disease.

The nurses and a few people in the waiting room stared at the screens, expecting the punch line of a joke or some sort of reassurance that everyone would be fine.

"Authorities ask that you do not panic," the weatherman continued. "We currently do not know what caused the storm or why it's spreading so rapidly, but we do know that its size and strength far exceeds that of 2012 Superstorm Sandy, the hurricane that years ago brought our eastern coastal cities to a halt. Our regions' preparations since then should allow us to handle the storm effectively. It is best for everyone to stay indoors and remain calm."

Before the weatherman could sign off, chaos ensued in the hospital. Moans and wails echoed through the halls. The faces on all the nurses and people standing around the televisions dropped. Some shed tears. Others cried out in shock and fear. Shell didn't understand. It just seemed like a rainstorm. The words "Armageddon" and "apocalypse" bounced around the room. She recalled her history lessons about several false end-of-the-world predictions that lead to mass hysteria during the earlier parts of the twenty-first century.

Everyone scattered, and visitors demanded to see the patients they had waited for immediately. People groaned in frustration as their cell phones only responded with busy signals. Nurse Janie spotted Shell and rushed up to her.

"Get home! Get home now, Shell!" she ordered.

Shell considered asking why, but did not mind the command to end work a little early. She grabbed her things and headed for the bus stop. Once outside, her eyes floated west, catching the day's last rays of sunlight. They followed the cottony wisps to the east and the ominous skies just beyond. The instant the sun said good-bye, a flash of lightning made her jump. She instinctively reached into her backpack, where her hand fished for the childish pink umbrella her mother always made her carry. Instead of pulling it out and facing embarrassment, self-inflicted or otherwise, she opted to tuck herself further under the bus stop overhang to avoid the impending rain. She considered running over to the nearby parking structure, which only stood a dozen or so feet away, but the bus arrived as soon as the rain did.

Shell took a seat next to a window on the uncharacteristically empty bus, stared out at the mysterious storm that looked like none other she had seen before, and rode home to a symphony of thunderous roars amid flashes of sky-illuminating lightning strikes. A cornucopia of colors accented the charcoal stormy clouds. Stains of crushed plums, apricots, kiwis, and berries streaked the sky with an array of beautiful, yet foreboding, hues.

Heavy rain pelted Shell's pink umbrella as she stepped off the bus a few blocks from her house. She didn't realize how cold the air had become until she noticed her breath puffing out of her mouth as she ran home.

She fumbled through her bag for her keys when she reached her front door. After snagging them, she extended her hand to unlock the door when she saw what seemed like a drop of red paint land on the doorknob and then drip down to the ground. She paused as she watched the drop float away in the stream of water rushing down her steps, over the walkway that led up to her house, off the curb, and into the street, wondering why paint had nearly fallen on her.

After readjusting to avoid the raindrops, especially the weird paint-looking ones, Shell unlocked the door and went inside before slamming it shut behind her. "I'm home!" she called as she stepped into the foyer.

Her parents' home had most of the same bells and whistles as the other homes in the area, minus the swimming pool. Her family could afford it but, as her father liked to say, "Invest in the things you need, and spoil others before yourself." Apparently her grandfather coined that phrase and "others" did not mean "your children."

"Excellent," Mrs. Wayburn called from the kitchen down the hall. "Go clean up, okay, sweetie? Dinner will be ready in five minutes."

Shell headed upstairs to her bedroom, when another loud crack of thunder rumbled through the house. Once she reached the top of the stairs, she heard the rain beating against a windowsill.

"Oh no!" She sprinted down the hall, burst into her room, and saw what she dreaded. She had left her window open. Her plants liked the fresh air, despite the fact that the open window upset her mother. She's going to kill me, Shell thought as her feet squished the damp part of the carpet by the wet windowsill.

She leaned outside to pull the cottage-style windows shut, extending a hand to each pane, planning to pull them closed in unison. She leaned out against the sill, wetting her shirt. The rain pounded on her head and arms. As she pulled the windows toward her, another peculiar drop landed on her right hand. The violet paint-like glob spread over the back of her hand like an inkblot. Instinctively, she jumped back from the window and tried to shake it off by waving her hand furiously, but it settled like a stain.

She tried to rub it off and even scratched at it. Still it remained. She grabbed a T-shirt lying on by her bed in hopes that drying it would make it go away, but before she could try, the mark began to fade. Shell could only stare at it. Relieved that it did not stay forever like the birthmark she already disliked, it did concern her that the mark had soaked into her skin.

Standing there, wet and confused, staring at her hand, she heard her mother call her down for dinner again. Calmly, she reached back out into the rain and pulled the windows shut. She changed her clothes and went downstairs for dinner.

Chapter 3 - Elsewhere

Music whistled through the thick vegetation of dry leaves. The wind played a familiar tune, but a new melody whispered on the horizon. Through the brush, the broad head of an African elephant appeared, shaking its ears free from the grasping branches. Its gargantuan body pushed through the forest and into a clearing. Its long trunk unrolled like a fire hose, stopping just short of the ground. Its dry tip hovered over the crackling grass—reaching, examining, and searching through the crusty casks of dead meadow for the slightest remnants of nourishment. Its hungry mouth opened to greet the long sought-after sustenance, but quickly rejected the rotten vegetation it found and dropped it to the dead earth below.

From out of the distance and high in the air raced a blanket of darkness speckled with twinkling colors. The storm swarmed around the elephant before it had a chance to find cover in the dying jungle from which it came. As the sun withdrew from its battle against the impenetrable clouds, a mighty wind rushed through the elephant's clearing. The storm's ominous arrival insinuated a much-welcomed intrusion.

On cue, a long-desired drop of water fell atop the aging elephant. The oh-so-foreign liquid was almost completely absorbed in the crevices atop the elephant's crown, creating a large, temporary, tattoo. A crescendo of dancing leaves rolled from the north and the east like an army of tiny soldiers, then a shower of epic proportions bathed the caked dust off the elephant's entire body.

As if the elephant had just awoken from a dream, it focused on the ground, its head swaying side to side. The animal's trunk stretched like an old man in the morning, rejuvenated by the unexpected present. A light brightened from deep within the elephant and shone through its eyes; a quivering lip appeared to almost smile.

The elephant reared its head back, readjusting its spine, forced its chin high in the air, unrolled its trunk like a flower in bloom, and drank in every fate-guided drop it could. The creature's tired eyes clapped on the falling drops as it fought off instincts to close its lids, wanting its every sense to enjoy this moment. Appearing to almost gulp down the air of the world in a single breath, the mighty elephant inhaled and then trumpeted an eardrum-shattering sound, seeming to suspend the raindrops above its trunk.

For nearly a minute it sung over the splashed canopy of the forest and the moaning wind of the sun-suffocating storm. The elephant's song quieted to a peaceful undertone, and its mighty horn kneeled upon its brow, bowing thanks to the heavens. Its mouth remained open; its eyes relaxed, then closed. Its ears flapped and its tail wagged with joy in the wind.

ELSEWHERE

From right above the soaked elephant fell a raindrop unlike the others that had fallen before it, landing in its wetted mouth. Common colors for any drop ranged from translucent shades of blue to white, but this raindrop fell like a spill from an oversaturated sponge just dipped in yellow paint.

The drop's uniqueness went unnoticed to the blissful beast, as it drank its fill before resting its entire body under this magical shower. It lay there a while, still, until finally it opened its eyes to the vision of a mud-puddle building before it. Now aware that great things could get even better, the elephant rested on the mire.

Chapter 4 - Just Dessert

Shell sat down at a picturesque circular wooden dining table set for four. Flashes of lightning from the storm outside brightened the shadowy trees, shrubs, and a manicured garden that danced in melodic disarray, swaying in a chaotic rhythm of wind and pelting precipitation. Her eyes focused on the storm outside, wondering why she had never seen colored raindrops before and if this storm really did differ from all other storms.

A collection of casserole dishes filled with mashed sweet potatoes, string beans, and two separate types of lasagna adorned the table. One, Shell could tell, belonged to her and her mother; the greenish tint gave away that her mom added spinach to their signature vegetarian dish for the evening. Shell had chosen vegetarianism only recently after accidentally watching a graphic video of poultry processing online. Mrs.

Wayburn considered lasagna her specialty. The other lasagna she stuffed like a meat lover's pizza, with pepperoni, ground beef, and chorizo. Olives, warm bread, a dipping concoction made of olive oil, cracked pepper, and Parmesan cheese, along with homemade biscuits and a large bowl of apple-walnut salad, decorated the rest of the table.

Shell sat between her parents and across from her brother. Her beautiful brunette mother reached to her and her freckle-faced brother, Skitch, inviting the family to hold hands around the table. She and her brother grabbed a hold and reached for their balding and surly-looking father. "Happy Dinner," they all said in unison. Then they each extracted the folded napkins from their matching napkin holders and began making their own plates.

No one spoke. The only noise came from the clanking of spoons into serving dishes preceding a cacophony of metal clanging against porcelain plates. Then followed the clicking and grinding of teeth as mouths dislodged food from utensils. The staccato-like dotting of rain against the windowpane and the explosions of thunder from the storm accompanied the familiar clatter, but resonated with comfort more than intimidation.

Mrs. Wayburn attempted to draw her feeding-focused family's attention with her tired and intense, though still inviting eyes. She forced herself to liken the clamor to an indication of overwhelmed appreciation for her culinary efforts.

"This looks great, sweetie," Mr. Wayburn stated, not looking up from the feast in front of him.

A long-awaited smile crossed Mrs. Wayburn's face, as if her lips had held their breath awaiting acknowledgment or some semblance of family interaction.

"Well, it's Sunday. We should get ready for our big week," she explained. Mrs. Wayburn, Victoria to those outside her home, aspired to live the life of the model modern woman. Beyond having her profession as a news anchor on an internationally televised network, she hoped to excel at everything a professional woman could do while still upholding the traditions beset upon women from generations ago. Regardless if her love for cooking came from social pressures or fortunate coincidence, Mrs. Wayburn used dinner to show off her skills. "So, kids, are you ready for school tomorrow?"

Shell glanced at her mother disapprovingly. Skitch, Shell's taller but younger brother by three years, responded with a mouth full of food. "Oh, yeah. Can't wait," he muttered as food fell from his mouth.

"Don't talk with food in your mouth," Mr. Wayburn instructed.

Lightning struck outside and the immediate thunder vibrated the house like a subwoofer, shaking the fork out of Shell's hand. It clanked against the plate. She picked it up quickly and glanced around to measure an appropriate level of embarrassment, but no one noticed. "How about you, mi Shell?" Mrs. Wayburn redirected. Shell cringed when her less-than-fifteen-percent-Cuban mother said her name like that. Shell believed that if her mother wanted to caller her "mi Shell" she should have just named her Michelle.

I'm finally out of middle school and I'll get to join all the kids who think I'm the idiot that had to repeat eighth grade, she wanted to say. "Just thrilled," she replied.

"Now, dear," Mrs. Wayburn replied, aware of her daughter's sarcasm.

"I'm gonna miss you, sis. It was fun riding the bus with you. You were like that lame eighth grader that had to hang out with sixth graders to feel cool." Skitch laughed at his own joke.

"I hope Mom and Dad keep you in middle school forever," she retorted from across the table.

"I bet you'll still be shorter than a sixth grader no matter what school you go to," Skitch snarled.

Fury, rage, envy and embarrassment coated Shell's face. The past year raced through her mind as she recalled each event that culminated in her current disapproval with the rest of the table. First came her mother's surprise announcement that she would repeat the eighth grade, telling her she needed to show more social development. That led to the duplicative year wasted on lessons she already learned and the ironic further development of her anti-social behavior as her new classmates referred to her as "the old kid." This added insult to injury since her birthday came before most everyone else's amongst her original classmates. Finally, her father's suggestion, which became her mother's mission, of a summer spent candy-striping as a résumé-slash-character builder seemed to indicate their lack of confidence in their daughter's ability to make responsible decisions. Everyone's lower opinion of her fueled her lack of respect for everyone else.

"I hate you, Skitch!"

"You two!" The smile disappeared from Mrs. Wayburn's face. "No arguing at the dinner table." Silence resumed for several minutes as they all resorted back to their own plates.

Mr. Wayburn, always the fastest eater, scanned the table as he prepared for his second helping. "Any fun stories coming up tomorrow, my love?" Asking his wife about work always served as an easy icebreaker and guaranteed an extensive stream of dialogue.

"Well, I'm sure this storm will cause enough damage. The weather reports right now are calling it a global event. I'm sure we'll have several conversations with our meteorologists. We'll interview some experts, take some stories from our affiliates, and see what we can put together. We'll probably cover some back-to-school stuff, too. Shopping. Clothing. Oh! That reminds me," she redirected her pending question to Shell. "Did you see the GNN bag I put in your room? Some designers came by the studio today with some of their back-to-school fashion lines. I brought you some things they had in your size that you can wear to school tomorrow. What did you think?"

I think, awesome! I'll be the oldest freshman in the class and the only one still getting dressed by their mother, Shell considered for her response before saying in a less than enthusiastic tone, "I didn't see the bag. Sorry. I'll check it out."

"You mean to say thank you, right young lady?" Mr. Wayburn bellowed. Skitch chuckled. Shell shuddered.

Thank you for the bag of free stuff to make up for the fact that you didn't take me back-to-school shopping or thank you for holding me back and setting me up for a very embarrassing first day of high school, she wondered before giving a reluctant "Thank you."

"You're welcome," Mrs. Wayburn directed to her daughter. Sensing Shell's uneasiness, she attempted to lift her spirits. "You made great strides last school year, sweetie. I think you've put yourself in a great position to really succeed in high school.

"Succeed? Anything I do, you're just going to tell me it's not good enough." Shell surprised herself. *I shouldn't have said that.*

"Calm down, Shell," her father warned.

"We just want to make sure you are ready for opportunities when they present themselves," Mrs. Wayburn added.

"Chance favors the prepared mind," Mr. Wayburn quoted for the millionth time in Shell's life.

"Have you locked down your career path, yet?" her mother asked. Shell resented the barrage of parental advice aimed at her from both sides of the table and cut her eyes at the question. After sixth grade, students selected their career path and tailored their class schedule accordingly. Shell had changed hers every year since then and her mother asked her about it on what felt like a daily basis.

"You're not still stuck on mythology, are you?" Mr. Wayburn pressured. "There's no future in history. Especially fictional history.

"I'm going to be an astronaut," Skitch chimed in, excited to share his recent decision.

"See," Mr. Wayburn presented to Shell. "Your brother made his decision."

"Can I be excused?" Shell muttered under her breath as she dropped her silverware on her plate.

"Yes, you may," Mrs. Wayburn answered, surprising her husband.

Mr. Wayburn huffed in disapproval. "Check that attitude, young lady, or you won't last a day in high—"

"You don't have to wear it if you don't like it," Mrs. Wayburn interrupted, "but it's there for you if you want."

Shell made a noisy exit from the dinner table. She placed her plate in the sink and stomped up to her room.

Posters of boy bands and professional athletes decorated her yellow-painted walls. Trophies from tennis and basketball camps and tournaments, along with ribbons of all colors from horseback riding and gymnastics, lined the shelf facing the foot of her bed. Figurines of horses and an old jewelry box with a ballerina draped in bracelets and hair bands sat on her nightstand. She noticed the GNN bag by her door. She must have walked right past it when she first got home.

Despite her attempts to ignore the bag because of her anger toward her mother, her curiosity eventually overtook her. She ran over to pick it up, avoiding the damp area of the carpet, and dumped the contents on her bed. A bright blue yoga top with a matching vintage long skirt looked pretty impressive. Shell felt even guiltier when she picked up the top and felt the weight tugging on the left sleeve.

No way, she thought. She placed the top back down on the bed and reached for the sleeve. She nearly gasped. "amginE Armer!"

She fought her urge to run to her door and yell an apology downstairs to her mom.

Shell pulled out a change purse from her semi-wet backpack and dumped it out onto the bed. Her ID, Visa Allowance card, a few coins, and some bills lay scattered on her comforter. She gawked over her new Armer. The forearm fashion-tech accessory took the world by storm a few years ago and she had asked for one repeatedly. Now she could access all of her smartphone features on a purse that wrapped around her arm. It was her ticket into the amginE Games. She marveled at how seamlessly it integrated and coordinated with the outfit. She began to place the items on her bed into the accessory and synced it to her wrap phone. Even the sleeve of the shirt had slots for cards to slide through it and into the Armer and a flap that could snap shut to cover the control screen.

"So cool," Shell said out loud as she unsnapped a couple of the buttons, separating the Armer from the shirt. It looked even cooler on its own. With its bright gold croc-embossed patent leather and black accents around the seams; Shell knew she had the coolest Armer she had ever seen.

Refocusing her attention on getting ready for school, she snapped the Armer back onto the sleeve of her new top and placed everything on her charge pad to make sure her batteries did not die. She loaded her backpack with a few smart pens, her tablet, and her reader. While peering across her room, making sure she had everything ready, she noticed a damp pile of pink and white clothes on the ground. She didn't remember changing out of her work clothes, nor did she remember leaving them on the wet part of the floor.

"I think they'll need this back," she told herself as she held up the apron. "Although, this could come in handy one day." Shell threw the wet clothes in her hamper and hung the apron on her doorknob to dry.

She hopped in bed, but still felt too excited to sleep. She grabbed her Scroll, a laptop computer with a keyboard made for typing with one hand that rolled up into a tight little cylinder. She laid the detachable screen on her propped up legs, rested the touch-pad uni-board on her stomach, opened her books app and scrolled through all the books she had read over the summer, most of them assigned reading. She paused in admiration of her favorite book, one her grandfather wrote more than fifty years ago.

She skimmed through a few of her favorite amginE Game sites and tried to narrow down the events in which she wanted to simul-play. With her new Armer, she could finally watch shows, play along, and impact the story with millions of others. After checking out some news alerts about the storm, the riots it seemed to incite, and a video showing a series of lightning strikes that appeared to spell out words, she sedately rolled up her scroll and went to sleep, unaware of where her dreams would take her.

Chapter 5 - Thump in the Night

The storm outside raged out of control. Water streamed down windows in countless unending snake-like dances. Constantly refilling puddles overflowed in the streets and spilled into the many places water disappears.

Shell tossed and turned all night in her sleep. Beads of sweat dripped down her furrowed forehead from her tangled hair as she rocked about in her bed. Every crash of thunder made her jump, though she never woke. She breathed in heavy pants, as if running. Her chest heaved rapidly, in and out, in and out. Shell dreamt a dream not experienced by anyone for countless ages. However, on this night; hundreds would share this dream with her. In the nights to come, thousands more, and later, millions would all recollect this exact vision.

***

B.E. HOWARD

Like white flakes floating on the black placid surface of a massive unnamed, unvisited, and unseen lake isolated by steep, barren, and desolate cliffs, an endless spattering of cosmic clusters swayed atop gently lapping watery curves as a dark cloudless sky gazed upon the mirrored image of its own vast void.

From a distance beyond reckoning, that which is occasionally felt yet rarely seen approached with unwavering fortitude toward the serene setting. The invisible force, massive only in its comprehension, converged upon the lake with the subtle ferocity of a pelican diving to dine. The formless body whispered, "Find me," before crashing into the water, but without the slightest splash. The water remained still and the stars shone uninterrupted.

Moments after, the lake transformed into a cauldron, bubbling as steam slithered above the surface and collected into a sight-sucking fog that blocked out the sky and rose to the stars, blemishing the clear night with the birth of clouds. The bubbles multiplied and swelled until they popped all over the lake, splashing against its rocky border, turning dust to mud. From that mud grew green blades like feathers reaching for the new cloudy canopy. And still the water boiled. Ripples turned to lapping waves, masking the happenings beneath the water's surface. The stars could only share silhouettes of the slithering, hopping, flopping, and crawling creatures that emerged from the murk. When the percolating ceased, the lake's tranquility returned to its familiar tranquility. Yet, life had come and life remained—above, below, and all around.

***

THUMP IN THE NIGHT

And that's where the similarity of Shell's dream to the dream experienced by many others that night ended and a new, unique dream began.

***

A lion with a red-glowing mane of fire approached the lake. Relaxed and at peace, it bent over, closed its yellow eyes, and drank from the serene water. The beast's silent gentle lapping of the liquid created subtle ripples that made the lion's reflection sway. When the lion had its fill and gazed upon its likeness in the water, it reared back in shock that the once bright and burning mane it had gazed upon its entire life now seemed to blaze a purplish haze. The lion instinctively roared and clawed against the threatening reflection as it watched its face transform into that of a hawk with striking white eyes. A piercing screech reached to the stars instead. Though they twinkled, the stars appeared to shudder at the creature's call. The amalgamation galloped from the lake in great haste and tore through the brush, digging its mighty claws into the ground, ensuring its path. The earth seemed to wince at every stride.

Unexpectedly, the four-padded plowing through the eye high reeds turned into a two-footed frolic as the beast transformed again and Shell ran through the brush instead of the lion. Ahead of her she made out a massive cave, camouflaged by a dark dense forest of tall twisted trees and vines. Urged by a panic that something chased her, she kept running. She knew not what it looked like. The vegetation beneath her steps burned like coals on her bare feet. Noises resonated from all around her: chirps, squeaks, squawks, croaks, moans, roars, and every other sound imaginable.

She stopped at the forest's edge. Light, hurried, frightened steps approached her from behind while slow,

37

heavy, thunderous steps advanced from the forest ahead. Yet she saw only the open spaces of the foggy field and the blanket darkness of the woods. The climaxing cacophony throbbed like a prey's heartbeat trapped between competitive predators. A chilled wind froze her bones, locking her in place. She sensed that whatever approached her from behind halted that instant and reached out to touch her shoulder. She dared not look and braced herself for the threat behind her who roared in a hushed tone, "Fear me." As she did, the trees parted in front of her, inviting her into the darkness.

***

Shell awoke breathless. Drenched in sweat, she sat up in bed. Clammy, she rubbed her forearm across her brow, wiping off enough sweat for it to drip off her arm. She exhaled and steam wafted from her mouth. The cold surprised her; the room seemed darker than normal. *The light that shines in from the lamppost across the street must have burned out,* she thought. The storm had not subsided.

"Or maybe the power has gone out around the neighborhood," she continued. The shadows in the room looked familiar, but they did not feel that way to her.

She lay back down and listened to the storm. The soothing consistency of rapid tapping against the roof and windowsill relaxed her. Even the thunder seemed to strike at regular intervals, as if intentionally. Shell continued to listen as the thunder rolled in at a quickening pace. It sounded more like a bass drummer from a marching band stood outside her house and banged out a slow, deep, beat. THUMP. THUMP. THUMP.

The more Shell listened the more it started to remind her of the beating she heard in her dream. She remembered the trees parting in the shadowy forest and wondered if the monster she assumed had approached her had come for her again.

Goosebumps replaced the blanket as Shell slowly removed it from on top of her, exposing her legs to the cold air. She stepped out of bed and made her way toward the window. THUMP. THUMP. THUMP. She walked in step with the ominous rhythm and slowly reached for the latch to unlock the window. The coldness of the metal reminded her of a fence pole after a snowfall. She lifted it and peered outside as she grasped the handle. Despite the intensity of the rain hitting the windowpanes, she pushed the windows open easily. The ground looked black below her window, as if oil spilled over the grass, the walkway, and the street by her house. She saw no drummer.

Without warning, a great force sucked Shell through the window, lifting her off the floor, out of the room and into the storm. At the last moment, she grabbed onto the window ledge. Her legs kicked as she screamed and cried for help. She looked back hoping to find the source of her predicament, expecting to see a giant tugging at her ankles. Instead, she saw a massive twisting whirlwind of infinite colors stretching higher than the clouds, devouring buildings as it headed right toward her. She screamed louder, pleading for someone to save her. Closer and closer the radiant tornado came. Her fingers strained to keep hold. Just as the pain consumed her hands and she nearly lost her grip, a burst of wind sent her flying back into her room, throwing her against the wall.

Chapter 6 - Lunch Money

Christopher woke to the start of a truck engine. Living on the first floor of an apartment building in a unit right by the outdoor parking area made him quite accustomed to using an Express Mail truck for an alarm. He heard it every morning at six-fifteen, except for Sundays.

Staying in bed for a few extra minutes with his eyes open, Christopher thought about the day ahead of him. *The sun's shining. That's a start,* remembering the words his mother whispered to him when things got him down. Not that he could see the sun or the sky or the weather outside, but the fact that light came in through his dirt-stained, filthy-film-coated, bar-protected window looked promising.

In zombie-like fashion, Christopher got out of bed and dragged his feet across the hard, matted, brown bedroom carpet to his door. He pulled the loosely hanging doorknob less than gently to dislodge the doorframe-filling wooden plank and stepped barefoot onto the dim hallway's cold linoleum floor. The only light came from an old projection television in the living room and a bit of sunlight that bounced in and out of the kitchen.

Christopher made his way through the narrow paint-deprived corridor, already numb to the marks and scratches that gave the apartment more of a warehouse feel than a home. He tried to see the imperfections as lame attempts at decorating.

The noise of the television and the city outside barely masked the creaking floorboards beneath his feet. Traffic played like static on a radio station. The horn honking, engine revving, breaks squeaking, and jackhammering blended together in a swirl of white noise. It permeated the apartment's thin walls, while a stench that only a barkeep could love stuck in the apartment's every crevice. Cans and bottles of beer (some empty and some with warm day-old remnants of beverages past) overloaded trashcans, the sink, and the unwashed kitchen tables and counter. Nervously, he peered down the hall to the living room straight ahead, where the footrest end of the peeling vinyl recliner peeked back, but he didn't see any feet hanging over the edge.

"Maybe he made it to bed last night," Christopher wondered.

A few steps later and Christopher finally reached the slightly nicer than expected in-door outhouse. He pushed the door open, but the rough texture, odd creaking, and soft thud the door made against the bathroom wall surprised him. He flipped the light switch to the lights, but the buzzing hum he had grown to expect over the past eight months never began. He tiptoed his way to a crusty plastic shower curtain and pulled it back to let light in from the small window inside the shower, looked back at the door, and saw a cheap piece of plywood where the knob-less door once swung.

Redecorating? He mocked silently. Under the faint lighting, he turned a squeaky hot water knob at the sink. After some rumblings from the pipes behind the wall and under the sink, water trickled out of the faucet and drooled on to his stiff and matted toothbrush. He rubbed it on the Colgate paste bar that sat next to the soap by the sink before brushing his teeth. "Back to school," he muttered, forcing himself to feel uplifted.

As he reached for a hardened washcloth, loud harsh coughing reverberated through the wall. Christopher stopped brushing and turned the water off. He flinched as the metal faucet handle squealed, then stood motionless, toothbrush still lodged in his mouth full of bubbly suds. Sheets rustled around in the next room. After a few seconds passed and he heard no indication that his cloud-belching uncle had made his way out of his room, Christopher finally spit the toothpaste out of his mouth. He held the washcloth and stared at the rusty knobs straddling the faucet.

"It's not worth it," he told himself as he hung the dry rag back on the towel rack and left the toothpaste suds to dry in the sink basin. He tiptoed back to his room, despite feeling sticky and dirty, and got ready for school.

He grabbed his old yellow backpack with its big blue stain on the bottom corner from where a pen had exploded, worn out straps, and leftover remnants of a once sewn-on cartoon character, and headed to the front door. He expected that his aunt and uncle had remained asleep in their bedroom, so Christopher jumped when he stepped into the hall and nearly ran right into his Uncle Jack.

With a voice groggy and reeking of skunked beer and morning breath came, "Where are you off to?"

"I've got school today."

"School? Already?" Jack continued on with some inappropriate and unnecessary mumbles before he shoved his hairy knuckles into his jeans pocket. Loose change clanked around before he pulled out a few wrinkled bills. "Pick me up some cigarettes and some buzz gum on your way home." He handed Christopher two wadded up dollar bills.

"This isn't e—" Christopher tried to reply before Jack walked past him and into the bathroom.

As Christopher turned to leave the apartment, he saw his Aunt Leslie lying on the bed; barely covered in the only article of clothing he assumed she owned—a bathrobe. He left the apartment, closed the door behind him, and looked down at the two dollars. He made his way to school wondering what he should do about lunch.

Chapter 7 - Dis-Orientation

Shell woke up screaming, tears streaming down her face as she bolted upright. She finally opened her eyes to a room filled with sunshine, surprised to find herself sitting on her bed and not the floor. She swung her head around to read "six twenty-nine" on her alarm clock. She watched the numbers turn and listened to the ensuing buzzing.

"What the heck?" she demanded. Her eyes ping-ponged back and forth between the window and the wall she recalled getting slammed against just moments ago. She rubbed the back of her head, but felt no pain. She checked her arms and legs for bruises, then her hands for scars from hanging onto the window ledge. Nothing. She felt her clothes and her forehead. "Did I even wake up sweating?" She remembered the drumming, or a drummer, and had the vague recollection of something sucking her out of her room, but almost nothing at all about the dream she'd had before the other craziness began; except the phrases 'Find me' and 'Fear me.'

A door closed downstairs. Shell finally got out of bed, walked over to her window, and peered out in time to see her dad get into his car and pull out of the driveway. Shell's house sat on a hill across the river from New York City, not too far from where the Hudson River emptied out into the Atlantic Ocean. Towering skyscrapers glistened in the distance, brighter than usual this morning.

It looks like all that rain gave the city a good washing.

She watched her dad drive away, down a semi-storm-decimated street, through the puddles and past the debris where everything dripped. She half expected to see a marching band drummer walking down the sidewalk.

After turning away from the window, Shell perked up when she saw her new outfit awkwardly lying on her desk with the phone and Armer resting on the charge pad. She dressed quickly, excited about her new clothes; posed a bit in front of her full-length mirror, then headed to her closet to rummage for a few accessories to spice up her outfit even more.

She felt a little nervous as she headed to the kitchen, but she also felt a little older than she had the day before. High school had always seemed like such a far off place for her, full of cool kids that knew everything, where everyone stood tall and dressed well, and soon she would walk the halls with the beautiful giants. But it turned her stomach to think that now she looked up to the people with whom she once felt equal.

"I'm older than most of the entire sophomore class. Heck, I'm going to be sixteen in a month." The thought had upset her on numerous occasions, but today it made her angry to think they would all seem older, wiser, and better than her. "Maybe I could go to a different high school. That way, no one would know me. I'd probably blend in better with the freshmen. No one's ever going to take me seriously here."

Her mother's voice echoed in her head. *No, Shell. We moved to this neighborhood years ago just so you could go to these schools. Your father and I put a lot of planning into this, so you're going. This is a great school and you'll become a better person for it.*

Better how? She always wondered.

Shell entered the kitchen just in time to catch Skitch inhaling his last little bit of oatmeal. Not even on the first day of school did he bother to brush his hair. He started middle school a year ago with a buzz cut that earned everyone's ridicule and his vow to never cut it again. His hair had not seen a pair of scissors in a year, but Shell thought he looked messier than usual. With his mouth still full of food, Skitch waved to the refrigerator, "Thanks, Mom."

"You're welcome, sweetie," a slightly digitized voice said somewhat louder than necessary. Shell turned to the refrigerator to see a transmitted image of her mom waving at Skitch. Mrs. Wayburn made sure to see the kids off every morning before school. Normally, that meant scanning in. No matter what time she left for work in the morning or where she worked from, she always had some sort of camera ready so she could make sure her kids ate their breakfast and left for school on time. "Good morning, Shell," Mrs. Wayburn said with a smile through the flat screen monitor on the refrigerator door.

"Morning, Mom," replied Shell with deliberate minimal enthusiasm. She sat down at the island in the kitchen in front of a bowl of dried instant oatmeal that her mother had set out for her before she left for work.

Skitch grabbed his backpack off of the counter and whizzed by her in a blur. "Later, squirt," he joked.

Shell curled her lip in disapproval. "Have fun in middle school, dork," she mockingly hollered at her brother as he shoved a protein-loaded, sugar-coated Breakfast Bomb down his throat on his way to the front door.

With his mouth full of food and one foot outside he snarked, "Aren't you coming? Mom said you need to try eighth grade again." He slammed the door shut before Shell could reply.

"Here, let me heat some water for you," Mrs. Wayburn interrupted while nodding to the electric kettle on the island.

"I got it," Shell interjected before her mother could heat up the metal kettle remotely from an app on her phone. It annoyed her that everything seemed within her mother's reach.

"Are you ready for your big day?"

Shell picked up on the familiar tones of desperation and forced excitement in her mother's voice as she attempted to extract a positive emotion out of her daughter. Still, Shell did not answer. The kettle clicked as steam billowed from its top while Mrs. Wayburn waited for a response, watching her daughter prepare breakfast.

"You look great. Do you like the outfit?"

Shell ignored the pleas for conversation while she stirred the water into her cereal. Frustration dulled Mrs. Wayburn's face amidst Shell's silent protest.

"Are you okay, baby? Are you nervous? It's okay, you know, to be scared. It's your first day at a new school. But don't worry, it's a great school and all of your friends will be there."

It bothered Shell to listen to her mother fill in both sides of the conversation. She stopped listening once she noticed an advertisement running on the side panel of the Refriger-Vision for the latest blue-tooth earrings for girls and blue-tooth studs for boys. The ad finished by explaining how well the earrings paired with the amginE Armer. Shell looked back at her mom, who had conceded to simply staring at her, and considered making a request for the additional accessory.

"I'll be fine, Mom." Shell took it as a 'lose-lose' situation. Whether she entered into the conversation or not, Mrs. Wayburn wouldn't stop talking.

"If you say so, honey. There's a lunch waiting for you." Mrs. Wayburn gestured toward a red tote bag at the other end of the island from where Shell sat.

"Thanks," Shell whispered as she mentally predicted the contents of the bag with her name on it.

"And take your umbrella today. The weatherman said we could see some residual rain from yesterday," Mrs. Wayburn added while hands filled with makeup-applying tools swarmed her face.

Shell gazed outside the kitchen window. She had never seen a more picturesque morning. Nothing gave her an inclination that she would need an umbrella today. Grateful for the distraction the people surrounding her mother provided, Shell enjoyed some pseudo-privacy during her breakfast. She ate her hot oatmeal in peace as she thought about her dream again. She glanced up in between bites, catching her mother staring at her while she ate. So, she stared back.

"What is it?" she demanded, perturbed by her mother's inquisitive look. "Fine! I'll bring my umbrella. Gah."

"So, do you like the Armer?" Mrs. Wayburn asked.

Shell tried to hide her pleasure with a nonchalant response. "Yeah. It's cool."

Her effort to sound unimpressed did not fool Mrs. Wayburn. Excitedly, she bantered, "I knew you'd like it. It's got all of the latest upgrades, extra battery, and extra memory. They did a whole segment about it yesterday. Did you see how it detaches? I thought that was really neat."

The word echoed in Shell's head like a puffer fish trapped in a balloon. *'Neat'? Who says 'neat'?*

Mrs. Wayburn continued on. "Are you going to volunteer at the hospital after school? I hope you don't give up on your social obligations."

"Does it make sense to feel obligated to do something I'm volunteering for?" Mrs. Wayburn never appreciated it when Shell attempted to mask witty, and sometimes rude, comments behind intellectual quips.

"Now, now. Have fun at school today. Say hello to all your friends for me."

"I wouldn't call them friends, exactly," Shell mumbled under her breath.

"Is that Christopher still making it into school?"

"By Christopher, do you mean Topher, Mom? And why wouldn't he be going to school?"

"Yes. Topher. Of course. Just be careful around him, dear. I met his new parents and I'm not sure what sort of bad habits Christopher may have picked up from them."

"Topher?" Shell retorted with disgust. "You want me to be careful around *Topher*?"

Mrs. Wayburn backtracked. "I don't mean it like that. I love you and I always want you to be careful."

Shell interjected, "They're his aunt and uncle. And because his real parents died, I should be careful around him? You really do see the worst in everyone." She dropped her spoon in her bowl and pushed it down the island, away from her. She grabbed her lunch from the island, picked up her book bag, and started out of the kitchen.

Mrs. Wayburn called after her, "Shell, that's not what I meant. Christopher, I mean Topher... he's a great kid. Things change sometimes. Some people can't help it."

Shell did not acknowledge her mother's 'I love you' as she stormed out of the kitchen. "Have a good day, Mom."

It hurt Shell a little to hear her mom say she loved her and then not say it back herself. She stood at the front door for a moment to gather her composure. She turned on the house alarm and opened the door to a beautiful, sunny Monday morning. The sun seemed brighter than usual. She reached down and picked up her pink umbrella, closed the door, and locked it behind her.

It took Shell about fifteen minutes to walk to Riverside High School. She had seen the inside of the school a couple of times, but knew her way there largely because of the frozen yogurt shop across the street. All of the streets along the way had sidewalks, so getting to school would not prove too difficult.

She took the residential route, winding through neighborhoods and staying off the busy streets. Mostly cars and school buses drove by, along with the occasional post office delivery truck. The journey seemed slightly odd to Shell, because she had never made the trek this early in the morning. The relatively quiet and somewhat lonesome walk did much to calm her nerves.

The weather felt perfect. The sun shone and everything had a glow about it. The trees, the grass, and the bushes radiated a brighter green. It brought a smile to her face. She tried to put the anger toward her mother behind her, though she did not like having her friend judged like that.

Now is my chance. My old class will think I'm weird for staying back. My current class thinks I'm weird for being older than them, but I can be the new me. I'll be like one of those girls in the movies who gets a makeover and the next day, I'll be cool. Guys will like me because I'm smart. And once the guys like me, the cool girls will like me. I'll be the freshman who has the in with the upper classmen, just like Betty said. I already know a bunch of sophomores. Now that I've got the trendy clothes and a new amginE Armer, I'll definitely fit in.

As the neighborhoods faded away and Shell started to pass more shops and stores, she started seeing more people walking in her same direction. A block away from the school she still hadn't recognized anyone—not that she expected more than the occasional familiar face. It concerned her more so that she really couldn't see very well. People looked blurry. She glanced around at other things—street signs, store names. She could make out all of the words.

Her eyes glanced at a few of the scattered trees along the sidewalk and the glow she noticed earlier seemed a bit exaggerated. "Should trees be that green?"

Shell rounded a corner and saw hundreds of kids piling in through the front gates of her new school. Her anxiety skyrocketed. She breathed heavily as her chest heaved in and out, and she rubbed her eyes until they turned red. The thought of high school gave her enough to worry about, but this new development with her vision only made matters worse.

As she joined the herd and entered the school's gates, she heard a pounding coming from inside the school's front entrance. The bright sun made the double doors and halls beyond them appear cavernous. *Thump. Thump. Thump.* A repeating beat that echoed over the crowd took Shell back to a vision from her dream. She knew a swarm of students trudged behind her, but she felt an eerie presence. "Fear me," echoed in her mind.

First came the memory of the noise she had heard outside her bedroom window. Her face paled as she recalled her fears of someone approaching, of getting sucked out of her window, and the pain of getting thrown up against the wall. Dream or not, it felt real then and felt real to her at this moment.

No longer did she want to go into the school. She tried to stop in place and turn around, but the corralling crowd of people forced her to move closer to the cave's mouth. The thumping grew louder and louder. Screaming came from inside the building. Overwhelmed by the situation, she started to cry, certain that some massive monster from her dream would devour her as soon as she walked inside. People stood outside the door, facing her. She could not make out their faces either, though she could see them ushering people to their doom.

Step by step, she inched closer to the school's mouth. Claustrophobia set in as the masses squeezed her through the funnel. Facing the inevitable with only hope to protect her, Shell closed her eyes. As soon as she did, another vision came to her from her dream about the ominous trees in the frightening jungle parting in front of her.

Thoughts lapped one on top of another like a dog's tongue at a water bowl. *If I scream, maybe I can stop everyone behind me. Then I won't have to go to school and satisfy the appetite of an unspeakable beast. But no one else is scared. Maybe I'm seeing things. Maybe I'm hearing things. It was just a bad dream, right? If I scream, everyone will think I'm crazy.*

She kept her eyes shut and stepped across the threshold.

The thumping continued. The cold breeze from the school's air conditioning washed through her hair. She held her breath, waiting for the thumping monster from her dream to fulfill its purpose. Then, the screaming she heard started to make sense, and could detect words and laughter.

Chapter 8 - This just in...

Sitting in her studio with cameras and bright lights pointing at her from every direction, her three-dimensional image projected on televisions, second screens, and third screens around the world. Mrs. Wayburn sat confidently, smiled, and greeted her audience.

"Good morning, I am Victoria Wayburn. If you are watching this, then I am glad you survived last night's worldwide catastrophe. In the history of recorded weather, never has a storm encompassed the entire planet at one time. Never before have we collected readings of more than seven hundred tornadoes touching down in a twenty-four hour period. Data continues to pour in, but many lakes and rivers have flooded, dams and levees have been destroyed, thousands have died and countless more are without basic necessities.

"Hours of footage and hundreds of stories have been brought to our attention from both professional and amateur sources. While the validity of some pieces cannot be confirmed, the sheer volume of contributions is overwhelming. Videos like this tree in Washington that appears to bend at the trunk to avoid a lightning strike, or this camera phone footage of what appears to be a bear with eight legs crawling on top of a cabin in North Dakota represent some of the questionable information we've received. Some reports are more positive, like the boy who caught a baby that had been thrown by one of the tornadoes in Texas. We are still filtering through the international stories, but we did come across an apparent snowstorm in Dubai after the rainstorm ended, a woman who drove a motorcycle on top of the ocean off the coast of Japan, and we still remain skeptical of an often-reported flying alligator in Thailand.

"We are hosting all of our submitted stories and videos on our sister WeTube site under the hash tag 'Great Storm.' Feel free to upload your own or comment on the listed stories.

"While it is not our place to draw comparisons to religious doctrines, it is hard to deny that several miracles, miracles by many definitions, did take place around the world just hours ago. The storm's impact remains to be seen. Just know that we will be with you every step of the way to keep you informed as we move forward, together. I am Victoria Wayburn and this is the GNN."

Chapter 9 - Elsewhere

"Mommy! Mommy!" A toddler yelled while standing on the Cadiz shore. "There's a man in the water." The toddler pointed to an unconscious man strapped to a plank of wood who lay in the surf with waves gently rocking his pale body. The mother rushed to her child, scooping him up before he could touch the body as it washed ashore. Her actions drew the attention of the lifeguard on duty, who blew his whistle frantically when he spotted the toddler's discovery.

The whistleblowing echoed down the shore to the nearby docks, where several men dressed in white jumpsuits rummaged through the remains of a severely damaged submersible, disconnecting and collecting computers, cameras, hard drives, and all forms of information-gathering equipment from the critically damaged vessel.

One of the men in white looked up from his scavenging to see a crowd of people form a circle around a body on the shore. He pointed the site out to his

Elsewhere

similarly dressed counterparts, one of whom instantly made a phone call but did not speak, only nodding several times before hanging up.

Chapter 10 - After Math

Shell slowly opened her eyes to a river of blurry faces. "Brown squirrel. Brown squirrel. Shake your bushy tail!" People sang and danced and chanted all around her, motioning to the words of the song. "Crinkle up your little nose. Shove it down between your toes." Bigger, older kids, one of whom Shell saw beating a drum, all wore matching shirts, lined the sides of the hall and sang the loudest, ordering the younger, smaller freshmen to join them in the singing. "Brown squirrel. Brown squirrel. Shake your bushy tail."

Despite the festiveness of the unexpected pep rally, Shell remained quite freaked out. A hall full of blurry faces she couldn't make out did little to ease her mind, but she did not scream or run away. Her face turned a bright shade of red and she may have stopped breathing on occasion, but at least no monsters tried to eat her.

"Hi, Sea Shell. Long time no see," two voices laughed in unison.

AFTER MATH

In Shell's current state, she had to guess at who stood in front of her. From the similarly styled attire along with their high-pitched nasal-heavy accent, Shell had a pretty good idea who she had run into. She played along.

"Hey," she embellished. "Yeah. I guess it has been a little while."

"We didn't think you'd ever make it to high school," one of them said as the two girls only pretended to hold back their laughs.

Irritation infiltrated Shell's chest. The Miller twins had served as the bane of most of her education and it looked like it would continue in high school. *I guess not everyone matures with age.*

"So, welcome to Riverside," said one twin.

"Took you long enough," the other chimed in.

"I know you're a little slow, so let me explain something," the first one began. By now, Shell could tell the two apart. Veronica, the bossier and meaner of the two and who typically did most of the talking, slowed down her speech as she delivered an overly thought out insult. "You're still a freshman and freshmen have to pay dues. So, you're going to be the school mascot and," before Shell could see the hands moving toward her, Veronica ripped her necklace off with a *pop*, "instead," Veronica continued as she placed some other cheaper necklace around Shell, "you can wear a turtle shell."

The twins' roaring laughter bounced off of the cinder block walls of the hallway, echoing around Shell in surround sound. The itchy, brittle yarn around Shell's neck and the heavy weight of the box turtle shell hanging from it tugged on Shell's spirit. The burden of embarrassment made her want to collapse to the ground. The memory of her picking out her necklace in Hawaii, running it over to her dad and asking him to buy it for her played like a 3D movie in her mind. *My shell...*

"Daddy, please? Can I have this one? It's so pretty," *pleaded a happy, younger Shell.*

"Now's not the time Shell," responded a somber Mr. *Wayburn. He tugged at the soaking white collar snuggly wrapped* *around his neck.*

"But I've never seen one like this before. Where else will I *be able to get one like this?" She hopped up and down at her* *father's feet. The oversized pearl necklace she wore bounced* *awkwardly against the collar of her black dress. "Please, Daddy.* *The lady said I could have it for forty dollars. She said it was a* *special price, just for me." Shell extended the necklace she wanted* *in her hand with the beautiful white shell up for her father to see.*

Mr. Wayburn turned and snatched the necklace out of her *hand. His tears nearly turned to steam in his burning eyes. Shell* *pulled her hand away and took a frightened step back from the* *man she hardly recognized.*

Witty comebacks ricocheted inside Shell's head like spit balls, waiting for her mouth to pull the trigger. But the Millers' cruel trick left her flabbergasted.

"Roni!" Shell boomed over their laughter, attracting more attention to their spat.

"Oooh," Veronica grumbled. "Don't call me that."

"Give me back my necklace right now or I'll..." Before Shell could get the words out, she was interrupted.

"Get to ya classrooms," bellowed Mr. Hollis in a deep, intimidating Bostonian accent. The tall, slender teacher towered over the three girls with a demeaning look in his eyes.

AFTER MATH

"Yes, Mr. Hollis," the Millers recited as they scampered off, leaving Shell standing in front of him with a turtle shell hanging from her neck.

"Do ya know where ya going, young lady?"

"I think so," Shell responded bitterly.

"Well get there quickly and quietly and take that shell back to Mrs. Hughes afta class."

The rest of the morning did not go well for Shell. She spent the entire fifty minutes of each period staring at inanimate objects, especially the clock, afraid of the blurry faces and especially afraid of how she might embarrass herself if she told others what she saw. During lunchtime, she found a seat that faced a wall and sat alone while she ate.

"Way to go, cool kid," Shell taunted herself. "It's the first day of high school and you're already the weirdo."

A familiar voice asked, "What are you doing over here?"

She looked up and stared directly at the person asking, but she could not make out who was speaking, so she said nothing.

"Really? Now that you're in high school, you don't know me anymore?" said the young male voice.

"Topher?" Shell pleaded.

"Wow," he exclaimed, exasperated. "Freshmen." He took a moment to express his disappointment. "I get it. Well, enjoy your private little lunch," Topher stated as he began to walk off.

"Please!" Shell blurted with pain and desperation. "Please sit."

Topher paused for a moment before sitting next to her, facing the wall.

"Making a lot of friends today?"

61

"It's been a nightmare," she replied. "I think I'm going blind."

"It's your first day. You're probably just nervous." He tried to ease her fears. "How was your summer?"

Shell continued to stare at the wall while she caught up with him, still trying to temper the anxiety of losing her sight. She filled him in on her days at the hospital candy striping and the people she met. She went on about how annoyed she felt that her parents made her do it and how she didn't learn anything that could help her through science classes.

"You? Volunteering? Really? I never would have guessed," he remarked.

"I know, right? I didn't really volunteer for it, but it wasn't all bad. The nurses were pretty nice." Shell smiled for the first time since school started. "How did you spend your summer?"

"I think the word is 'grounded,' " Topher said with all sincerity.

Shell couldn't help but chuckle. "Seriously?" She asked through a smirk.

Topher's blank stare revealed a young man who dreaded his memories. She guessed by his silence that she should stop smirking.

"Yeah. Jack…," he hesitated before continuing. "Jack, he, I guess… I don't think he really wants me around, but he didn't want me leaving much either."

"I'm sorry, T." Shell felt bad for laughing.

"I simul-played a lot, though."

"Ooh, I just got a Armer. What are you playing?" Shell asked eagerly.

"Nice. You gotta play SWE. 'Social Wrestling Entertainment'," he detailed. "You vote on who you want to win. Both wrestlers wear these gravity bands on their wrists and ankles and the one with the least votes has to wrestle with the bands weighing him down. It's crazy when the guy no one wants to win still does!"

"Got anything less… violent?"

Topher chuckled. "amginE lists all the game shows on-line. They've got Regional Feud. It's trivia and you can help your town or your city win. There's some books that have all kinds of games you can simul-play along with. *Kingdoms of America* is pretty awesome. It's this story where America gets all medieval and each city has a king and ruined buildings become their castles. There's the book you can read, but they have this cool app that will show you what that world would look like from wherever you're standing. Sometimes characters from the show appear and you can chat with them. They'll ask what you think they should do and you can watch the decision they make on the TV show. I play along with the battles, mostly. Halfway through the show, you can join the big battle and depending on who wins, you'll see a different scene after the break."

"Don't they have those major events where people all meet up in random places and play against each other? So now that I have a Armer, I can play too, right?"

"Yeah, but you could have played without one. It's just more fun with one." Topher chuckled as the school bell rang, indicating the time had come to head to class again. "Are you walking home after school?" Topher asked with a shy smile.

"Wow, we haven't walked home after school since—," Shell stopped her response short. Reminders of her mom holding her back aggravated her more than she expected. "I actually have to stop by the hospital today. I forgot to leave my candy-striping apron with the nurses. What are you doing?"

"Probably just heading to Jack's; do my homework, get on-line, nothing special. Do you know where your next class is?"

"No idea. I'm looking for Mr. Hollis. Algebra II."

"I'm sorta headed that way."

And with that, Topher and Shell headed out of the cafeteria. Shell noticed as she passed the trashcans that he didn't have anything to throw away. *Maybe he ate earlier.*

They walked down one hall for a ways, past the school library. Shell continued to rub her eyes, wondering why she couldn't make out any faces. She started to notice that their clothes began looking grayed-out and blurry as well. She kept thinking her eyes had gone bad, but she could see so many other things clearly.

"Down that hall to your left," Topher guided, pointing in the general direction for her to head. "You'll see the room numbers and teacher names as you get closer."

"Thanks, Topher. If I don't see you the rest of the day, I'll see you tomorrow."

"Sounds good. See you soon."

Tick-tock-tick-tock, taunted the clock.

Day one of high school and, if you asked Shell, time had already found it amusing to mock her with the reward students never long for—the slower passing of it.

She squirmed in her one-size-fits-all school chair-desk. Nothing the teacher said registered. Large animated digital maps could not pull her eyes from the one-hundred-year-old analog clock mounted and encaged on the wall. Her assignment flashed unnoticed on her touch-screen desktop. Only the clock could garner her attention.

Stress had already taken enough of a toll on her for the day. With her condition worsening as the day progressed, blurred faces were now contorting and she knew the second she looked at anyone else, the images would come again, making the people she looked at appear even weirder than before. Despite the inevitability that what she wanted most would bring what she wanted least—to be surrounded by a crowd of shadowy people, not knowing if those shadows hid whom she should 'fear'—she still longed for the school day to end.

Brrrrrrrrrring. Shell wriggled from her desk, having prepared for her abrupt departure the second she sat down. Unfortunately, she had to make her way out from the back of the classroom. Her eyes fixated on the door and she dodged the slower students who showed far less urgency to get out of class than she. Ignoring the blurry visions all around her that oozed from their seats, Shell beat everyone to the door, except for one person—Mr. Hollis.

"Please be sure ta submit ya assignments via tha intraport by tomorra morning; no later than seven o'clock." Mr. Hollis yelled over the blaring school bell and rustling students. "And don't forget ta have ya parents digi-sign it fa confamation."

Shell froze in fear, as her visions appeared more severe than before. Kids bumped into her from behind. The teacher stood twice her height. His attempt to dress modern in the 1920s "retro-reborn" style of the day peaked distortedly through the rippling clouds that funneled around his body. It disturbed her that she had no idea what he looked like.

Mr. Hollis finally freed the mob and let pour the masses from their period-long captivity. Students swarmed out of the rooms like bees from a hive. The swelling crowd of chaos behind Shell funneled her down the hallway. She kept her eyes closed and bumped her way along until the force behind her subsided, leaving her washed ashore like an inept jellyfish. Her eyes found peace once she opened them and realized she faced a brick wall. She needed to make her way to the bus stop, but could not tell which direction to head. Timidly, she turned around, testing her courage. A sea of hazy, wavy, blurry-faced, cloud-covered mini-tornadoes spun all around her.

Shell took in a deep breath, tucked her chin into her chest, and charged her way through the crowd. She could scarcely breathe as she bounced off students, immersing herself in the flow of traffic, hoping that she would eventually be led to the exit.

"Where's your shell, Shell?" Veronica's squeaky voice asked rhetorically before her obnoxious laughing attracted the attention of everyone in sight. "It looked so good on you."

Shell peered through the fog surrounding Veronica, searching for her necklace. She could not see it, but she knew Veronica would wear it as if she owned it. She did not know if she saw something small and white around Veronica's neck because she wanted to see it or if she truly did see it, but something inside of Shell exploded. Without saying a word, she lunged toward Roni's neck, aiming to take her necklace back by force. Unnecessarily loud and exaggerated screaming ensued. Shell grabbed and reached blindly, not letting go of anything she got her hands on.

"What's going on?" A voice boomed from down the hall, nearly drowning out the circle of cheering students surrounding Veronica and Shell.

"The principal's coming. The principal's coming," voices repeated.

Nothing made sense to Shell, she looked away from Veronica for just a moment to take in the surroundings of her very first fight could not understand how a day she had so looked forward to ended up with her surrounded by cloudy figure after cloudy figure. *This is what it looks like inside a tornado.* Shell saw a taller figure step into the circle.

Instincts took over. Shell looked around the circle, back to Veronica, at the principal, and then around the circle again. Behind her and past the crowd, beyond the school doors, she spotted trees waving in the distance. She turned back around, pushed Veronica into the principal and ran through the crowd.

"Stop that girl!" Principal Turnsnip shouted, to no avail.

Stupid Roni! Shell screamed in her head. *Just when I thought today couldn't get any worse.*

Chapter II - Sore for Sad Eyes

Exhausted, dejected, and on the verge of tears, Shell waited at a bus stop several blocks away from Riverside High School and thought about her fight, the likely suspension waiting for her, and the punishment she would get from her parents. It all made her feel like an absolute failure. *I try so hard to make everyone happy and it doesn't matter.* She raised her chin skyward; stretching her cramped neck after a day's worth of cowering, and embraced the sun's energy. The world did not look the same as it had before the storm. People especially. Plants, animals, and even rocks—a haze shrouded everything, but she found a beauty in it, as if someone had unlocked a hidden part of the world that she wished everyone could see.

Cloudy mists smeared her visions like a bright foggy morning. Hues bled and blended together. A large yellow school bus passed by, driving under a lush tree and created a soft shade of blue where the green leaves brushed against the painted roof of the bus. Even the sun had a magnificent light-green aura as it radiated through the light blue sky. She noticed something new in the people walking by. Shallow, waterless puddles pooled around people's feet, gently rippling translucent waves outward from them.

Quietly sitting on the city bus brought Shell her first peaceful moment of the day. After walking past a clutch of blurry, grayed-out strangers, she took solace in her unobstructed view of the passing scenery and the blanketing white noise around her. She stared out of the window the entire ride to the hospital, wondering why all of the plant life seemed to glow with such vibrancy.

The lobby appeared in stark contrast to the pandemonium from the day before. Shell casually walked past the security desk, and headed up the elevator to the third floor where she found the situation a bit more hectic.

Doctors and nurses scampered up and down the halls. Their shoes clomped and squeaked over the linoleum floors. From all the noise and panicked conversations, something serious had everyone's attention. Shell squinted and strained, trying to see through the gray and cloudy concealments to make out faces and expressions. She found it frustrating that everyone at the hospital looked the same without a face; each nurse looked like every other nurse and the same with doctors.

This is why everyone needs to wear their own outfits with their own style.

She headed for the nurses' station, where she could see a woman sitting behind the counter, taking phone calls. Shell approached her, whose voice started to sound familiar, and pulled out the apron she brought in to return, using it as an excuse to join the fray, and plopped it on the counter in front of the woman.

"Hey," Shell said, unsure of whom she was greeting.

"Shell!" the woman exclaimed, giving her good reason to believe that she had found Nurse Janie. "What are you doing here?"

"I forgot to leave my apron so I brought it back."

"You are the best. We've got a box of extras, but thank you for returning it," said Nurse Janie as she continued to juggle work on her computer, a constantly ringing telephone, and a pile of tablets.

"Of course," Shell responded, not sure of what else to say. "So what's going on? Is everything okay?"

"Oh, don't you worry. We've got things…" Nurse Janie took a deep breath and forced a smile, "under control."

"I'm happy to help out if I can," she offered, surprised by her own generosity.

"It's still visiting hours," Nurse Janie replied with a sly tone. "If you'd like to say hello to a few of your old friends, I don't think that would hurt."

A smile crept across Shell's face.

"But if you see a bunch of doctors in any of the rooms, it's best to leave them be."

"Got it," Shell replied before she skipped down the hall, dodging doctors, nurses, gurneys, and various hall cluttering computerized mobile medical monitors.

The rooms on the third floor seemed fuller than usual. *Storm victims,* Shell thought. She peeked into the first room and regretted her offer to help out. With everyone looking blurry, she couldn't tell if she recognized the patients or not. It occurred to her then that she remembered patients better by face than by name. She also couldn't tell if going into a room would wake up a patient or not since the patients appeared asleep in their reclined beds.

Shell worked her way quickly down the hall, ignoring anyone that didn't call out to her. She had nearly finished her lap when she noticed two doctors and a nurse rushing inside the room where she remembered meeting Betty. Shell approached the door slowly to avoid attention, peeked inside, and saw the makings of a living horror show. Dozens of machines, tubes, and wires were connected to the older woman like an inside-out computer. Some sort of tarp covered her body while the wires poked through it. Shell had looked in on operations and emergencies over the summer, but she never saw such chaos. The blurry images of the doctors swirled like phantoms around Betty as they poked and prodded their twisting and lurching patient. Her arms and legs had been strapped down to the bed and she screamed into the plastic mask that covered the nose and mouth on her discolored face. *Why does her face look like that? Why can I see her face and no one else's?*

Shell spun back and covered her mouth to keep from screaming. She doubted the doctors and nurses would or needed to do all of that to Betty. She clicked on the iChart tablet on the wall outside of the room to confirm the patient's name. Betty Harmony popped up. Next to the word diagnosis, it read Alzheimer's. An empty box below her name asked for a passcode to see patient's details. Shell tried the code the nurses gave her during her internship. 'ACCESS DENIED.'

Poor Betty. Shell wondered what happened to cause all of this. She peered back into the room. She couldn't help but watch the horror unfold. All of Betty's convulsing shook aside a portion of the tarp covering her, revealing to Shell more of what she could not explain. The same discoloration Shell had seen on Betty's face existed on the exposed portion of Betty's arm and leg. The colors appeared quite clear to Shell. She did not see the grayish blur around Betty that she saw around everyone else. Betty's hand looked like it had a colorful glove on it with each finger and her palm a different color. The colors on her legs reflected a similar random arrangement to those on her face.

The odd sight transfixed Shell. She almost forgot about the torture Betty was experiencing. Amidst the chaos, Betty's eyes connected with Shell's. A long, slow, pleading stare of desperation from the older woman sent a chill down Shell's spine and nearly brought her to her knees. Shell knew Betty wanted her help, but instead took a step back. She couldn't break eye contact with the sad old woman who looked more confused than anyone around her, but she took another step away from Betty, and continued to do so until she made it all the way home.

Chapter 12 - Indigestion

Shell bolted through the front door of her home and slammed it behind her. She felt tired, distraught, confused, and overwhelmed as she leaned her back against the door, as if keeping out an army of evil that had her home from the hospital. Her chest heaved in and out as she caught her breath, inhaling the aroma of lemons and capers from her mom's chicken piccata.

"You're just in time for dinner," called Mrs. Wayburn. "I'm glad you're home. I was getting worried. I thought you were coming straight home after school."

Shell's stomach dropped immediately. It had not dawned on her until now that the principal may have called her parents. *Do they know? Did someone tell them already? Who gets a call home from the principal on the first day of school?*

"I'm not hungry," she replied with a residual tone from their squabble earlier that morning, desperate to escape to her room. She snuck toward the stairs, which

73

stood closer to her than the kitchen, hoping she would meet no resistance.

"Now, now, Miss High School Freshman," her mom played the cute, friendly, inviting card, "we don't skip dinner. And we're dying to hear how school went."

"It sucked," she snapped as she gave up on tiptoeing and started her rapid ascent to her room.

"Shell!" thundered Mr. Wayburn. "Join us for dinner."

Shell stopped in her tracks as a bead a sweat formed on her brow. *They know.* She paused for a moment before heading back downstairs. *He never used to sound this angry.* She turned the last step toward the kitchen, her head down, eyeing the metal strip on the floor that separated the wooden floor of the hallway from the ceramic tile of the kitchen. She lifted her chin like a scolded child forced to look into the eyes of an angry parent, afraid their eyes alone could inflict pain, and cringed as she walked toward the table.

The reaffirmation of the blurry visions that had plagued her all day made her more self-conscious than she had felt all day. She inhaled deeply and took her place at the dining table, staring down at her decorative place setting until her mother interrupted her view with a plate of food. She felt everyone's eyes resting on her. She could sense Skitch reveling in her misery.

Shell loved chicken piccata, especially when her mom made it with spaghetti. She loved it so much that she used to order it at every restaurant she could find it in, just to prove her mom made it better. Even Topher said he never tasted better. But now the meal smelled sour and her stomach turned at the thought of eating it.

"Excited?" Mrs. Wayburn asked. "I had a feeling you needed a little pick-me-up."

INDIGESTION

Shell realized that staring at her plate made her look eager to dig in. Playing along, she looked up toward her mom, closed her eyes before she could see her blurry face, and gave her a big smile. Mrs. Wayburn sat in her seat and then the customs commenced.

"Thanks for dinner, Hun. It looks amazing," Mr. Wayburn said.

"Thanks for dinner, Mom," Shell and her brother echoed in unison.

"Oh, everyone is welcome." Mrs. Wayburn smiled as she sat upright in her chair, observing everyone's reactions to the meal.

Mr. Wayburn, in keeping with standard operating procedure, asked rather nonchalantly, disregarding Shell's comments just before dinner, "So, how was everyone's day?"

Really?

Skitch blurted out, "I'm going to get to kill frogs this year. And we're taking a field trip to Washington, D.C."

"Well, that sounds like someone will be working part-time to save up for that trip," Mr. Wayburn replied.

Mrs. Wayburn turned to Shell. The two of them always exchanged glances when they saw Dad getting sarcastic with Skitch, only Shell didn't look up this time.

"Dad! Come on! I've got school."

"It's a good thing your weekends are free," Mr. Wayburn quipped.

"No one else in my grade has a job," Skitch whined.

Their father chuckled. "Then it should make it much easier for you to find one."

Skitch probably knew he didn't have an excuse for not working. Shell giggled as she imagined the bulging vein that always ran down the middle of Skitch's forehead whenever he thought hard.

"What are you laughing at?" Skitch demanded with a glare in her direction.

She only shook her head and avoided looking up.

"Well, things have been crazy at the station," Mrs. Wayburn began. "More and weirder stories keep coming in. I'm thinking about putting together a piece on how they seem to be related."

Shell had a hard time believing anything could top how weird her day had gone. "Stories about what?" she whispered, though no one noticed her sarcasm.

"Our blog sites exploded last night and they kept coming in all day today," continued Mrs. Wayburn. "Everyone seems to have something to say about that crazy storm. Tons and tons of posts about it being a sign and people shouldn't drink water, and should stay out of oceans, rivers, and lakes. The list goes on. But our affiliates fed us some interesting stories too about really peculiar events from around the whole world."

Shell perked up. She recognized the "news angle" excitement in her mom's voice when she got all 'broadcast-y.' Working as an anchorwoman, her mom always had her eye on tomorrow.

"And I think you'll like hearing this, too, honey," Mrs. Wayburn went on, directing her attention to her husband. "A medical development compound in Africa was running a trial to combat a viral disease that infected every patient at the facility. Well, the storm hit them at night, and when they woke up the next morning all of the patients were cured. It's a miracle! The doctors said they hadn't administered anything that could have cured everyone overnight. They're skeptical, but the people in the village believe it was the rain. The funny thing is, not everyone was exposed to the storm. Many of them had been quarantined, but somehow everyone was cured."

"I heard about that," Mr. Wayburn replied, sounding somewhat down about it. "That was one of our research facilities. We were treating a new form of cancer. It's rather painful and disfiguring. I'll spare you the details, but we diagnosed it over ten years ago and haven't been able to do much more than help prolong lives. It's been tough for our staff over there."

While Skitch had moved on to making a second plate of food, disregarding his parents' deliberation about other events and their relation to science, Shell sat at full attention. Each story she heard filled her with more curiosity and more hope. Her head swiveled like a spectator at a tennis match. Her eyes strained as she tried to see past the impenetrable fog surrounding her parents.

Her mother noticed. "Are you okay, dear? You're squinting. Do your eyes hurt?"

Shell flinched, as she had never considered what she looked like to everyone else with her new predicament. She refocused her attention on the untouched chicken piccata. She wanted to tell them what she had gone through all day. She wanted to tell them about all the blurry visions and about what she saw at the hospital. She considered downplaying the whole thing and just saying she thought she might need glasses, but figured that would just make her look weaker in her parents' eyes. "I'm fine."

Mrs. Wayburn, directing her remarks to her husband again, said, "I bet the staff was excited to see everyone doing better, right, honey?"

"Oh, um, perhaps. Shocked mostly. From a research perspective, not knowing the cure is still the obstacle, which is why we're there. We've got so many questions. Everyone is pouring over the data and retesting everyone now to figure out what happened. Technology like that can change the world."

Shell chimed in. "Dad, how can technology make a miracle? Why can't it just be a miracle?"

"Technology makes miracles happen every day. The ability to connect with people through phones, computers, and televisions, or being able to witness events from around the world in real-time are miracles that we make happen. We've cured diseases in the past and we'll cure more in the future. We just have to figure out how to do it."

She had no rebuttal, so she sat back in her chair and slowly began to eat some food while her father continued.

"When miracles happen, we typically just accept them as miracles, but if we dig deep enough, we figure out the truth. There's always an explanation. That's what science is all about."

"And if anyone can figure it out, Shell-bell, it's your father," Mrs. Wayburn said with a smile as she beamed across the table at her husband, proud of his genius and accomplishments.

Getting back to the facts, Mr. Wayburn continued, "If we can isolate the solution, we'll be able to replicate it and provide cures for the millions of others who suffer from this disease."

Skitch jumped in, proving he had some sense. "If the rain fixed them, could the rain fix people with different problems?"

"Possibly," their father replied. "Supposedly, it rained all around the world, but we didn't get any reports from other facilities about overnight cures. We still need to check, though. All we know about that location in

INDIGESTION

Africa so far is that Sunday was a typical day with patients and treatments, but when the storm hit, it was night time and most of the patients not in quarantine along with many of the doctors at the compound came out of their tents and started dancing in the rain. According to reports, that area had not seen rain in over two years, and everyone played in the mud until the storm got too dangerous."

"Isn't that amazing?" Mrs. Wayburn asked. "And I heard another story, a little scarier, about all of the animals in a zoo disappearing. Witnesses say that one of the tornadoes," then, interrupting her own thought, "— by the way, did you know that we recorded over seven hundred and twenty tornadoes last night? There may have been more, but that's never been seen before."

"So what happened at the zoo?" Shell pressed.

"Oh, right. The witnesses say that one of the tornadoes blew straight through the zoo. Ooh, I made a rhyme!" She giggled, typically the first to laugh at her own jokes. "Anyway, some think the tornado sucked them all up - but the buildings and cages remained intact. All of the snakes were housed in a locked building and inside secure glass tanks, but they were all gone. Not a bit of damage anywhere. It's a bit of an enigma."

"Do you think someone stole them or could it be another miracle?" Skitch asked.

"I don't know, sweetie, but our staff is tracking down as many miracle stories as we can. If there are people out there who can explain these miracles, it would be beneficial to have them come forward and share their tales with the rest of the world, don't you think?"

Shell could hardly contain herself. She yearned to share her story, but doubted anyone would believe her. Nothing miraculous had taken place. She never heard of

79

a day more opposite to miraculous than hers. So, she bit her lip and kept quiet, but it excited her to hear about so many crazy things going on in so many places.

Then, a thought occurred to her. "Do you think people are making the miracles happen?" Her voice came out as a whisper, as if speaking louder would have revealed too much about her own situation.

"I mean, it's kind of farfetched that people could suddenly do these amazing things," Mrs. Wayburn responded, tapping her chin. "But if they could, imagine the good they could do."

Skitch nearly jumped out of his chair with excitement. "You mean people with powers?"

"I doubt you're going to see people flying around like super heroes," Shell said with a smile.

"Why not?" Skitch countered. His thoughts avalanched from his mouth. "If people had powers, they'd totally be heroes—unless they're bad guys. That would be spazzy. Imagine if they just went around blowing stuff up and sucking the life out of people."

"What would you do if you came across someone with powers?" Shell asked.

Skitch replied first. "I'd ask if they were good guys or bad guys. Then I'd ask to see their powers and maybe for an autograph."

Shell swung her head around to her mom, silently asking for her answer.

"I'd love to interview them, ask them how they feel, what it's like to have powers, what they would want to do with their abilities. I think it would make for great television."

Last, she turned to her father, who shared his reluctance to participate through his hesitation to respond.

INDIGESTION

"I guess I'd strap them to a chair so I could run some experiments to see how they're able to do what they do, and figure out if we could replicate their abilities somehow."

His answer struck Shell like a spike to the chest. *That must be what they were doing to Betty; strapping her down and experimenting on her.* She felt transported back to the hospital, back to Betty's room. She could feel Betty's eyes boring into her soul.

Her voice quivered. "But what if they're scared? What if they think they're cursed?" she asked. "What if they don't want to have their powers or want other people to know there's something different about them?" Her emotions escalated and her face blushed.

"Calm down. Let's not get carried away," Mr. Wayburn interjected. "No one has any magic powers, so there's nothing to worry about."

"That would be so cool," Skitch blurted.

"I think so, too," Mrs. Wayburn whispered, inciting Mr. Wayburn to shoot her a disappointed glance.

"Did you kids do all of your homework?" he asked, changing the subject.

After some grumbling about schoolwork, everyone finished their plates and helped clear the table. Shell felt worse after dinner. *Would dad really strap me to chair and run experiments on me?* She wondered. *What would he do if he found someone that could make these miracles happen? What would his company, or companies like his do with someone like me?* She ran up to her room after cleaning up and hopped on her Scroll, searching for any stories she could find about the previous night's storm.

Hours passed like minutes. Shell came across weather sites talking about the storm, blogs reporting updates on disasters and unexplainable events, conspiracy theory sites talking about the end of days and government cover-ups, and religious sites from around the world sharing their interpretations of the great flood. She ran searches for miracles, and Africa, and zoo disappearances. Everything her mom said seemed true. She narrowed her search down to local news, and mostly came across stories about looting in Manhattan during the storm.

She did not find much information for miracles nearby, but just as she considered rolling up her Scroll, she came across a gossip blog posting about a woman in a hospital causing quite a ruckus. Apparently, an elderly woman being treated for Alzheimer's had become temporarily untreatable when doctors tried to draw blood and give her I.V. fluids. The blogger wrote about overhearing nurses say things like, "the needles are exploding," "the solutions are solidifying," and "solids are turning into liquids."

What if they're talking about Betty? Shell speculated. *What are they going to do with her? Are they going to torture her? Are they going to force her to do things? Evil things? What would they do to me if I were like Betty?* Her mind flooded with the terrifying possibilities until she drowned in sleep.

Chapter 13 - Elsewhere

Carl Matheson woke up to a foul stench. Having grown up in New York City, he likened himself to a chef in terms of his ability to identify odors. Given his current situation, the stench of homelessness served as the most prominent of aromas he reckoned with on a day-to-day basis. It radiated from any homeless person seven to ten feet in every direction and lingered for at least forty-five minutes after they left. It recalled the aroma of a misused and forgotten sock left crumpled in the dark corner of a dirty bathroom long enough to spawn its own living organisms. Its unsightliness and stench encouraged everyone to avoid it at all costs.

Carl knew all of this and considered himself an expert on the subject since he became homeless three months prior to this particular evening and now lived in a damp, musty alley, hidden behind some trashcans in a light-deprived corner next to his old apartment building. Fortunately for him, just after he got evicted and before he ran out of money sleeping in overnight motels, he caught an episode of *Surviving the Wild—New York City*, a show that gave directions on how to live as a homeless person. The warped reality show became applicable after the Economic Hindenburg forced the closing of three-dozen blue chip companies and much of the United States became unemployed. Carl had lost his finance job late into the crash. He didn't think he'd wind up on the chopping block the way his friends had, so he found himself at the end of the line when the Wet Debt rebound hiring took off. Despite his claims to the Wet Debt concept of restructuring the investment world to a borrowing-only format, Carl walked away from interviews to the sounds of laughter and rejection.

He came to homelessness somewhat prepared. He had a strategy for staying as clean as possible, avoiding starvation, using the bathroom, and the best way of brushing his teeth. Back when he had his own apartment, he prided himself on how clean he kept his place, bragging about how he never had a cockroach step foot in his home. In the world of homeless abodes, Carl ran a pretty tight ship. He saw his current predicament as a temporary bump in the road.

This evening, however, Carl did not wake up to the smell of homelessness. Initially, he found the putrid stench of his body odor both shocking and appalling, but this stench nearly choked him with its acidity. He looked around, trying to find the source. The sun had yet to rise and the distant street lamp shed a cloudy haze near Carl's cardboard mattress, revealing nothing but the garbage he fell asleep looking at the night before. Despite his propensity for clean living, he had never lived a healthy lifestyle. The habitual smoker and binge eater literally ate himself out of house and home when he lost his job and spent the majority of what he had left on food, so it took him a while to roll over his large, bloated frame and see if the stench radiated from behind him.

The crunching, cracking, and popping began instantly. By the time Carl turned himself around, he heard more squishing and squashing than an army marching through a movie theater with a floor covered in popcorn. Then the clicking, hissing, and chirping began. The streetlight did little to help him see the cause of the heinous smell and annoying noise.

Carl fumbled for his lighter through his trash-filled pockets. He always kept one on him in case he scored a cigarette. His fat fingers stroked the spark wheel and pressed the fork repeatedly, but he could not get the flame to hold. The noise became louder as the odor grew stronger, until it surrounded him. Wildly, he flicked his lighter. Useless spark after useless spark teased him until, finally, he got a flame to hold. He extended the lighter into the darkness, searching for anything to reflect the light of the flame.

A glint—Carl saw the tiniest reflection bounce back at him. He squinted; adjusting his eyes, and saw more tiny reflections. Once his eyes started to comprehend the sight before them, his mind refused to believe it. The small flame revealed much in the dark alley that he had recently become his home, and in that light, he spotted hundreds and hundreds of small heads with whisker-like tentacles waving and little stick-like legs dancing while beady black eyes stared back at him.

He panicked. Still waking up and starved from days of rummaging for scraps, he struggled to get to his feet. Crunching and squirting accompanied every move he made. His hands smashed exoskeleton after exoskeleton as he pushed against the ground to stand up. With the lighter still in his hand, he noticed that his flame caught the cardboard he used for his bed. He tried to stomp it out, crushing bugs as he panicked.

"What the heck is going on?"

Then, almost predictably, his foot ignited like a Cub Scout campfire. The flame was small, but it reminded him that he had fallen asleep with his shoes off and only had a crusty old sock on his foot. He ran deeper into the alley, stomping on bugs along the way, kicking and flailing as he pounded his burning foot, trying to put out the fire, but the movement only incited the flame. It grew up to his ankle and the larger flame shed more light in the dark alley. Bugs skittered in every direction. They sat on the ground, on the walls, on the piled up boxes and old discarded family items that came to the alley to die.

Why are they all here? Why are they just staring like that? Then he felt the heat of the flames and yelped. *Stop, drop, and roll!* Carl remembered an old lesson on what to do if you caught on fire. He dropped to the ground and started rolling back and forth. He couldn't tell if the fire had gone out, but he had killed at least another hundred bugs. His clothes grew damp from the squashed bugs. The smell he noticed when he woke up still remained the most prominent thing in the alley, more overwhelming than the bugs themselves or the bite of the fire.

"What is that stench?" he asked out loud. Still rolling, having finally lost his temper, he yelled, "I wish these bugs would leave!"

Unsure of any progress, Carl continued rolling back and forth and did not stop until he felt cooler air around his foot. He propped himself up on one elbow and checked out his foot. With only the scarce light from the streetlight to aid him, he could barely see the charred remains of the bottom portion of his pant leg and a blackened sockless foot. He sat still a moment longer and noticed that the bugs had disappeared along with that putrid smell. "Did I really see all those bugs?"

He felt his shirt. Sticky ooze clung to his hand like honey, and he looked up, wondering where all the bugs had gone.

That was when he heard a faint buzzing. It sent a chill up his spine. It remained too dark to see what made the noise, so Carl crawled along the ground, reaching blindly for his lighter again. He had a vague idea of what he might see, but had to know. He found his lighter, flicked it on, and saw a swarm of flying roaches, flies, gnats, bees, crickets, and other insects he couldn't classify hovering above him. The wind from the swarm of flapping wings made the lighter flame flutter.

"This isn't happening," he muttered. He swatted at the bugs, hitting several, but not scaring any of them away. *What do they want with me? And what is that awful, awful smell?*

"Leave me alone!" he screamed. He darted out of the alley, tripping over the trashcans, and just kept running.

Chapter 14 - Different Strokes

Shell slept more peacefully that night, but dreamt still. This time, she swam through the streets of Manhattan. While everyone walked on the sidewalks and drove on the streets, to her, the ground had changed to a deep body of water. She swam everywhere. She could dive down and peek through the ground like a snorkeler. She watched the subways running underneath her and people walking above. She recognized a few monuments and familiar buildings, like the one where her mom worked. Buildings looked much taller and the water felt gritty, like the air in the subway on a hot summer day.

No one noticed her. She swam by strangers and familiar faces, like the Miller twins. Roni had on her necklace. Shell whispered to a school of swimming sewer rats that turned and swarmed Roni, biting and scratching only her before finally ripping off the necklace. The shell, on its leather string, sank out of sight until a dolphin the size of a seahorse caught it and swam it back to Shell before swimming away.

DIFFERENT STROKES

She swam on silently, even to the edge of the island, where the East River separated Manhattan from Brooklyn and Queens. She peered up and spied the bridges gleaming in uninterrupted sunlight. Yet, when she looked down at the water, the reflection was of multi-colored clouds that looked like quilts floating in a black sky. The image confused her, even beyond the confines of her dream, so she swam on as though to flee.

Her fun romp through the city was quickly transforming into something quite unnerving. Sensing evil lurking behind her, Shell started to pick up her pace. Without looking back, she knew someone chased her. She raced through the city, swimming with the speed and grace of a seal. She darted through the streets, swam through buildings, up and down stairs, through garages and restaurants. Yet still, no one saw her and she could not see her menace.

Next, the waters grew rough and the waves pushed her about. It became harder to navigate. The current built momentum and twisted into rapids like a river. Shell no longer had control of where she went. Faster and faster the waters swept her north through the city and what seemed like Sheep Meadow in Central Park. Trouble clung to her heels, so she swam with the tide, speeding past traffic and pedestrians until the river brought her to a roaring and foamy waterfall. The deafening rush of water ensured her demise. Shell wanted to turn around and swim against the force, but her fear would not let her look at what chased her. Something tugged at her ankle, but it did not feel like the current. She felt fingers wrap around her foot and pull sharply until it had her shoe. She screamed, but no one could hear her and no one came to her aid. She felt the hand again and this time it pulled her below the water.

She reached up for help and saw a young boy sitting on a rock staring back at her.

Shell reached for the boy, but the boy did not reach for her. Her hand made contact with the boy's rock and she used it to pull herself up. She pulled and pulled at the rock, still feeling the hand around her foot. She kicked and struggled and finally made it breathlessly onto the rock where she found the young boy holding his knees to his chest, rocking back and forth.

The scared little boy, no older than about eight, despite not appearing wet, shivered uncontrollably. Shell tried to talk to him, but no words came out of her mouth. Still, he would not stop staring. Shell consoled him, hugging him, trying to keep him warm, and felt no desire to try to escape their isolated rock. They sat embraced, surrounded by the flowing river at the edge of the waterfall for a few moments when the boy turned to her and, with a solemn face, screamed at an ear-piercing decibel, "FIND ME!"

Chapter 15 - Gut Reactions

Shell woke up. Her heart raced. The clock read six twenty-nine and, before she could ask herself what her dream meant, she wondered why for the past two mornings she'd woken up in time to watch her alarm go off. It only took a moment for the dread she had gone to bed with to return. She had to do something about her and Betty, she had someone to find, and she had to do both immediately.

She dressed quickly, putting on a bright purple sweatshirt and a pair of thin, black, tribal-patterned jeans that looked more like dressy workout clothes. Rummaging around her room, she grabbed her charge pad, some yoga pants, one of her dad's sweatshirts that she never gave back, and a few other items, cramming everything into her book bag. Thirty minutes ahead of her routine breakfast session with her mom, she made it to the kitchen before Skitch came down for his breakfast and her mom logged in to the fridge. Shell scavenged the pantry for a few snacks, and then headed out the front door, walking directly to the hospital.

It dawned on her as she left the house that what she had in mind to do might get her in trouble, so she had to do as much as she could not to get caught. She avoided any public transportation that would track her whereabouts when she swiped her allowance card. She had never walked all the way to or from the hospital. She assumed it would only take her twenty minutes since the bus typically took less than ten, but underestimated her shorter legs. Forty-five minutes later, her Armer rang.

"Shell. What's up? Where are you?" asked Topher after Shell answered.

"It's a long story."

"Do you know why everyone's asking me if you're coming in?"

"People are asking about me?" Shell asked excitedly.

"Well, apparently, Veronica Miller wants to fight you and the principal wants to suspend you."

"Awesome!" Shell bemoaned as she continued her hike to the hospital.

"So where are you?"

"I'll be in later."

"It's a little early in the year for skipping. You're going to wind up in detention."

"I'd be lucky to only get detention after what happened yesterday."

"Really? What happened?"

"I got in a fight with Roni. She stole my necklace. I tried to get it back, but Principal Turnip showed up."

Topher laughed as quietly as he could. Even Shell knew he could get in trouble for talking on his phone at school.

"I don't think that's funny," she exclaimed.

"I'm not laughing at you. It's just that you called him Mr. Turnip," Topher explained.

"Turnip. Turnsnip. Parsnip. I'd like to nip that Roni in the bud."

Topher chuckled a bit more and Shell couldn't help but to giggle with him.

"Anyway, I ran out of school before he could talk to me. I was surprised he didn't call my parents, though. I figured I'd be busted as soon as I got home. So, no. I'm not going into school; at least not this morning."

"What's that supposed to mean? What do you have going on?"

"I don't know where to start. There's a lot going on. I'm headed to the hospital."

"What for? Are you okay?" Topher's impatience and concern encouraged her to get to the point.

"Something bad has happened, and I'm afraid it could get worse for…" she paused. "For a friend of mine."

Topher took a moment before he spoke sullenly. "Shell, it's a hospital. Sometimes you can't stop bad things from happening to people."

"It's not that kind of bad. It's actually worse. Well…" She paused, wondering how much of this story she had to share and unsure of how he'd handle the whole truth. "You know how my mom's a news reporter and my dad's a scientist?" She continued after Topher's acknowledgement. "Well, they both came home last night talking about how all these crazy things have been happening since that rain storm and how there was this camp in Africa where everyone was sick, but after the storm, they weren't sick and they think that either the rain cured everyone or one person, potentially affected by the rain, may have cured everyone. The thing is, though, if it was one person, they're looking for them. And if they did cure everyone, then my dad's company is going to try experimenting on them to figure out how they did it so his company can do it themselves."

Topher asked, "Did all this happen at the hospital?"

"No! Africa."

"So why are you going to the hospital?"

"There's a woman there named Betty. I think she's like the person in Africa, if there was just one person that cured all those people there."

Confused still, Topher asked, "What makes you think she's...like that?"

"She, uh... I, uh," Shell held back. "Someone posted about her on a blog site. Now there are all these rumors about her. I went to the hospital yesterday and I saw doctors doing all sorts of scary things to her. My dad's company is going to treat people like her like frogs in science class. You remember what we did to those frogs, don't you? And the look in her eyes, she begged me to save her. I have to help her."

"So what are you going to do?"

"She can't stay there. It isn't safe. She can't check herself out, so I'm going to sneak her out. I have a plan."

"And you're going to do all this on your own?"

"Yeah, why not?"

"Because..."

"Because I'm too small? Because I don't know what I'm doing and I'm not smart enough to figure it out.

"No. Well... You are small and you don't know what you're doing, but because you're going to get yourself caught. You're going to wind up with fighting, skipping, and kidnapping on your record, and all of it in less than twenty-four hours."

"I'll be fine."

"Sure you will. Just wait for me at the hospital."

"You're coming?" Shell couldn't hide her enthusiasm. "I said I'll be fine. I don't need any help."

"There's no way you're going to pull this off on your own."

"Of course I will. It's easy. I'll sneak her out, put her on a bus to New York, and then catch a bus to school. I'll be back by lunchtime."

"Yeah, right. Just wait for me. Which bus do I take?"

Shell's Armer read eight forty-five. Thirty minutes had passed since she got off the phone with Topher. *He should be here by now.* Bus after bus came and went with no sign of Topher. Shell checked her Armer, but had received no messages from him. *There's no way he went to school, right?* She called his cell, but he didn't answer. Another ten minutes went by before she spotted him in the distance jogging toward her.

"Where were you?" Shell scolded.

An out-of-breath Topher apologized. "Sorry. I got lost. I took the wrong bus."

"I see high school hasn't helped your sense of direction," Shell commented to her grinning friend.

"Now, you're sure this friend of yours is worth all of this trouble? I mean, what if you're wrong? What if she isn't...? What if we get caught?"

"First of all, I know she's special. Second of all, we can't get caught. If we do, the bad guys will take her and we'll get grounded."

"You'll get grounded; I'll probably wind up in a foster home."

"We just won't get caught then," Shell stated with false confidence.

With that, they headed for the front door of the hospital. Shell gave Topher an overview on the hospital and staff. She felt like a hero from one of those old *Mission: Impossible* movies.

"Just follow my lead and they won't even know we're here," she suggested. They walked in through the automatic spinning doors of the lobby and headed for the elevator.

"Excuse me," boomed an unfamiliar militant male voice from the security desk. Shell kept walking, assuming and hoping that no one wanted her to stop. "Excuse me, young lady."

Shell froze mid-stride.

"Yes, sir?"

"Everyone needs to sign in," stated the security guard.

"Oh. I'm sorry. I used to work here. They all know me on the third floor," she explained. *So much for sneaking in,* she thought.

"That's fine. I still need you to sign in," continued the security guard.

Shell walked back to the desk and looked down at the tablet. She saw columns asking for her name and the guest she came to see. She did not want to leave any traces of their visit, and thought about her options. *Are they going to ask me for ID? Can I get caught for putting down fake information?* Shell could feel the guard's suspicion rising. *He's going to have us kicked out. This is not going to work. Betty's going to wind up a lab rat.*

Slowly, she reached for the pen when Topher whispered in her ear, "You're kinda new at this, huh?"

He grabbed the tablet, scooped up the pen, and started scribbling in the blanks.

"Thank you, sir," he said as he nudged Shell past the guard and to the elevator, dropping the tablet down on the counter, and not giving the guard another opportunity to ask any questions.

"What did you write down?" asked Shell as he ushered her onto the elevator.

"Roni Miller," he replied.

Shell laughed nervously and took a deep breath as she hit the button for the third floor. When the doors opened, she felt relieved to see less chaos than she had seen the day before.

"Follow me," she whispered as she took an immediate left out of the elevator, hoping to stay unnoticed. She turned the corner and saw someone headed their way. She could not tell if the figure was a nurse or someone else. She could only see white shoes, as the grayish wavy whirlwind around their clothes masked whatever else they wore.

"Hey there Shell. Just can't get enough, huh?" asked a nurse.

She stiffened and stuttered out an awkward response. "Ha ha. Yeah… I… you know. Just showing my friend where I spent my summer."

"Shouldn't you be in school?" the nurse asked.

"Yeah. This is for school. We're working together on a report." She felt like an idiot and a failure all at the same time. Now people would know she had come to the hospital and she also admitted to having an accomplice.

"Sounds good. Have fun," the nurse said in passing.

"Oh, yeah!"

Topher groaned and Shell knew she had sounded excited to the point of suspicious. They waited for the nurse to walk farther down the hall before Shell pulled Topher a few more feet and through a door marked 'Staff Closet.' The close quarters pressed the two against each other.

"Ummm," uttered Topher. Their close proximity made him physically uncomfortable while his encircling tornado gave Shell a slight, but peculiar rush she never felt before. She could not explain it or understand it, but it energized her.

"Put these on." Shell pulled some folded white scrubs off of a nearby shelf.

"Do these go on over your clothes?" he asked.

"They can, but you'll probably look weird," she explained as she started to take off her clothes.

"Is there another place I can change?"

Shell stopped as she grabbed the bottom of her sweatshirt. "Don't worry. I prepared for this." She lifted her sweatshirt above her head revealing a black spandex tank top. She took off her jeans, showing she had bike shorts on underneath.

"You really did prepare for this," Topher commented with a bashful grin.

"Do you want me to wait outside while you get dressed?" Shell mocked.

"Yes, please," he replied.

She smirked, finished dressing, and went outside. She tried to look busy so no one would get a good look at her and, a minute later, Topher came out. "Where are you putting your book bag?"

Shell gave him a once-over and chuckled when she saw the fuzzy outlines of his navy blue 'distressed' skateboard shoes that did not fit the hospital attire at all.

"We're going to use that gurney over there. We'll put our stuff underneath it."

They scurried down the hall and grabbed the gurney.

"Now what?" Topher whispered.

"Now we get Betty out of here."

Shell felt pretty good about her plan thus far as they wheeled the bed down the hall on their way to Betty's room. They came to a screeching halt when they turned the corner. Just a few doors down, a darkly dressed figure sat in a chair in front of Betty's room. "T, who's that sitting in that chair down the hall?"

"You tell me. It looks like a cop. Is that the room we're supposed to go in?"

"Maybe. Just play it cool." Shell started pushing again and Topher pushed alongside her.

"I don't know, Shell. I hate cops. I'd rather not do this."

"You said you would help me. Plus we're already here. Just follow me."

They wheeled the gurney right up to Betty's room and pushed the carted bed inside. The young and somewhat hefty police officer stood up from his chair.

"You two. What are you doing here?"

Chapter 16 - Shell Shock

"Just making our rounds," Shell replied while Topher shot a fearful glance back at the officer.

"No one is to see this patient. I have strict orders to keep everyone out of this room."

Topher redirected his gaze back toward Shell. He started to reach for his bag, the nervous wrinkles on his forehead revealing his desire to run away. She cut her eyes at him, expressing her disapproval of him reaching for his bag, ordering him to keep cool.

"We're just here to keep the patients comfortable. You know, adjust their blankets and the temperature, get them to move a little bit so they don't get bed sores, clean them up so they don't smell, take them to the bathroom or clean out their bed pans. Did you have someone taking care of that for you, officer? I can leave it to you if you prefer. If you need, we can show you how. It's not hard." Shell reached under the gurney and pulled out a kidney shaped plastic bowl. "First you look for a bedpan. If it's full, clean it out and

100

put it back where you found it. If it's empty and they need to use the bathroom, then you can help them. Sometimes you have to hold their arms when they try to sit down. It depends on the patient. Also, when you get them out of bed—"

The officer stopped her. "Okay. Fine, but make it quick."

"Will do, officer," she responded. As she closed the door behind her, she politely mentioned, "We're going to need a little privacy."

The morning waned outside of Betty's window as the sun rose over the trees. Betty rested, somewhat inclined in bed, covered in thin, stiff, over-washed white blankets. She had more sensors stuck to her than a bird had feathers, and her limp body reminded Shell of a decorative sock puppet.

"Oh my," Betty said surprised. "I have guests." She beamed as Shell walked toward her. "I weren't expectin' no one."

Shell stood at her friend's bedside.

"Your friend is older than I expected," Topher whispered.

"Hello to you, too, Betty. How are you feeling?" she asked pleasantly, tapping into her candy-striping experience.

"Just dandy. Sorry for the mess. I was fixin' to tidy up. How do I look?" Betty said in jest before her emotions sank. "Well, I am rather uncomfortable. You know, I came here for a spa treatment. Are all of these wires really necessary? I got more holes than a paper snowflake. And I haven't slept too well for the past few days. Perhaps you have a room with an ocean view I can move to?" She paused to look Shell and Topher over. "I normally prefer a male masseuse, but I think two at once sounds just fine to me."

Shell stood dumbfounded. It surprised her that Betty did not appear as disturbed by the horror show from the day before as she felt. "Betty. It's me, Shell. I came to see you yesterday."

Betty paused again. Shell could see the confusion on Betty's face and so could Topher.

He tapped Shell's shoulder. "What's going on, Shell?"

She ignored him. "Betty. It's Shell. Shell Wayburn. Do you remember seeing me yesterday or speaking with me the day before? We talked about my first day of high school."

Betty sat still for a moment. "Oh! Boys! That's right. Is this Topher?"

Shell blushed, as did Topher.

"Yes, Betty. This is Topher," she admitted. She pulled a chair next to the bed and sat down while Topher stood awkwardly behind her. "How has today been?"

"Well, the doctors gave me more tests today. Or, they tried to anyway. I mean... I know things don't always make much sense. It's probably the Alzheimer's. I mean, I'm not as far along as I could be. My Nana, she used to make breakfast twice a day. No reason to be upset about that. I love eggs. I could eat eggs for every meal. Don't see why not. Momma always called me a hypochondriac. I just thought I'd get ahead of it. But either way, this science stuff is confusing."

Shell enjoyed Betty's ramblings, but she found herself trying not to look at any portion of the older woman. She stared at the sheets instead of Betty's exposed hands and face.

"But the doctors looked as confused 'bout what was happening as I did."

"What was happening?" Shell asked. "Was it like yesterday?"

"I dunno. What happened yesterday? Or was it yesterday? All I remember is they tried to draw some blood, and I hate needles, but the needle went limper than a wet noodle. Then, they tried to give me a shot, but I could have sworn the glass part melted and everything just spilled everywhere. So they tried again, and this time, the liquid in the syringe turned into glass and when they pushed that little plunger-majig, the whole thing shattered. At some point, I passed out. I remember a gas mask, but that's about it. When I woke up, I was covered in tubes and wires, and all these sensors." Tears started to build in Betty's eyes; her cheeks tended to jiggle a bit when she got choked up. "I just think the Alzheimer's is kicking in, or maybe I truly am going crazy."

"But the doctors said they saw it, too, right?" Shell asked.

"I don't know. They ain't tellin' me much. They didn't exactly say they saw it, but they looked as shocked as I felt," Betty responded between sniffles.

Shell looked up at Betty and all the feelings she had tried to hold back finally bubbled to the surface. Her impassioned thoughts almost flew right out of her mouth. She wanted to say so many things, to tell Betty everything she had seen. She thought, *before the storm, you were just a normal lady. Now, you look like a walking, talking tangle of multi-colored yarn. I see red for cheeks green for your nose, yellow for your chin, and on and on.* Luckily, Betty had her eyes closed when Shell nearly opened the floodgates.

"I'm sure you were not seeing things, Betty, and even if you were, I don't think you were the only one,"

Shell reassured her, doing her best to suppress her emotions.

"Oh, good. Those straightjackets neva looked very flatterin'."

Betty chuckled for a moment, but Shell only smiled, ready to tell Betty the true severity of their situation.

"We'll save crazy for later," Shell said, knowing she had her own crazy story to tell. "But, the thing is, Betty, I don't think you're safe here anymore."

A grave expression crossed Betty's face.

"I don't know what's going to happen, and I could be making this all up, but I think if people find out about what happened to... you, they might try to take you somewhere else."

"You mean like n'other hospital? Because of that syringe thang?" Betty asked with growing concern.

"I don't know. My mom and dad were talking last night about all these weird things going on all around the world since the storm the other night. These things that are happening, they're happening to people or because of people. Either way, they're looking for everyone that could be tied to the storm. If you're one of those people—" Shell paused, sensing Betty's concern and fear. "I just don't want anything bad to happen to you."

"You are such a sweetheart, little angel." Betty's voice quivered while she tried to remain calm while she collected her thoughts and considered her options. "I don't think anyone's gonna come after an old lady 'cause of a few mishaps."

"Did you know you have a policeman outside your door?"

"Really? That's who's tellin people not to come in? Am I under arrest?"

"I don't know, but I would guess they don't want you leaving your room. Maybe they're keeping you here until someone else comes. Maybe they're sending some sort of scientist to examine you. My dad's a scientist. He says that they're always doing experiments, trying to figure out how things work. What if they do experiments on you?"

Shell turned around to talk to Topher. "We're going to run out of time soon. Can you go outside and tell the cop we had a bit of a spill? Grab as many towels out of that closet and tell me what you see going on out there."

Topher flew out of the room without questioning the orders. Before he closed the door behind him, Shell heard him give the officer the story.

"He's cute," Betty admitted.

"Betty..." Shell's blushing and loss for words made the older woman smile. "So," attempting to get back on track, "do you want to stay or should we get you out of here?"

"Oh, Shell. Many things happen in a lifetime. Not all of them can be what you want them to be. Maybe I deserve these things that are happenin' ta me now. Maybe it's for a better cause and they'll find something that can help others."

"But what if you wind up in some sort of lab where every day is like yesterday?"

"Yesterday? Yesterday I was with my daughter, her husband, and my two twin grandchildren. We went pumpkin huntin' for Halloween. It was wonderful. Oh, I'd love another day like that."

Pumpkins? Halloween? It's August. Shell forced herself to look into Betty's eyes and recognized the same frightened look she saw the day before. She questioned her purpose, knowing that even if she did get Betty out of the hospital, she might not even know what to do on her own. "I'm scared, Betty."

"Don't be, my child. Everything'll be jus' fine."

"I'm scared for me." The words flew out of Shell's mouth before she realized what she said. She had not planned on revealing anything, but her inability to share with others finally overwhelmed her. "Something happened to me that night of the storm. You were out in the rain, too, weren't you?"

"I think so, but it was just rain."

"Something landed on me, like ink or something. All I know is I've been seeing things and having weird dreams ever since."

"What are you seein', darlin'?" Betty asked. "What have you been dreamin'?"

Before Shell could respond, Topher ran back into the room. He could barely speak through his panicked breaths. "They just said, 'Betty Harmony.'"

Chapter 17 - Elsewhere

"Left. Right. Left. Right. Left. Right." The commands echoed off of the towering cement walls. "Left. Right. Left. Right. Left. Right." Men walked in step with the orders along the inner perimeter of HCA Private Correctional Facility in Alabama, each step accompanied by the jingling of the ankle chains attached to their yellow jump suits. The institute, named after a collection of semi-educated founders and fat cats, established itself as the holding facility for all the life sentence inmates. It lived up to its nickname, "One Way," for a few reasons.

The facility's first inmate came in the year 2020 and set the precedent for its future inhabitants. Convicted of a crime and sentenced to a life in prison with no parole, HCA became his final home. That inmate lived 37 years inside those prison walls, longer than any other prisoner. The shortest stint came from a prisoner who only lived for two hours after his arrival.

The crimes committed by these men ranged from the mundane to the insane. How any of them managed to coexist behind these walls warranted special appreciation, as the warden, a religious man, preached at every opportunity in an attempt to keep the prisoners in line. Some of the inmates became his followers, others played along. Among those who despised him was one man who made his opposition to the warden and his beliefs quite clear.

This man, who never downplayed the severity of his crimes and pleaded for no solace from the punishment set before him, stumbled during his walk around the prison yard this evening and fell to the ground. With his hands and ankles semi-bound, he could not break his own fall, and fell face first to the ground. The common occurrence drew little attention from the guards barking orders and monitoring the herd, and neither they nor the falling prisoner noticed the puddle he would fall into contained a peculiar solitary red drop of water floating, waiting, in the puddle.

A guard picked up prisoner 927694 by the back of his jump suit like a pup. He saw the red mark on his face, assumed it to be blood from the fall, and told him to keep moving. Prisoner 927694, also known as Tussin Jussin, thought nothing of his fall or the nightmares he experienced that night (which scared him but little), but after his incident the next day in the library, he went on to prove to the warden the power of his own beliefs and became the first man to escape HCA.

Chapter 18 - Time To Go

"Who did?" Shell and Betty asked Topher in unison.

"A guy in a white suit just said 'Betty Harmony' to a doctor. They just went into an office and shut the door," Topher explained.

"Maybe it's another doctor," Betty proposed.

"The guy in the suit flashed something in his wallet, like the cops do."

A grave look crossed Shell's face. "It's happening. This is what I was afraid of."

"What have you been seein' and what have you been dreamin', Shell? Tell me," Betty urged.

"What's she talking about?" asked Topher. Shell ignored both of their questions.

"I don't know if you remember what happened to you yesterday, but when I came to see you, there were doctors all around you with all sorts of needles and they had to strap you to the bed. You looked at me and your eyes told me that you wanted me to help you get out of here. That's why we're here now. We came to get you out. Do you want to come or do you want to stay?"

Betty hesitated and Shell continued. "If something did happen to you, and there were people looking to take you away, and you were about two minutes from becoming a guinea pig, and you had the choice to make a run for it, what would you do?"

Betty took a moment. "I really don't like needles... What do ya have in mind?"

A smile crossed Shell's face. "Let's just get out of here for starters." She went to the closet, found Betty's overnight bag, and threw all the clothes she could find into it.

"Are you gonna properly introduce me to this young strapping hero of mine?" Betty asked coyly.

"Oh. Topher, this is Betty. Betty, Topher."

"Nice ta meet ya, Topher," said Betty. "I've heard many a wonderful thang about you."

Topher responded with a quick, "Hello, ma'am."

Betty offered a flirtatious nod, and Topher leaned over and whispered to Shell, "So, are we going with the same plan? There wasn't a pit bull staring at the door when you explained this earlier."

"Just grab her things. I'll think of something."

"Getting arrested wasn't something I thought I'd have to worry about when I woke up this morning," he whispered as loud as he could as he took over packing and Shell moved to Betty's bedside.

"Don't be a baby," Shell snapped as she stared dumbfounded at the all the wires connected to Betty.

"Is everything okay?" Betty asked. "Maybe it's not such a good idea for me ta try an' sneak away. I don't wanna get ya'll in trouble. I'll be fine."

"Just stay right there, Betty," Shell said, softening her tone. "Topher is going to pack your bag. Don't touch any of those..." A thought popped into her head.

She walked over to the machine that connected all of the wires to Betty. It had a tablet attached to a blue box that had all of the wires coming out of it. The infusion control portion of the blue box hung from a metal pole on wheels with pigtail corkscrew-like hooks protruding from its top to hold IV bags. One power cord connected the blue box to a power outlet in the wall.

Betty's eyes nearly popped out of her head. "You're not gonna mess with that, are ya?"

"I think I am," Shell admitted with a slight grin.

"Won't the alarms go off if you pull them off of her?" Topher asked.

"They might." Shell traced the wires and tubes to and from the blue box. "Are we ready?"

"Yeah," Topher fibbed as he grabbed the last few items.

"All right, Betty, when I say *go*, I'm going to need you to walk over to the gurney. Can you do that?" She asked gently.

"I'm not that old," Betty replied.

"Are you sure this is the best idea?" Topher asked with a quivering voice.

"I think it's the only idea that might work."

She scrolled over the screen on the tablet. The battery sign on the screen showed a lightning bolt and the Wi-Fi arches.

It's charged and the wireless connection should hold so long as the tablet stays on, she thought. As she reached for the plug in the wall, she could hear Topher and Betty taking a deep breath with her. She closed her eyes, pulled the plug out of the wall, and waited.

No one moved or made a sound while the hum of the florescent lights above droned unaccompanied. They waited to hear alarms and an overhead code blue sirens accompanied by the rapid pounding of squeaky shoes heading toward them, yet heard nothing of the sort. Shell opened one eye and could feel Betty and Topher staring at her, awaiting her next move.

"Sweet. I think that worked. Now, let's get you on that gurney."

Betty eased out of her hospital bed.

"Careful," Shell cautioned. "I'm not sure what could happen if any of those sensors came off, so let's try to keep them on you."

Betty took her cue and moved cautiously. Shell and Topher maneuvered the IV pole and the wires to make sure nothing got caught or disconnected while they eased Betty down onto the gurney. Shell placed the blue box in a metal basket that hung from the frame under the thin mattress, and placed the IV bags by Betty's side.

"Are you okay like this?" Shell asked. "You've got to stay flat."

"I'm fine, but how am I gonna hide like this?"

Shell took all of the blankets off of the bed and covered Betty, the bags, and the wires completely.

"We're going to have to keep you under these blankets. I'm going to pile more sheets and stuff on top of you so it looks like we're just dropping off laundry. Try not to move or make any noises, okay?"

Betty nodded with the slightest flinch of her chin, already following Shell's orders. Shell then took the other towels and blankets in the room and piled them on top of Betty in scattered bunches. Topher followed her lead until they stripped the entire room of linens they could place on top of Betty.

Shell and Topher exchanged glances as they stood on opposite ends of the gurney.

"You ready?" she asked.

"Don't have much of a choice now, do I?" He responded with far less confidence than Shell would have appreciated.

Shell led the gurney toward the room door while Topher pushed from the other end by Betty's feet. She reached for the handle and opened the door, hoping the guard left for some reason. Unfortunately, there he sat, staring right at her, seemingly perturbed, though she could not clearly see why. Since her last wish didn't come true, now she hoped the officer would not stop them or notice Betty on the gurney.

"That took forever," Shell admitted, sounding tired and exasperated, but still pleasant. "There was a lot to clean."

The officer's expression remained stoic.

"We'll be back with some more linen. Do you want anything? I can get you soda or juice."

"No, thanks," replied the officer.

"Okay. See you in a sec." Shell led them down the hall in the direction they came from just a short while ago. Topher kept his eyes down as he pushed past the officer, avoiding eye contact at all costs.

No more than two doors down from Betty's room they heard, "Hey, wait a sec. Whatcha got?"

Topher stopped pushing the gurney. Shell strained to pull it alone and knew that he had frozen under the questioning. She turned around, primarily to express the severity of the situation and the necessity for Topher to keep moving with a sharp glance, but her efforts failed. She could only tell that nothing she did short of yelling at him to run would get him to move.

The officer stood up from his chair. Shell's eyes dodged back and forth between Topher and the officer.

"To drink," the officer specified.

"Oh. We've got Coke, Orange, Sprite, and we might have some root beer. That one goes pretty quick, though." Shell rattled off the options like a waitress.

"I'll take root beer if you've got it," the officer said as he sat back down in his chair.

"Sure thing," responded a relieved Shell.

Topher exhaled as they rounded the corner, out of the officer's line of sight, and wheeled the gurney to the closet.

Shell spoke in a low voice. "I'm not sure if we can make it to the emergency room elevators."

"This may be the last time I listen to one of your plans," Topher commented. "What's wrong now?"

"The elevator we need is past the nurses' station and all the way down this hall," she pointed as she explained.

Topher estimated the distance. "We made it this far."

"Yeah, but if they recognize me, we're busted."

"I can push it down. They shouldn't recognize me."

"Those nurses know everyone who works here. I'll create a distraction. Wait for my signal and push the bed to that elevator. Don't let them see you" she directed as she grabbed her bag and headed to the closet again.

"What are you doing?"

"Changing. I'm not supposed to be wearing this. They'll think I'm crazy or something."

Shell disappeared into the closet and came out less than a minute later dressed in her sweatshirt and jeans from earlier. "All right. Here we go."

She scampered off to the nurses' station, where she could see a nurse sitting at the phone. A few feet from there, in a small office, she heard the baritone voices of two men having a conversation. She eyed the dry erase board just across from where the nurse sat that listed everyone on duty. All four names were familiar, including her favorite, Nurse Janie. Shell debated on her plan of attack as she moved toward the nurse sitting by the phone.

"Back again, I see. Shouldn't you be in school?"

Shell recognized Nurse Janie's voice and smiled.

"You sure you don't want to come work here? You're two for two now, aren't you?"

"Hi, Nurse Janie." Shell beamed. "I realized yesterday that I never got to say 'bye to everyone."

"Oh, that's sweet of you. Things have been kinda crazy around here lately."

"Did everything from yesterday get worked out?"

"I think they've almost got everything taken care of," Nurse Janie replied.

Shell couldn't tell, but it looked like Nurse Janie motioned to the doctor's office behind her. She assumed she meant working things out related to Betty.

"I wanted to tell everyone 'bye, but it looks like they're all busy." Shell waited for Nurse Janie to offer to call all the nurses to the desk so she could see all of them at once. After an awkward silence, Shell tried something else. "Well, since I'm here, is there anything I can do?"

"I think we're all set here, but you're always welcome to come visit."

Shell started to retreat. "Ooh! What if I put in orders for lunch?" She blurted out.

"You know what? That would be perfect." Nurse Janie picked up the phone, hit a couple of buttons, and said over the floor PA system, "Will all nurses please report to the nurses' station at this time?"

"Yay!" Shell smiled as she ran back to the nurses' station.

"Shell?" A nurse called in excitement. "What are you doing here?

"I came to say 'bye and figured I'd handle the lunch order while I'm here."

Another nurse joined the jubilation. Shell smiled and hugged everyone, weaving her way through the interactions without saying anyone's name. She noticed one of the nurses had to have passed by Betty and Topher, but she assumed all was well since no one seemed alarmed. The blurry images and little tornadoes continued to unnerve her, but she did not let on how freaked out she felt. Each time she hugged someone, though, she felt a rush of energy like she did when she bumped into Topher in the closet, but different... weaker.

"Party over here!" Shell yelled awkwardly and slightly too loud, though none of the nurses seemed to mind. Shell watched out of the corner of her eye the blurry figure pushing a gurney by the nurses' station. *It's working!*

"So who's having what, Nurse Janie?" Shell began as she made a spectacle of herself to divert everyone's attention as Topher snuck by. "Pass me a note pad, please!" Shell took the orders from the four nurses and once she saw Topher had made it past told them, "I'm going to miss you ladies! You've really taught me what it means to care about others and to do all you can to help them." Shell felt like a liar. "I'll take the orders down before I head out."

TIME TO GO

She waved goodbye and made her way toward the emergency room elevators, but before she turned the corner, she saw two men leaving the doctor's office. The doctor's long, white lab coat gave him away. The other person the doctor left with appeared to have on a white woolen suit, white shoes, and he carried a white hat.

The two men whispered too quietly for her to overhear with the nurses still chatting away. Shell hid around the corner, out of their view, and eavesdropped on their conversation. She heard the words "Betty" and "research" and then heard the clomping of heeled shoes against the hospital floor. Shell decided not to stick around for any more and sprinted down the hall toward Topher and Betty.

"Push the button," she whispered loudly and somewhat out of breath as she ran.

Topher punched the down button a few times with his fist.

"What happened?" he asked as Shell finally reached him.

"They're going to look for Betty now. We've got to go."

Chapter 19 - No Faux Pas

The elevator door opened and they wheeled Betty inside. Shell and Topher stared down the hall toward the nurses' station, hoping not to see anyone chasing after them. The doors closed and all of them, including Betty through the towels and blankets, let out a loud sigh of relief.

Shell chuckled a little. "This is crazy."

"Yeah. I told you it was," Topher replied.

"Okay," Shell prepared for her next set of instructions. "Betty, come on up. You and Topher change back into your normal clothes. We can't wheel a gurney out of the emergency room. We'll sneak toward the waiting area and then walk out the main door."

Betty sat up, knocking the towels and blankets onto the floor. Shell looked at her and realized she still had the sensors and bags of saline attached to her.

"Dang it! I totally forgot about those."

The elevator dinged. They had descended to the second floor.

"This hospital needs more floors. We don't have time. Get back down," Shell directed Betty as she started putting the linens back on top of her.

Topher helped.

"Push her and follow me."

The elevator dinged again for the first floor just before the doors opened to a hallway with an overhead sign to the right that read for the *Emergency Room*. Shell led the way and Topher followed.

A murmur filled the rather quiet emergency room. The screams from ambulance sirens wailed in the distance. Doctors ambled between a desk by the exit and patients on hospital beds that lined the perimeter. ER nurses walked in and out of the same exit doors where another large security guard paced like a British sentry. Shell pointed to an empty bed near the back of the emergency room, and Topher pushed the gurney next to it while Shell pulled the drape around to enclose the small area.

She couldn't tell if anyone watched her, but she didn't feel the presence of a watchful gaze and no one ran toward her. With the drape closed, Shell whispered, "Coast is clear, Betty. You can get up, but be careful and be quiet."

Topher removed the blankets from Betty again while she maneuvered her way out from under them. Shell eyed the sensors and the machine connected to Betty's body, not sure where to begin.

"Is this thang gonna make a ton a noise?" Betty asked in a hushed tone.

"Probably."

"What if I get dressed as much as I can, then we take 'em off at the last second?"

Shell didn't acknowledge Betty's question. She heard the familiar ding of the elevator doors and wondered if the nurses and the man in white had followed them down to the ER. She heard feet scamper off of the elevator and froze, waiting for a hand to swipe away the drape.

"She could wear my sweatshirt," Topher offered a moment later.

Topher and Betty looked at Shell who stood awkwardly, listening to the noises outside of their cramped enclosure. A few more seconds passed before Shell finally replied, "You mean walk out of here with the whole thing?" Shell asked, sounding optimistic. "Do you think it will all fit?"

"I can't think of anything else to try," he answered.

"Let's do it quickly," she urged as she hastily but delicately pulled the box off the gurney and collected the bags of IV fluid and placed them into Betty's overnight bag.

Topher yanked his sweatshirt out of his bag and handed it to Betty, who sifted through her bag and pulled out some jeans. She started to put them on underneath her hospital gown, when Topher blushed.

"Should I leave the room?" he asked bashfully.

"Such a gentlemen," Betty winked at Shell. "No darlin'. You're just fine," she said, zipping up her jeans.

He looked at his clothes, not sure of what to do, and tried to find a corner in the small semi-circle he could hide in, but had no luck.

Betty tried to gently pull the sweatshirt over her head but stopped, as the weight of the thick cotton garment tugged on the wires attached to the sensors on her head. "I don't think this is going to work. I don't think I can get my arms down the sleeves without yanking out the tubes."

"Don't put your arms through the sleeves, just stay like that," Shell suggested as she heard another elevator door ding. "Shhh. Don't move."

They each froze and waited several moments before reconfirming their safety and continuing their preparation. Shell readied Betty's bag and grabbed the empty sleeves of the sweatshirt. She paused, curious about the tingly surge she felt, like excited butterflies in her stomach, and then tucked the sleeves into the front pockets of the sweatshirt and slowly pulled the hood over Betty's head. She struggled a little, since Betty stood about six inches taller.

"You should probably keep your head down until we're outside. How's that?"

"Well, I feel kinda useless, but I guess I'm good to go," Betty answered. She turned to Topher to see him still in his nurses' outfit with his clothes in his hand. "Oh! Young man…" she started in motherly fashion. "Shell, dear, you face that way. I can't turn around myself, so go change over there and I promise we won't look," she ordered Topher, who obediently went to his corner and changed his clothes while Shell giggled.

Once dressed and ready to go, he and Shell strapped their book bags to their backs while Shell picked up Betty's bag and laid out the plan.

"Betty, you just keep your head down and that hood on. I'll walk next to you and keep these wires hidden." Shell pulled the curtain back and peeked toward the elevator. The emergency room remained quiet with doctors continuing to go about their business.

"Let's go," Shell whispered.

They walked in a tight pack. Shell kept her eyes forward, staring at the security guard, hoping that they would make it out with no trouble.

"Speed up, guys. We look weird walking this slow," Topher chimed in anxiously from behind them.

All of the sudden, chirps and beeping echoed around them. Doctors started turning up their forearms, reading their Armers. Shell could see the screens glowing in the gray haze that surrounded them.

"Keep moving," said Shell as if the thought had not occurred to the others.

They all picked up the pace. Just steps away from the security guard, now leaning on the doorframe of the massive sliding exit doors, they heard his walkie-talkie chirp. They could only hear a static, jumbled message. Neither Shell nor Betty could gauge the officer's reaction. Fortunately, Topher could.

"We really need to get out of here," he emphasized.

It looked like someone put defibrillators on the ER and shocked it to life. Doctors and nurses raced frantically about as they yelled orders in code to each other across the room. It became harder to hear everything. Panic set in on the trio. Collectively and simultaneously, they feared talking to each other, feared stopping, and feared the sense of evil they felt nipping at their heels, so they kept moving forward.

We're looking for an older woman possibly with two teenagers. One male. One female.

Despite the commotion around them, they all heard the message over the walkie-talkie loud and clear. The security guard raised his head and scanned the emergency room for matches to the descriptions. Shell saw his head turn, but could not tell if he stared at her or not. Topher tucked his chin to avoid eye contact with him.

Just as the three of them came within ten feet of the ER exit and the security guard, a siren-blaring ambulance pulled up. The back doors to the ambulance flew open. Doctors ran past them and up to the back of the silenced vehicle. An orchestrated fire drill proceeded as the paramedics rushed a gurney inside. Doctors and nurses came to their aid, surrounding the new patient, carrying bags of fluid and calling out vitals as they rushed into the ER.

Over all of the commotion, it only took a few words to force Shell and company to strongly reconsider the decision they made to sneak Betty out.

"You three! Stop!"

The guard posted by the emergency room door must have suspected Shell, Topher, and Betty of fitting the description he heard over his walkie-talkie and started to approach them. The guilt-stained threesome did a poor job of pretending not to notice the hulking guard moving toward them and gawked at the enormous man who seemed to grow taller and wider with every step. Topher instinctively nudged the group to the right as the guard approached from the left side of the exit. Topher accidentally caught the man's eye, which triggered his full pursuit.

The ambulance coming in made for a well-timed distraction. Though they did not blend in with the doctors, nurses, paramedics, or patients in the emergency room, the triad did manage to keep plenty of bodies between them and the security guard, staying out of arm's reach and breaking his line of sight long enough to sneak outside, round the ambulance, and then sprint for a place to hide fifty yards away. Even after putting some distance between them and the man set to ruin their plan, they could still hear him yelling on his radio, "They ran into the parking deck!"

"Betty, you can rip those things off now. They know you're not in your room."

Betty reached her hands through the sweatshirt and started yanking the sensors off of her face and head. She struggled pulling the IV tubes out of her arms, especially while walking at the same time, but grimaced her way through it.

"This way," Shell directed as they ran up a small incline to the next level of parked cars.

"I think that's it," Betty told them as she wound up the mess of wires and sensors into a ball before handing them to Shell. "Ouch!" Betty yelped. "Forgot one." She pulled off the last sensor, put her arms through her sweatshirt, and picked up the pace.

They were running to the next level in the parking structure when Shell pointed toward a staircase to their left. "Wait at the bottom of that staircase for the bus. I'll be right there."

"A bus?" Topher asked. "We're going to get away on a bus?"

"Was this a part of your grand plan, my dear?" Betty added.

He and Betty made their way toward the stairs while Shell ran off to the right. She pulled the blue box, the tablet, and the wires out of Betty's bag and slung it underneath a parked van. She caught up with Betty and Topher at the bottom of the stairwell. The three of them waited in the drafty door-less opening, staring out to the bus stop.

"So, what now?" Topher asked as they panted and wheezed.

"We wait for the bus," she explained as she heard a metal door slam and feet clomping on the parking levels above her.

Given the circumstances, everything they just went through, where they wound up, and their options going forward, Betty could only laugh. She covered her mouth quickly as Shell tried to shush her, but that only made the woman laugh more. And she laughed hard. She laughed so hard she couldn't breathe, which wound up better for the three of them, because she barely made any noise.

Topher could not help but to join in on the laughing. He cupped his mouth with his hands to keep the noise down. Shell took a little longer to consider the fact that taking a bus from the scene of the crime sounded like the slowest getaway ever, but she eventually joined in.

"Think about it, though," Shell whispered between the laughs, "they'll spend all their time looking for us in a car."

Betty laughed harder and looked even sillier by trying to keep quiet about it, which infected the others.

"You don't happen to have a bus schedule on you?" Topher managed to squeeze out the question in a single breath before he started to crack up again.

As the laughter trailed off and reality set back in, they heard footsteps slightly closer than before, only one level from the alcove where they hid, but it sounded like only one set of feet. The three of them remained still. For a moment, it seemed as if someone had entered the stairwell as the clomping grew louder. They held still and silently begged for the bus to arrive. Topher nudged Shell, suggesting they move, but Shell sat firm. Eventually the steps faded and shortly thereafter, a bus pulled up. Shell made a dash for it with Betty and Topher on her heels.

Shell's Armer read ten o'clock in the morning. She hoped that traffic would be light this time of day so they could get to the city faster. The three of them shared another nervous smile as the bus trundled along.

A few hours, a seemingly infinite number of stops, and a couple of transfers later, Shell, Topher, and Betty rode into New York City, where Shell hoped Betty could hide and she would find whoever, or whatever, wanted finding.

Chapter 20 - Brighter Lights Bring Darker Shadows

The 159 bus emerged from the Lincoln Tunnel in Manhattan when the sun shone high above the mega-metropolis. The buildings of the big city played their roles as sun dials while the bus bumped along a shade free 39th Street. Row after row of hunched shoulders and exhausted faces stared out of dirty windows or down into glowing electronic devices. Amidst the drab and bored-looking riders sat an older woman with a hood pulled over her head. Across the aisle from her sat a young man aging with worry and fret who sat next to a stressed-out, guilty-looking young lady named Shell.

The bus soon pulled in to a multi-level parking structure and drove down a cylinder shaped ramp, passing other buses, until it pulled into a slip in front of a numbered door.

"Last stop," the bus driver yelled in to his microphone with a raspy voice as he opened the vehicle's door.

A faint hum of city noise floated into the bus and mixed with the stomping, chair squeaking, and general grumbling people made as they exited. Shell, Betty, and Topher hesitated to get off. Without sharing their thoughts with each other, they all feared that they would walk right out into the hands of the police the second they stepped into the garage; that somehow, the authorities knew what bus they took and where to find them.

"I'll go first to make sure no one's looking for us," offered Topher. His voice quivered, exposing the fear they all felt.

"Be careful," Shell barely uttered.

Shell watched as Topher threw his book bag over his shoulder and cautiously walked down the bus aisle, peering through all the windows as he looked for the welcoming committee of police. He tiptoed down the steps and peeked out of the dual sliding doors like a mouse hoping to avoid a cat.

"Hey!" the bus driver hollered. "This is the last stop, so y'all gonna have to get off!" He shook his head as he continued to mumble under his breath about crazy people and trying to get home and no one appreciating him.

At that, Betty and Shell tripped over each other as they stumbled to catch up with Topher in the garage of the Port Authority on 42nd Street. The dank, poorly lit bus terminal emanated an old stench that tasted like metal.

BRIGHTER LIGHTS BRING DARKER SHADOWS

"Where are we?" Shell asked as a group of cockroaches scampered by her foot. She shrieked and jumped toward Topher.

"Pretty sure it's a bus station," Topher answered while laughing at Shell's reaction to the bugs. She jabbed him in the shoulder. Topher rubbed his arm while spinning in a circle, trying to understand how he wound up in New York instead of homeroom. "We're not going to school now, are we?"

"I don't know," Shell replied as they followed Betty through the numbered doorway.

"What was your plan once we made it to New York?" he asked, his agitation rising.

"I don't know."

"Are we just going to live at the Port Authority forever like that guy over there?" he demanded with a considerable amount of anger in his voice as he pointed to a homeless man digging through a trashcan.

"I don't know!" she screeched, loud enough to attract the eyes of a few bystanders.

"Follow me, you two," Betty interjected. "And stay close."

Shell, who had portrayed such confidence earlier, now looked like a lost child. Regret tried to take over her thoughts. She wondered if she should have dragged either Topher or Betty into this. She considered the idea that maybe she blew all of this out of proportion.

Shell could barely keep up with Betty's urgent pace. Despite the oddities of the quasi-subterranean life of the bus station underbelly that she rushed past, she found herself intrigued by the variations in the cloudy whirlwinds and the gently lapping layer of waves that flowed over the ground like the shallowest river. She saw specs of colors of the clouds around an elderly couple holding hands and small, but frantically crashing waves at the feet of a second homeless man digging through a trashcan.

Betty continued to haul Shell and Topher through the dirty red-bricked hallway of the station like an angry mother. Finally emerging from the subterranean tunnel, they climbed a stairway toward the traffic and noise of the city to let the fresh, gritty air wash over them. Up the subway exit's steps they clamored until they found themselves across the street from the Port Authority in a chaotic cornucopia of electronic stimulation. Billboard after billboard radiated bright, animated images advertising everything from beverages to real estate. The streets looked like something out of NASCAR with taxicabs and buses covered in Enter-Paint showing advertisements on every visible surface.

The cool air refreshed them, despite arid hints of asphalt, steel, and rubber. The companions found themselves standing next to an interactive bus stop with a filthy touch-screen map of bus routes and nearby restaurants. People whizzed by them in all sorts of bright ensembles. Executives on lunch breaks donned curve- and muscle-accentuating formfitting power suits. Tourists and locals alike wore the spectrum of class-indicative fashion trends: twenties retro, tattooed yoga sport, sleeveless grunge, and faux naked chic, with a heavy emphasis on loud colors.

They had no plan. Even worse than at school or on the bus, Shell saw so many little spinning tornadoes that she thought they would suck her in. She did not visit the city often. Probably because of her size she had never liked crowds, so her desire to mingle in the most crowded city in America remained minimal. She always felt seconds away from getting stepped on or kidnapped.

BRIGHTER LIGHTS BRING DARKER SHADOWS

Quite some time had passed since her last trip when she came to visit her mom at work, but her dad drove her and her brother in that Saturday. They had a whole plan for rescuing her mom from working too hard and taking her to Central Park for a picnic. Of course, they wound up staying in her office, but Mrs. Wayburn let them play with all of the computers and gadgets. Before that day, Shell came for a field trip to one of the museums during her first stint through eighth grade. This visit felt nothing like the other two. She had no idea where to go or how to get there.

"I don't know about you two, but I haven't had real food in days." Betty patted her stomach as she tried to ease the fear and the tension in the two children. "Let's get something to eat before I start missing hospital green gelatin."

A smile crossed Topher's face as he nodded. Shell shrugged in reluctant agreement as Betty led them again with slightly less haste.

After weaving through crowded sidewalks of fast walking, uninterested pedestrians and strolling window shoppers for a few blocks, the three walked stumbled into the first inviting diner they could find.

"This is one of those ASPOTA places," Shell explained with some excitement as her eyes danced around the chic restaurant. The earthy ambient music gave the crowded establishment a tranquil vibe and the plush seating seemed to drown out the murmur of engaging conversations happening.

"I've heard of this place, but I've never been to one," Topher answered.

"Me neither," added Betty. "What is it exactly?"

"It's amazing," Shell began. "My mom brought me once. They have everything here. The whole place is integrated. The tables are giant tablets and the menu pops up when you sit down. You order right from the table and you don't have to wait for the check when you're done. You can pay from the table too. They even have the BLink cloud. It scans your eyeball so you can sync your e-print to the table and access your music, nearby shopping options, and your favorite apps."

"It sounds overwhelming," said Betty.

"The best part is, they only serve breakfast," Topher chimed in.

"Breakfast only?" asked Betty. "Well, I'll be... Sounds like my kinda place."

They chose a booth with large green leather seats, deep into the restaurant, far from the large windows by the entrance.

"Just don't use retinal scan," suggested Topher. "The police can use that to track us down."

Shell and Topher tapped away on the icons in front of them while Betty struggled with the menu. Shell opened and an app to bring up the news while Topher opened a Role-Playing-Puzzle-Game. The three of them sat in silence.

"How does this thing work? I can't tell what I clicked on," Betty commented. "How do you know if you're food's coming?"

Shell and Topher glanced at one another and giggled. "What do want?" Shell asked.

"You two put your orders in while I try to find something."

Betty looked up at Topher and Shell and noticed their blank stares. "Go ahead, ya'll. Lunch is on me."

Topher and Shell shyly gazed at their menus until Topher finally blurted out, "I'll have the pancakes with apples and whipped cream and a hot chocolate." Shell tapped on the menu and watched images of Topher's order appear on the table.

"What about you Betty?" asked Shell.

"I think I'll have the French toast, scrambled eggs, and an orange juice." Shell entered the order.

"I'll just have a blueberry muffin."

"Goodness, sweetie," Betty remarked. "You'll stay little forever if that's all you're gonna eat. Give yourself an egg-white omelet with…," she paused. "Do you like mushrooms and cheese?"

Shell nodded.

"Good. Add some mushrooms and cheddar with a blueberry muffin on the side and an orange juice." Shell tapped on the screen and watch the ingredients come together as if she had made the meal herself.

Shell thanked Betty with a smile she forced through her troubled eyes. Again they sat silently, each lost in their own thoughts until Shell finally spoke up.

"I'm sorry, guys. Maybe it wasn't the best idea to do all of this." She looked longingly toward the collection of colors she now knew as Betty. "I really thought you were in trouble," she said, her eyes red and watery. "I can't help but think that the man in the white suit may have been somebody that could have helped."

Shell took a minute to choose her next words and began again just before Betty spoke up. "Topher, I'm so sorry if this gets you in trouble. You can probably go home now if you want. I probably just need to face the music and deal with my parents and the principal and everything else. I don't know what you want to do, Betty. I don't even know where you're from. Does it make sense to go back to the hospital?"

"Listen, love. I'm an adult. I made the choice to follow you, so don't you feel guilty at all. They had done so much pokin' and proddin' already, and I could tell it was only gonna to get worse. Maybe the man in the suit was some sorta specialist familiar with things like this, but the police officer outside of my room was a little scary. I feel like they was more scared of me than I was of them and their needles. I think I'm better off outta that place and I'm glad you came. Don't worry about me. I have a friend who lives in the city."

A look of relief washed over Shell's face.

"And—" Betty paused as a waitress arrived with their food. Everyone's eyes lit up, especially Topher's. Betty waited for the waitress to leave before continuing.

"And if you decide that you'd rather stay here," Betty continued, "I'm sure he can accommodate us."

Shell gave a sad smile. She glanced over to Topher, hoping he could help her with the decision, but as far as she could tell, his face hovered just inches above his syrup-flooded plate of food as he vacuumed the meal into his mouth. Shell and Betty exchanged a glance of understanding and then ate their meals. For Betty, this meal had become more challenging than she would have liked.

She had just finished a bite of food and began wiping her mouth when her napkin felt cold, heavy, and stiff on her face. She looked down to see the napkin had turned into a thin sheet of metal. She eyed her fork and instead saw a limp piece of fabric that looked cut out in the shape of a fork. Betty quickly glanced around to see if anyone noticed, and felt relieved that neither Shell, nor Topher noticed. She finished her meal with her spoon. Later on, when she took a sip of her beverage through her straw, she watched her straw turn into liquid and fall into her drink. She played it off and drank with nervous caution straight from her cup.

BRIGHTER LIGHTS BRING DARKER SHADOWS

Minutes passed and Topher finished eating first. Before Betty and Shell ate more than half of their meal, he blurted out again without looking up from his plate, "First of all, thank you for lunch, Betty. Secondly, I'm sorry for yelling at you, Shell. Third of all, I don't think we'd make it back in time for school today, so can we call your friend," directing his comments to Betty, "so we can at least make sure you're all set and then figure out what to do next?"

Betty and Shell exchanged a smile that they shared with Topher, once he finally looked up from his plate and saw Shell and Betty staring at him with huge grins on their faces. "What?" he asked.

Betty rummaged through her bag, pulled out her cell phone, and scrolled through her contacts. Topher put his hand over the screen so she couldn't press any more buttons.

"Just in case they are looking for us, we shouldn't give them any calls to trace," he said.

"Oh no," blurted Shell.

"What is it?" Topher and Betty asked in unison.

"My mom is texting me!"

"What did she say?" asked Topher.

Shell read for a moment. "She's asking where I am since the school called and said I never went in."

Topher thought for a moment. "Don't reply. Quick; hand me your phone."

Shell did as he asked without hesitation. She pulled her wrap phone out of her Armer and handed it over. Topher rapidly tapped on the screen before handing it back.

"I logged you into the city's Wi-Fi. Since they probably know we're in New York anyway, this will make it harder for them to find an exact location.

Although, once we pay, they'll know we were at this diner… Unless we pay in cash." They exchanged dubious glances. We should go as soon as we pay."

"But what should I say?" Shell asked.

"Just don't reply," Topher suggested.

"I'll try usin' the phone here," chimed in Betty, rushing from the table.

Shell put her phone back in her Armer. Betty returned to the table a few moments later. They looked up at her with eager hope.

"No answer," said Betty. The weight of concern pressed harder upon their heads, dropping their chins to their chests.

"Maybe we can text him. Does he check his email regularly? Is he on Netbook or Social Plus or Digital Neighborhood?" Topher rambled with desperation.

"I don't know. I've never heard of any of those."

"Then we'd have to build a profile for you so you could reach out. That would take a few minutes." Topher looked at her phone. "How old is that phone? I don't think that phone can access those sites."

"Buck up. I know where he lives and he's always home. We'll just knock on his door."

Shell snapped her fingers, and grinned. "That's old school."

The three of them collected their things and headed for the exit. Betty paid the bill with her credit card, knowing that it would leave a trail for anyone looking for them, but she didn't have any cash. They left the restaurant and headed east on 42nd Street toward the heart of Times Square. Even during the middle of the day, the bright lights overwhelmed the senses. Billboards bigger than Shell's house displayed bright 3D images.

BRIGHTER LIGHTS BRING DARKER SHADOWS

One building had a television screen as wide as a city block showing a baseball game.

"I've seen bigger," Topher joked in regards to the massive display.

"Try to blend in, kids; and that means don't get caught staring at the lights and the tall buildings. Up here is the craziest area, especially." Betty noticed the book bags on their backs and Shell's sleeve rolled up, revealing her Armer. "Carry your bags on your stomachs and, Shell, cover up that doohickey. You don't want to be a target for some of the thieves 'round here." The kids didn't fight Betty on any of her suggestions. Shell felt a sense of appreciation that Betty cared about their safety.

The cohorts walked through Times Square expecting an attack from every angle. Fortunately for them, their odd assortment of an older woman in a sweatshirt and her two potential children or grandchildren with book bags over their stomachs blended in with the randomness of New York.

Passing the subway entrance they came from when they got off the bus, Shell realized they were once again across from the Port Authority and thought it curious they could access the massive building at the street level as well as via subterranean tunnel. She wondered how many paths traveled below the streets of New York.

Finally, after dodging a few dozen more aggressive walkers and sightseers, they came to Times Square, the massive intersection where Broadway met 42nd Street, full of movie theaters, wax museums, fast food restaurants, and a slew of shopping venues. The sidewalks overflowed to the point that people spilled into the streets and walked next to the taxicabs and bike couriers. They walked by street performers who danced in only flip-flops and board shorts. Another guy charged tourists to take pictures with him and his Australian pets. A woman speed-painted a caricature portrait of a couple using both of her hands at the same time.

Just as Shell peered straight up at the daunting skyscrapers, a swarm of police cars came screaming down Broadway right in front of her. Most citizens stopped to watch the action while others went on about their business. Shell had seen cops speed by before, but not this many. The siren noise dominated the area as if nothing else existed. She did not expect the two gunshots that came next.

Chapter 21 - Signals Crossed

Everyone in the area instinctively ducked. A woman nearby screamed. Betty clutched Shell and Topher to her chest, trying to shield them from any danger.

Cars everywhere screeched to a halt just a few yards away from them. The ear-piercing noise sent a chill up Shell's spine. She shuddered at the thought that the police had found her already and sent an army to arrest her. Visions of armed men pointing guns at her froze her in fear until more gunshots and small explosions proved that the police had other things to worry about right then.

Topher nudged her and pointed to a black S.U.V. skidding through the intersection. Sparks leapt from its two rear shot-out tires as it slid toward a rather elaborate glass subway entrance. All of the bystanders braced for the impact, as if the S.U.V. headed straight for them.

Just as it nearly crashed through the glass, a series of automatic traffic posts rose out of the ground and stopped the vehicle just short of creating a disaster, crushing the front end and twisting its rear until it faced the subway entrance. In a choreographed maneuver, the police cars formed a semicircle around the crumpled S.U.V. Bolting out of their cars and using their doors as barricades against the criminals trapped in the steam-emanating, fluid-dripping, wedged wreck.

Officers taped off a large section to keep the rapidly growing number of spectators a safe distance from the danger.

Shell, Topher and Betty got a front-row view. The policemen and women dressed themselves in riot gear while in their defensive positions behind the open doors, hoods, and trunks of the police cars. They took aim at the smoking vehicle. The tinted windows of the S.U.V. prevented Shell and most others from seeing any movement within, raising the tension and intrigue of everyone in sight.

One buffed policeman waved his hand in the air. Without speaking, he organized his team with a few commanding hand gestures, pointed to the crashed vehicle, and they moved in. The gathering took a collective gasp of apprehension in anticipation of what might happen next. People, who couldn't see, hollered out questions and requests for details.

"They're moving in," Topher shared with the people around him. His message echoed throughout the crowd as if he had screamed it into the Grand Canyon.

The police team only took a couple of steps before two doors of the S.U.V. facing the subway station swung open. From where Shell stood, she could see only faint swirling clouds in the distance. A group of armed men dressed in black and gray camouflage jumpsuits hopped out, pulling a dark-haired woman in red high-heeled shoes with them.

"I see about five men. All with guns. And they've got a hostage," Topher whispered to anyone around him listening.

The policeman rescinded his signal to advance with a sudden sharp and forceful fist in the air. All of the approaching policemen stopped and held their positions. Behind them, more officers crammed into the previously empty glass-encased subway entrance, surrounding the presumed criminals. Topher continued to give everyone the play-by-play.

"We'll shoot her! We promise you that!" one of the criminals screamed with a deep, raspy voice as he held his position between the car and the subway entrance. "We'll shoot her, you, and all of the people watching." Their guns pointed at the hostage and out in all directions. The bystanders in their line of sight ducked and screamed, but refused to leave the scene. A massive spotlight shone down on the entire area once the police helicopter arrived with a half-dozen news choppers in tow.

"Drop your weapons and release the hostage!" said one older, rounder, unarmed policeman with a megaphone from behind one of the police cars.

"You drop yours! We're ridin' out of here," replied the presumed leader of the criminal crew.

Topher smirked. "This is just like TV," he whispered.

The stalemate ensued for what felt like hours. The initial response team had backed away and huddled alongside the officer with the bullhorn. The crowd behind the police tape swelled, filling the gaps left by those with better instincts for survival with those addicted to rubbernecking. More police showed up in an attempt to control the crowd.

"We're sending over a negotiator," hollered the man with the megaphone.

Shell's attention followed everyone else's as they watched a man in stained khakis and an off-brown non-matching jacket, beige loafers, a blue-striped button-up, and an undone red tie walk into the clearing between the ring of police and the criminals. He walked timidly but upright. Of average build and average height, he did not look intimidating, but Shell saw something she doubted anyone else noticed. The man's skin glowed with hundreds of pulsating blue marbles of light that seemed to dim and illuminate sporadically.

The negotiator proceeded into the clearing with his hands in the air. "My name is Glenn Watkins. I am going to remove my weapons," he yelled out to the criminals with a weak, slow, punctuated and octave-shifting voice. "Please do not fire your weapons."

Slowly, he took off his jacket and dropped it on the street as he tight-rope-walked toward the gunmen. He then undid the harness that held his gun under his arm. Someone from the crowd whistled. He eased the harness to the ground, stood up tall, raised his arms, palms out, navigated a three-point circle slowly, and then continued to creep closer to the criminals.

As the negotiator approached the gunmen, Shell lost sight of him behind the S.U.V. "Guys, this way," she urged as she took off, snaking through the gathered mob. Betty and Topher gave chase until Shell found a better view of the negotiator behind the crashed vehicle.

"This is getting' dangerous, Little Shelly. We don' wanna be near where they might shoot at us," Betty urged.

"There's something about that cop. I need to talk to him."

"Yeah. He's crazy," Topher sneered.

Glenn Watkins walked into the nest of guns, visibly nervous. One of the criminals snapped his gun up and pointed it at his face. All of the police re-aimed their weapons, ready to shoot. The throng gasped.

"Hold your fire," Glenn yelled, his voice cracking.

Sirens blared in the distance and grew louder as fire trucks and ambulances approached the police barricade. The gunmen shifted their aim to intimidate the gathering, drawing more screams. While Glenn attempted to calm them down, the lights that only Shell saw in him started to pulse faster and faster. The fire trucks and ambulances continued blasting their sirens as they parted the multitudes and maneuvered their way to the scene.

Glenn Watkins' comments to the criminals went unheard to the other police and onlookers in Times Square, while the tiny spheres of blue light intensified to a series of blinding white strobe lights invisible to everyone but Shell. She could not make out the shocked faces of the gunmen, but she did see their whirlwinds begin to wobble off balance like a dying top. As their hands weakened their guns trembled and eventually fell to the ground. Loud inaudible mumbling erupted out of the criminals as they each stumbled to the concrete.

Glenn gave the signal and the police emerged from behind their protected positions toward the criminals, tightening the vice around them while obstructing Shell's view. Moans of confusion emanated from the mob of spectators. People launched questions, wondering what happened, but cheered with applause when the police finally parted to reveal the criminals kneeling with their hands cuffed behind them. Some of the police maintained their poker-faced demeanor, but most of them relished in the crowd's appreciation.

Glenn Watkins and a few of the officers escorted the criminals into a transport vehicle to be taken to the police station a few blocks away. As he did so, other officers, including the one with the bullhorn, took turns shaking his hand and patting him on the back.

"How did you do that?" One officer asked Glenn Watkins.

"I guess I have a way with words," Glenn responded with a sly smile.

Betty breathed a deep sigh of relief. "Well, that was excitin.' Shall we venture on?" She suggested.

"We need to talk to that negotiator," Shell declared.

"I thought we wanted to hide from the police," Topher reminded her.

Shell took a moment to consider the outcome of both choices. If she wanted to talk to the negotiator, she'd have to go into the police station and they might recognize her, which would make everything up to now pointless. But, if she could talk to the negotiator and explain to him what she saw, maybe he could help her.

"Can we not make this day any crazier than it's already been?" pleaded Topher.

Shell hesitated before nodding in agreement, and they continued east on 42nd Street.

They walked several more blocks and started to wind their way down some of the dimly lit avenues and residential streets of Manhattan's eastern Midtown section where fewer people stalled their progress.

"How do you think they got those bad guys to drop their weapons?" Topher asked.

"They probably told them that they'd get in less trouble now than if they put up a fight," answered Betty.

They walked along silently after that. Shell wondered if they should turn themselves in. She eyed Betty as they walked, wondering why Betty looked like a kid's knit blanket and trying to piece together the reason behind the negotiator's appearance. She thought about the things that happened to Betty and the things the negotiator seemed to do. She caught glimpses of her own reflection in car windows as she passed them, but didn't see anything special about herself. No assortment of colors, no pulsing lights, and no masking tornado. She looked down at her feet and still saw the translucent, waterless waves encircling her feet, but it still felt uninspiring to her. She tried to convince herself that nothing had happened to her, that she didn't have anything special like she saw in Betty and the negotiator. The culmination of the past two days weighed heavily on her. She grew more frustrated than scared at her inability to see anyone's face. She felt more comfortable around Betty and Topher, but to not know what caused all of this made her worry. *Am I stuck like this forever? How am I ever going to fix this if I don't tell someone? Maybe I should tell Dad.*

"Are we getting closer?" Topher complained.

"Of course we are," Betty replied. "It's just a few more blocks."

Thank goodness, Shell thought. The odd noises of the city made her frantic. Bottles breaking, trash cans slam, high-pitched squeaks, the clicking of scampering bugs, and even paper crumpling all made her jumpier than usual. Whenever she looked to see where the noises were coming from, she wound up catching glimpses of small swirling winds scampering in the shadows.

"Keep ya eyes out for a church," said Betty.

"We've passed at least three already," replied Topher. "Nice big ones."

"Those tourist traps aren't what we're looking for," Betty rejoined.

They continued on for another half block when they came to the Catholic Church of Saints.

"Here we are!" exclaimed Betty to a doubtful Shell and Topher.

The church looked nothing like the others they had passed along the way, blending in with the storefronts and brownstones along the block. Only a sign with the church's name on it and a cross gave the building any church-like distinguishing characteristics. The doors stood behind a tall metal gate shaped to match the church doors. Betty grabbed the large, round, metal doorknocker and gently banged it against the gate three times. A moment later, a short balding man in a black robe with a black and white collar opened the door.

"Good evening," said the thin man. "How can I be of service?"

"Jon? It's Betty. Betty Harmony."

The priest looked Betty over. He smiled warmly and gave her a big hug. Without another word, he invited the mismatched bunch into the church and closed the door behind them.

"I am Father Jon," the man said to Shell and Topher. "I am the live-in priest here at the Catholic Church of Saints. If there is anything you need, please just ask. Betty and I have been friends since…" He turned to her. "My, how long has it been?"

"Since… Maybe elementary."

"My, my. It has been quite a while."

"It's been quite a day for the three of us already. I tried to call you, and hoped that you would be able to..."

"It will be my pleasure," Father Jon finished for her. "Are you hungry or thirsty?"

Shell and Topher shook their heads.

"We had lunch not too long ago," Betty replied.

"All right then."

He walked them down the aisle of the church. Shell took notice of all the unlit candles, the large cross hanging from the ceiling, and the organ up against the front wall of the chapel. Everyone took a seat, Betty on one of the pews at the front of the church, Topher and Shell on the floor in front of her, and Father Jon in a chair he pulled over from the pulpit. Betty gave Father Jon the recap on what brought them to him thus far, with Shell commenting along the way.

"So, what's next?" Father Jon asked after Betty and Shell finished their story, sounding as exhausted as the trio felt.

Shell and Topher exchanged dumbfounded glances. "Head back home I guess," Topher answered. "We're probably gonna get it for skipping school."

"Are you going to be okay here, Betty?" Shell asked.

"I'll be just fine. Thank you two so much for everything. Who knows where I'd be if you hadn't come for me?"

"I've got some protein bars and bottled water you two should take with you, in case you get hungry on the way home. I'll be right back," Father Jon commented as he left the room.

Betty gave Shell a big hug. "Thank you so much for all you has done. You're my hero, Little Shell." She looked up at Betty's yarn-like skin and smiled.

"Take care of my girl, kind sir," Betty directed to Topher while she palmed his head and ruffled his hair.

"Will do, ma'am," he replied with a country western accent.

"Are you two sure you'll be okay getting' back?" Betty asked.

"We'll be fine," said Shell reassuringly as Father Jon returned with their snacks. "We'll come back on Saturday to see how you're doing. If we're not grounded, that is."

The kids waved to Father Jon and Betty as they left the church. The sky had grown overcast over the past hour, giving the city a shade of gray only New York could create. The tall drab buildings seemed to imprint on the sky, giving the afternoon a duller shade than the vibrant blue Shell had grown used to just a few miles away in Union City. Yet the air felt surprisingly light and oddly fresh, like a wind had blown away all the yesterdays.

Chapter 22 - Channeling Discovery

Shell and Topher strolled through the streets a little less apprehensive than they had felt a few hours ago. Walking amongst the crowd of rat-racing businessmen gave them a sense of security. Two kids strolling around by themselves during a school day did not look as out of place in a busy city like New York, and it kept them below everyone's radars.

"I'm surprised you don't get stepped on more often," Topher joked. "No one around here seems to even notice us. Yet, somehow, they manage to dodge us without even looking."

"It's like they sense us, but don't notice us," Shell added loud enough for him to hear above the traffic, but quiet enough to not draw attention.

She tried to look up at the other pedestrians, but her inability to see their faces frightened her. She caught herself staring at Topher. She relied on her memory to imagine how his eyes squinted when he smiled, how his lips pouted when he was nervous, and how his ears moved when he raised his eyebrows. She missed his face, but having him with her all the time helped. *I hate dragging him through all of this, but I'm glad he's here. There's no way I could do this on my own,* she thought. *But I can't let him get in trouble. I don't know what Jack could do. He might send him away to another relative or to a foster home. I can't imagine not having him with me.*

"Shouldn't we be heading back the way we came?" Shell asked Topher.

"We are," he grunted.

She looked around. "I don't think we came this way."

"How can you tell?"

"I don't remember so many stores and bus stops."

"I think Betty took a funny way of finding the church. Either way, the city's a grid. So long as we're headed in the right direction, we'll be fine."

His words did little to comfort her, especially after his delayed arrival to the hospital earlier. His sense of direction had never impressed anyone, but Shell felt like they would reach their destination eventually. While weaving their way through the streets back toward Times Square and the Port Authority, Shell and Topher took a path that led them to one of the broadcast columns located around New York City.

Broadcast columns stood about fifteen feet tall and had four forty-eight-inch screens around their circumference. Each has five rows of screens stacked vertically one above another to make for one massive display. Coffee shops, restaurants, and media conglomerates typically owned and operated these giant

TV tubes so they could display several channels at once or multiple viewings of the same channel. The column Shell and Topher happened by presented the same show on every screen, drawing a large crowd.

"Is that your mom?" Topher asked, his voice pitched from excitement.

"Probably," Shell answered, sounding rather embarrassed.

She kept walking, but he stopped in his tracks. "Is that Betty?" he asked, stopping Shell mid-stride.

She whipped around to the broadcast column, glancing up toward one of the top screens not blocked by the dozens of people standing in front of her.

"No way!" she exclaimed before burrowing her way through the crowd to get a closer look at the column.

They played the audio over the speakers. Mrs. Wayburn delivered the following report:

"This just in: Reports on the aftereffects of the world-encompassing storm from two nights ago continue to pour in. Flooding and power outages across the U.S. and around the world are forcing people to abandon homes and seek refuse in shelters. Calls, Tweets, and posts continue to discuss the potential religious and environmental implications of the storm. One quotes stated, 'The Armageddon of previous generations was only a precursor, and this is the real one.' Another blogger claims, 'The apocalypse is now.'

"Maybe none of these recent events represent either scenario. Rumors abound that the storm is to blame, or to thank. That depends on which end of the story you hold faith in for the recent string of supposed miracles. All that can be quantifiably justified is that along with the number of unexplainable events, we are seeing increases in criminal activity.

"Just this morning in a hospital in Union City, New Jersey, the woman pictured here, Betty Harmony— a patient potentially impacted by the storm—escaped her minimum security room with the aid of two accomplices." Black and white video footage rolled of Shell, Topher and Betty dodging a mob of doctors and the security guard as they escaped through the emergency room. "Her daughter has stepped forward and shared that Betty Harmony has struggled with Alzheimer's ever since she caused a car accident that took the lives of her two children. Please call 9-1-1 with any details of her whereabouts. Betty's accomplices remain unidentified.

"In unconfirmed unrelated news, several gunmen were taken into custody after holding a woman hostage and threatening multiple people in a crowd in Times Square, New York City this afternoon. The heroic negotiator, Glenn Watkins, convinced the men to drop their weapons and release the hostage before any injuries were sustained.

"This story just in; apparently also in Manhattan last night, a bizarre case of vandalism took place when a swarm of bugs infested a grocery store, devouring nearly ten thousand dollars' worth of produce and foodstuffs. A recording shows countless insects flying into the store through the air ducts and crawling under the doors. The only suspect appears to be a homeless man peering through a window before the bugs filled the room and blocked out the cameras.

"We currently have no evidence to prove the relationship of these crimes to the storm, but officials can confirm that the storm has had an impact on the minds of people here at home and around the world.

Thus far in the online community, groups have formed in defense and in strong protest of those responsible for these events. While no hate crimes have been reported, national security does ask that everyone leave the handling of these circumstances to the authorities. We also ask that everyone work together to keep one another safe during these confusing times. We here at the Global News Network will continue to bring you the news as we learn of it. Until the next story, I'm Victoria Wayburn."

The security camera footage of them escaping the ER played over and over again in her mind. *I'm a criminal,* she thought. She stood in shock, confused by her mother's act; furious that she condemned Betty, but grateful she did not throw Topher and her under the bus. Shell assumed her mom recognized her in the video.

Topher tugged on her arm. "Can you believe that? We totally got away with it."

"You think we did?" erupted Shell. "They know we were at the hospital. They know I know Betty. By now, they've spoken to my parent. They'll have me pegged once they show my picture to that cop that sat outside Betty's room… They're gonna track me down!"

"Calm down," Topher pleaded.

"Easy for you to say. They don't have your name."

"Not yet, maybe. It's only a matter of time before they figure out I skipped school too and wonder if I was with you. Then they'll show my picture to that cop, too."

"So what do we do?"

"I don't know. If we go back, we're busted. If we don't go back, we'll be busted eventually." Topher's rational brainstorming made Shell feel better having him along, but it didn't help her feel better about their situation.

"I just wanted to help someone. She needed our help, didn't she?"

"Maybe. Probably. If we go back now, maybe we'll be in less trouble."

"But we didn't do anything wrong, really," whined Shell. "If we can prove that we did the right thing, we'll be off the hook."

"How are we going to do that?" Topher asked, to which Shell had no answer.

"I have no idea. We need help. There's gotta be someone we can go to who can prove Betty isn't a danger to others; that she didn't need to be treated that way in the hospital." A memory popped into Shell's head. Something from her dreams finally made sense. "Maybe there is someone. We just need to find them."

"You're starting to sound a bit loony again," Topher nagged.

"No, really," Shell stopped herself from explaining her dream. "There's someone out there who knows what's going on. We need to find them. They'd be able to fix this whole thing."

"What 'whole thing'? I still don't get what the big deal is. I mean sure, the storm, crazy events, but what's special about Betty? And why do you feel the need to figure this all out for her?"

Shell thought explaining her situation could help, but still felt unsure about it. "If you don't help people when you can, then what good are you?" It felt weird to quote her father. An icky feeling in her stomach alerted her that she may have offended Topher with her comment. "Sorry; I didn't mean it like that." She started to tap away on her Armer when Topher intervened.

"What are you doing?"

"I'm trying to find someone who has answers."

"Yeah, but if you use that thing, the cops will track us down even faster. We need to blend in, digitally. We need... a library."

It excited Shell to have Topher committed to the adventure. "How do we find the closest one?"

"Should we just ask somebody?"

Within minutes, the duo found themselves standing across the street from a massive stone building with two lions flanking the foot of its wide stairway. The sign in front of it read "Bryant Park Public Library."

"I guess this is it," Topher finally said.

They walked to the closest crosswalk and waited for the flashing hand to turn into the walking man. As they waited, several school buses drove past them and parked in front of the library. The light finally turned, allowing Shell and Topher to cross, but both of them had their eyes on the kids exiting the bus.

"Not even a week into school and they're already on a field trip," Topher commented.

"I could think of more fun places to go than a library."

"Anything to get out of class."

"I got you out of class," joked Shell.

Topher chuckled just enough to make her feel a bit better about their predicament.

"Let's sneak in with them," he suggested. "They look like they're in high school." He grabbed her elbow and pulled her in line with the kids walking toward the library. "We need to blend in. Try to look taller." He chuckled more than she did, but Shell felt better sensing a smile on his face.

"It's a public library, do we really have to sneak in?" she asked after growing more and more uncomfortable with all of the little tornadoes swirling around her that added to the standard teenage egos and penetrating judgments.

"Just go with it," replied Topher as he held her in line, doing his best to not draw extra attention.

She pictured his bottom lip sticking out, a clear tell of how nervous he felt. She would have seen it had the clouds not gotten in the way.

"Get in line you two!" a lady yelled from the front of the line of students.

Shell and Topher froze, almost causing a pile up of students behind them. Topher nearly tripped over his feet when he gave Shell an extra tug as they snuck in front of two kids playing a game on their Armers. Topher noticed two other buses unloading more students, offering them more of a crowd to blend into.

"I'm pretty sure we could have just walked in," she commented.

"This is way more fun," he replied, somewhat giddy.

They followed the crowd into the library and walked into a swarm of teachers funneling the students into the South Hall of the Rose Reading Room. Large windows and walls of books you needed ladders to reach adorned the perimeter of the enormous chamber while chandeliers illuminated the gold-and-copper-framed swimming pool-sized digital paintings on the ceiling. Shell focused on the massive oak tables lined with flat screen computer monitors and tablets. After spotting a camera that hung above the door she entered through, Shell quickly looked down and nudged Topher in the arm.

"Yeah," Topher said confidently. "That's why we need to blend in. We don't want to pop up on any more reality shows."

CHANNELING DISCOVERY

"Maybe the library was a bad idea," Shell whispered.

Topher ignored her and continued into the large room, the two of them taking seats at one of the large tables with the other students. The noise of a hundred kids walking, whispering, sliding chairs, and giggling, along with teachers shushing everyone, made for quite a disturbance in the typically and supposedly discreet domicile. A woman stood at the front of the room with her hand up, signaling for the students to lower their voices. It took some time for her to gain the attention of the majority of the crowd. She introduced herself as the head librarian and demonstrated to those paying attention to pull out the retractable earphones from a console in the middle of the table. Topher followed along sheepishly, urging Shell to play along.

Shell reached for the turn-of-the-century mouse and keyboard in front of her, but the computer did not turn on. Topher had his earphones in already, listening to the instructions given by the woman standing in front of the room, who seemed to be whispering into a headset. He noticed Shell pounding on the keys.

"I think the librarians should turn them on after she's done talking," he explained. "It sounds like all these kids go to schools where they don't have computers. They bus them here once a week. It's like gym class or something."

"That's wonderful for them, but we don't go to their school, so we don't need to sit here acting like kindergarteners." Shell stood up from her chair, looking around the room for an open computer.

Topher, who had been grinning at everyone he made eye contact with, turned to whisper, "Relax. Just play along. We'll—" he stopped when he noticed Shell making her way from the table. He stood up and grabbed her by the arm before she got too far away.

"You two, take your seats!" another teacher hollered in her loudest whisper.

Shell heard the request, but did not bother to look at where it came from. Topher finally pulled her back to their seats.

"Are you trying to get us caught? Now you've got the teachers staring right at us. If they find out that we're not supposed to be with them, we'll get in more trouble. Will you just trust me?"

Shell trusted him, but she also felt a bit pressed for time.

"Just be patient," he concluded.

Shell pouted for the remainder of the lecture, refusing to put in the earphones while Topher continued to act as the perfect student, smiling cordially to complete strangers. An echoing rustle of retractable earphones signaled the end of the librarian's lecture, and the computer monitors turned on.

Shell started typing away. Her hands felt awkward on the antiquated two-handed QWERTY keyboard, but at times like this, she appreciated the typing class her school forced on her in sixth grade. Topher pulled over one of the tablets and started scrolling through pages.

First, Shell visited GNN.com to see how much more they had on Betty. Fortunately, she didn't find more than what her mother mentioned in the report earlier that morning—just Betty's picture, her name, and a screen shot of that security camera footage.

Thank goodness it's in black and white or I'd need a new sweatshirt, Shell thought. She continued to scroll through the site, not finding much more than the stories she already had read or heard.

"Find anything yet?" Topher asked.

"Not yet."

"What are you looking for?"

"Anything. Blog sites. News sites. Anything."

"But for what? Storm? Weird events? Hospitals? I just realized that I have no idea what we're looking for. I'd like to help, but this is kinda your thing."

Shell paused. "I guess you're right."

After waiting a moment for her to respond, Topher sat back in his chair, glanced over at Shell's monitor for some clues, and then went about his own searches.

Shell jumped to a few sites she visited the other night. She typed in her first query, "hallucinations." The results populated on the screen. The first ten of over one million results gave her links to drugs, altered mind states, definitions, symptoms, and crazy-colored images. She decided to get a bit more specific. She entered "everything is surrounded by waves." Her results this time gave her a laundry list of articles and definitions associated with the ocean, radio waves, and airwaves. She scrolled down a bit to a video of an artist's interpretation of how people were made of waves, gave off waves, and were surrounded by waves. A few of the comments people left after viewing the video left the impression that most people did not believe what the artist tried to convey; that people, plants, animals, and even rocks all had life and gave off their own vibrations.

After everything Shell had seen, she felt the artist knew more about her ordeal than anyone else could have. She ran another search for "human vibration" and came across more articles about chakras, psychic healing, and the physics of energy fields. She knew nothing about any of these subjects. It didn't make any sense. Still, she did find comfort in that at least someone else had an idea of what she kept seeing.

"Look at this," Topher whispered. He had to poke her in the arm a half-dozen times before she stopped looking at her own monitor.

Shell leaned over in her chair to get a better view of his tablet. Her jaw dropped. Topher had found a blog site listing out crazy and supposed storm-related events that had taken place around the world. The two of them scrolled down the list, reading out the craziest of scenarios in disbelief.

"*BULL HOGTIES RANCHERS. BEAR HIJACKS RV. FLYING ALLIGATOR FLEES SWAMP. ELEPHANT DISCOVERS ANCIENT ARTIFACT. MASSACRE IN MEXICO. I SAW SHIVA. NEW BUDDHA. WIFE IGNITES HUSBAND. POLICE CLUELESS TO ROBBERY. TEENAGER DEFLECTS BULLETS.*"

The list went on and on. Just the first page had links to stories about events in China, France, Cambodia, Russia, Canada, Hawaii, the United States, Brazil, Africa, and Thailand. They clicked to the next page and saw even more headlines. They continued through a few more pages and finally came to a familiar story. "*OLD WOMAN DEFIES SCIENCE IN HOSPITAL.*"

They clicked into the news-reaction site story and read about how Betty created quite the stir in the hospital before two young teenagers helped her escape.

"We're so busted," bemoaned Shell.

"Not yet we're not. They still don't know where we are."

"They know we're in New York."

"Maybe, but not where in New York. It's a big city."

"So who do we go to for help?"

"Did you find anyone?"

"Maybe. There's an artist I came across and a physics professor."

"Where are they?"

"Let me see." Shell hopped back over to her computer and scrolled back through her history, looking for "Contact Us" info on the two sites she found. "It looks like the artist is in Australia and…" she paused for a moment while she checked the other site, "and the professor is in L.A."

"Both of those are going to be hard to get to," Topher acknowledged.

"Maybe we can web-convo," suggested Shell, who started typing furiously.

"Are you emailing them? What are you telling them?"

"Just that we need their help. What about your site?"

He clicked and scrolled to the end of the story before blurting out, "He's in New York!"

"Ask him if he can meet us."

"He's got Direct Connect. I'm asking him." Topher sent his message to a non-descript avatar. He and Shell stared at the blinking chat box. "Come on already," he snarled, a little louder than the other murmurings in the library. He drew a few requests for silence in the form of *"Shush!"*

Finally, the invitation popped onto the screen: *"Starbucks. 49th and Broadway. Four o'clock today. I'll be wearing orange."*

"Yes!" They celebrated with a high-five, drawing more disapproving noises from the teachers and librarians.

They slunk back down in the chairs, hiding from the noise monitors. "It's two o'clock now. And it should be close by," Shell whispered. "We can get answers and then he can help us with Betty." With that, they grabbed their bags and made their way for the front door.

Chapter 23 - Elsewhere

Dusty, dirty, and forgotten—the neglected streets of the trash-infested Mexican border town, Tijuana, looked both busy and desolate at the same time. The mixed crowd roamed like lost cattle. Locals paced the dingy sidewalks despairingly, as if waiting for fortune of any magnitude to come their way, while brightly dressed visitors hurried from one hole-in-the-wall souvenir shop to another.

Vendedores callejeros pushed two-wheeled food carts through semi-busy streets. Filthy rags wiped the brows of overly tanned inhabitants. Everything had a price in this third-world market. Jewelry, religious statues, and authentic delicacies filled the menu. Despite the courteous smiles of the business conductors, the town gave off a vibe indicating that all illegal activities could be gotten away with at the traveler's own risk. Desperation served as the common ingredient baked into the hearts and souls of all who came here, desperate for absolution in either moral direction. The look of longing on every face only paled in comparison to the unsightly animals that scavenged along busy streets and alleyways. Dogs, cats, rats—it's own circle of life.

Tag-less mutts roamed freely in this unlicensed territory. Only by sight and familiarity would a resident know the origin of a dog well enough to say its name or offer it a friendly pat on the head. Unfamiliar animals went ignored and they behaved as such, committed to the shadows and blind spots of would-be onlookers. A stray dog served no purpose but its own need to survive. Arid wastelands full of threats and leftovers could only be home to the most cunning foragers.

With the Great Storm just three days past, the memories of the dark clouds rolling in and the rain pouring down continued to inspire the masses with a level of reverence great enough to lift their spirits and their eyes to the sky. Despite the weight of the social and environmental burdens pressing upon their shoulders, hope filled their desperate hearts and gave them a respite from the impenetrable dryness of their vegetation-deprived wilderness. For now, people chose to ignore the overwhelming reality that optimism eventually dissipates like the last drop of water from a smoldering, sun-cooked metal basin.

However, they failed to realize that the tempest that brought them hope also brought to life a legendary nightmare. So while they waited for the precipitation to return, the bane the rain made crept closer, bearing the stain of rage and fury.

Chapter 24 - Breadcrumbs

An uplifting sense of hope and promise guided Shell and Topher to their next destination. The weather felt perfect as they walked from block to block amidst the shade- and breeze-inducing skyscrapers, and took in the majesty of the city. For once, they did not feel intimidated by the congestion. They strolled through Times Square like tourists with their heads on a swivel, marveling at the melting pot around them.

They arrived at the Starbucks and went inside, but the aroma of coffee made them both nearly gag. "I hate coffee," commented Topher.

"Me, too."

They headed back outside and took a seat on the grungy sidewalk next to the coffee shop's entrance, keeping an eye out for anyone walking nearby wearing orange.

"Maybe we'll catch him early. What do you think he'll look like?" Topher asked. "I bet he's an old professor with a beard."

"Totally. He's gotta be old. I'm guessing he works in a museum."

"What if he's, like, a fat lazy slob who lives in his mom's basement, like a hacker or some not-so-starving artist or a writer or something?" He grinned, as if he had solved the puzzle.

"What if *he* is a *she*, and she's like this grungy hippy revolutionist type who dresses like a gypsy and organizes protests?"

"What if it's a trap?" Topher continued.

He elaborated, while Shell's joy waned. She considered the reality seriously. It crossed her mind that anything could happen. The police could show up at the coffee shop and corner them, or it could be some kind of kidnapper.

"Did you tell them what we look like?" she asked with a serious tone.

"No. Why?" Topher's enthusiasm evaporated.

"Do you think it's odd that someone would want to meet us without knowing who we are or why we want to meet or what we look like?"

"I guess. Or they could just be willing to help and none of that stuff matters," he replied as his concern toward the people walking by heightened. "Just keep a look out."

The words stung Shell unexpectedly.

"Topher," Shell choked on the words she had to say next. "I have to…" She paused. "We should get out of here."

"There's a bathroom inside," he offered, confused by her sudden suggestion.

"No. It's not that. I think this is a bad idea."

BREADCRUMBS

"What are you talking about? We're finally going to get some help. If we leave now, how are we going to be able to go home without getting in serious trouble?"

"It just doesn't feel right. We should have asked the guy more questions. Do you remember the site?" She opened up the flap that covered the flex-screen on her Armer and started to type in a web-search.

Topher flipped it shut, slightly shoving her in the process.

"What are you doing?" she demanded.

"What are *you* doing? I told you, you can't use that thing."

"I just got this thing. Gah. I'm trying to look up that person we're supposed to meet and make sure we're not waiting here for someone to kidnap us."

"By telling the whole world where we are?"

"Sometimes the best place to hide is in the public eye. I just want to know who we're meeting here. I need to make sure it's someone we can trust."

"Trust, huh? You don't even trust me."

Her face turned somber.

"Please, Shell. Please tell me what I skipped school for. Tell me why I'm risking getting kicked into foster care by my deadbeat uncle. Please." At that very moment, as Topher flailed his arms with all of his exasperated 'pleases,' a stranger walked by and dropped some change in his direction. The coins clinked on the sidewalk by his feet. He and Shell watched with confused glances as the stranger walked away.

"You know what?" he continued, feeling rather fed up. "It doesn't matter."

"All right," Shell choked. "I'll tell you. I don't really know how to explain it. Everywhere I look, it's like... it's like..."

167

"It's like what?"

Shell started to mouth the words she had longed to say, but her voice choked on the thought of what could happen if Topher didn't believe her. "It's nothing."

"Seriously?" he exploded. "I can't believe this. You're keeping things from me? You've been keeping things from me since this all started. You're acting weird and I've been following you like an idiot. I thought you needed help. I trusted you. I don't know what you want or what you need, but if it's *nothing*," he mocked, "then I don't need to be here."

He stood; ready to leave the front of the coffee shop.

"I can't see you," she cried, and a sense of relief washed over her.

Topher heard her, but it did not register. Something distracted him. "What? What are you talking about?"

"I can't see you," Shell continued, frustrated, but she didn't notice him not paying attention to her. "I can't see your face, and I can't really see your body."

Topher wasn't paying much attention to her, as something appeared to preoccupy his thoughts. He stared down the block at a man approaching the Starbucks.

"I'm standing right here," he replied, noticeably uninterested in her comments.

Shell looked around, hoping to see what could distract him from hearing what she longed to tell him and what he must have longed to hear. Amongst the dozens of whirlwinds passing by, she noticed one that seemed headed straight for her.

"Is he wearing orange?" she asked. She opened the flap on her Armer. The screen had never turned off, and the clock on it read four.

"He's wearing a white suit," Topher responded.

"Is it the guy from the hospital?"

"I think so."

"We gotta get out of here."

They took off down the block, away from the man in white. Topher turned back and must have seen the man in white running after them, because he sped up and urged Shell to keep up, but her shorter legs struggled to do so. They dashed across an intersection while the warning hand flashed. By the time the man in white got to them, the light had turned green and the traffic separated them from their pursuer.

Topher turned around again to see that the man in white chose not to dodge six lanes of New York City cab drivers. That bought them thirty seconds. They continued down the block, crossed the next intersection, headed left down the next block, and made the first right they could.

"Did we…lose him?" Shell asked out of breath.

"I haven't seen him…for a while," Topher replied, equally exhausted.

"How do you think they found us?"

"I was wondering the same thing. Either they put up that website and set us up to meet them there, or they're tracking the Armers."

Shell fumbled with her Armer and turned it off entirely.

"If they tracked my Armer, then we better keep moving."

They ran down the rest of the block and made another left at the next intersection. The two had settled into a nice jog down a few more blocks when Shell came to a halt.

"What is it?" Topher asked.

She glanced around to make sure no one watched her. "This way."

"What?" His doubtful frustrations started to bubble again.

"Just trust me." She made her way toward a bus stop.

"What's going on now? And what is this about you can't—"

Shell put her hand up to cover his mouth and tried to stare into his eyes.

"I will tell you everything in a second. Just keep quiet."

A bus pulled up and the two got on. Shell paid for both of their tickets again, using up the last fairs she had on her metro-app, and they took seats toward the back. They rode quietly for a while, and Shell kept her eyes focused on the front of the bus.

"What's going on already?" Topher pleaded.

"I'm seeing things that don't let me see what I'm used to seeing," she explained in a whisper.

"Well, what do you see?"

"All sorts of things. Different things. Sometimes it's fuzzy. Hazy, kind of. Everywhere I look, I see some kind of wave. You know how on a hot day you look up a hill and it's all wavy, like everything is about to melt?"

"Maybe. I think so."

"Well, that's what I see around people's feet mostly, but I see it around nature too. I also see these little gray whirlwinds, like tornadoes, around everyone's body.

"So I'm in a wavy tornado and my feet are melting?" Topher's condescendence started to seep through the tone of his voice.

She fell quiet again. "I knew you'd think I was weird."

"I always thought you were weird. I just didn't know how weird."

Shell shoved an elbow in his ribs.

"Ow! I'm joking!" Topher chuckled. "I just think you're weird for hanging out with me. You're the only person I really get along with."

"So you believe me?"

"Of course I do. Wavy tornadoes. You see them everywhere?"

"Yeah. Around people, mostly. I think they show up around animals, too. I'm not sure yet."

"Were you born like this?"

"No. I don't think so, anyway. I think it was that storm. All I remember is this weird bright purple drop of rain from the storm landing on my hand. It looked like paint, but felt like every other raindrop. I even think I saw another one that was red earlier that day, but the purplish one landed on me and soaked into my hand. The next day, everything started looking weird."

"The night before school started... So that's why you've been acting funny. I figured high school just stressed you out. How could you tell it was me? I thought you said you couldn't see me."

"I can't, not really. I kind of recognized your voice, and then I figured you'd be the only person to talk to me."

"So everyone looks like that?"

"Well..." Shell considered how quickly strange would descend into ludicrous as soon as she told him

171

about the next part, but she dove in the deep end anyway. "There's Betty. She... She looks like a walking, talking ball of yarn."

He couldn't stop himself from laughing. "Yarn?" He tried to quiet down to a whisper. "Come on, Shell! You're kidding me, right? I just don't—"

"I know, right?" Her obliviousness to the absurdity she shared allowed her to ignore his disbeliefs. "I thought I was going crazy, but when they said all this bizarre stuff was happening around her, I knew I wasn't making it up. And that's why I knew there was something about that negotiator. He had all these strange pulsing lights in him. He did something to those bad guys. I know he did."

"Does any of that explain why we're on this bus?" Topher asked.

"Yeah. There's a kid up there. He looks like soda."

"Coke or Sprite?" Topher asked sarcastically.

"Sprite for sure. He's kinda clear, but there's a ton of bubbles. They just float up like soda."

"Why didn't you just go to your parents at the beginning? I'm sure your mom would have loved to help. Your dad could've figured this whole thing out and we wouldn't be doing all of this hiding."

Despite her insecurities, Shell gave him the recap on their dinner conversation.

"So why haven't you told your parents again?"

"Duh! If I tell them, they'll just treat me like they would if I wasn't their daughter. Mom will make a story out of me and Dad will put me in front of a bunch of doctors, and they wouldn't have helped Betty."

"Really? You think your parents would do all that?"

"Parents suck."

Topher fell quiet at the comment. When he didn't respond, Shell figured she said something wrong.

"I'm sorry."

"Have you told Betty?" Topher changed the subject quickly but could not hide the hurt in his voice.

Shell played along, but felt terrible about what she said. "Sorta. I told her I'd been seeing things and having crazy dreams. I think she's been having weird ones, too."

"What kinda dreams?"

Shell tried to explain that as well. She went on about how real they felt to her, how she thought the storm nearly sucked her out of the window and swimming through the city.

"What do you think it all means?"

"I have no idea, but I think they led me to New York."

"So what should we do about Soda Boy?" Topher asked as he turned to look at Shell, who laughed at the new nickname.

"We'll go up to him after he gets off the bus."

"And say what? 'Hey, I noticed you look like a walking carbonated beverage. By the way, my name is Shell and that crazy storm that covered the planet messed me up, too.' Are you going to tell him what you see? What if he tries to do something to you?"

"Good point." She thought about her plan and realized that she had none.

The sun began to set on that Tuesday evening. Commuters gave way to the night owls. Bars and restaurants filled with loud talking men and women who seemed to transform their work clothes into play clothes as they roared and jeered in disheveled revelry. The bus squealed to a stop and Soda Boy, dressed in a long black vest and a body-molded long sleeve shirt covered with silver holographic studded designs, hesitantly stepped off through the front door by the driver. Shell and Topher snuck off through the back door amidst a few other departing passengers.

"He doesn't look so bad to me," Topher commented.

"What if he doesn't know what he can do? What if he can't control it and he explodes all over us or something?" Her voice started to rise, potentially audible to anyone listening from nearby, but still not loud enough for Soda Boy to hear from a bus length away over the city's commotion. "What if he gets us caught?"

Topher tried to calm her down with more shushing.

"I told you what my dad said; they've already started hunting people that were affected and they're looking to study us. I could be a lab rat before the weekend ends. I need to be sure," Shell finished.

"Well, what if he's on a date?" Topher whispered.

Shell looked up and saw Soda Boy standing close to another whirlwind.

"Is that a girl?"

"You almost sound jealous."

"Oh, shut up," she said, flinging another elbow in Topher's direction. "Now what?"

Chapter 25 - Doc's Docs and Docs

Off the coast of Spain, in a Catholic hospital, a nun tended to a man who washed ashore the day after the great storm. Having already dressed his wounds and made him comfortable, she dabbed a warm, wet cloth on his head, whispered prayers, and hummed hymns.

The man lay unconscious under the watchful eye of Sister Amber, who looked at him in wonder of the events that brought him under her care. Sister Amber only knew that the man had been found along a beach and brought to her hospital wearing only a wetsuit with no forms of identification. She searched the Internet for missing persons and found few reports that matched his description. She held on to the hope that this man with disturbing vitals would wake up and answer her questions.

A doctor entered the room and asked for an update. Sister Amber explained that the patient's temperature still showed a core body temperature far colder than most warm-blooded species, yet his heart rate resembled that of a sprinter running for his life. His dilated pupils filled his eyes to the point of showing no eye color beyond black. The doctor left with a few recommended parting prayers that Sister Amber offered to recite for the ill patient.

Sister Amber retired for the evening having watched over him well beyond her shift and past midnight. She kissed his sweaty but freezing forehead, which always gave her lips an icy chill, turned off his light, and left the side of his bed. Alone, with only the moonlight streaming in from a nearby window to accompany him, the patient stirred.

His dreams took him to unexplainable places. From the depths of his slumbered journey, Dr. Hunter awoke. Neither groggy nor achy, feeling only confused, he sat up in bed wondering how he wound up in his current surroundings. He hopped out of bed with a youthful exuberance, walked to the window, and stared at the moon as if he had never seen it before. He stood for several moments before exploring the rest of his room.

The cross on the wall and the scriptures written in Spanish above the door reminded him that he had traveled to Spain previously. Coming upon a mirror in his bathroom, it surprised him to see the scratches, scars, and bruises over his face and arms. He looked down at his chest through the V-neck opening of the hospital gown he wore, and saw even more remnants of physical trauma.

Still unsure of his surroundings, yet sure of his desires, Dr. Hunter peeked outside of his hospital room in hopes of a clear path that would allow him to easily escape the hospital. He spied many people in the hall, but none looked like staff, save for a lone woman working at a desk with a lamp turned on.

Dr. Hunter walked down the hall in the other direction, passing by a few patients who sat alone in chairs in the hallway or stood solemnly against the walls. He tiptoed by them, hoping not to draw their attention, though he found them curious to observe. Initially, none noticed him, but the more of them he passed, the more of them took interest in him, as if their aspirations coincided with his.

Escaping his hospital confines proved rather simple. Still in his hospital gown, he walked the streets of the Spanish city, relieved when he found himself in the town where his journey had begun. He took a familiar cobblestone path through streets narrowed by nearly uniform two- and three-story wood and stone abodes, paying little attention to the street names. Muscle memory proved his most reliable guide.

After a few more odd stares from peculiar-looking people that roamed the empty midnight streets, Dr. Hunter entered into a hotel. The poorly lit lobby may as well have relied on candlelight, but likely used its lack of power as an excuse for ambiance. Dr. Hunter explained that he lost his keys in a boating accident to the barely awake innkeeper and received a new room key without any resistance or further curiosity.

He made his way up to his room to find things relatively normal. The unmade bed, a towel hung haphazardly over the doorknob leading into the tiny tiled bathroom, the flat-screen video display the hotel hung in the room in order to appeal to travelers seeking modern accommodations, and the antique wooden desk and chair

177

by the window all looked familiar, though the scattered notes on the desk felt uncharacteristic.

Walking around and picking things up helped to jog his memory of the events leading up to his dive, but the occurrences that took place after his submersible, Venator, descended into the ocean depths remained a blur. Only a curious sense of pride kept him from wondering why he felt so excited.

One small, rectangular-shaped, clean area on his desk reminded him of his computer. Still antiquated in his methods, he preferred the old-fashioned laptops to the new Scrolls, but he could not recall where he might find his laptop now. Understanding that he had a lot to recollect, he assumed it lost with a part of his memory. Despite the amount of information he could not remember, he did not feel overly concerned for its absence.

A small clock in the room read two in the morning. Dr. Hunter did not feel tired. One of his fondest memories of Spain crossed his mind. He got dressed and left his room, ready to find a place in town still serving dinner.

Chapter 26 - Still Lurking

Soda Boy exited the bus on Amsterdam near 93rd street to find a young lady dressed in a long, flowing yellow skirt, a white, lacey, tight-fitting shirt, a light-colored jacket with pearls hanging off it in all directions, and a tight yellow cap accented with more lace, awaiting his arrival. He approached her with a smile. She greeted him with a kiss on the cheek before they strode down the sidewalk away from Shell and Topher. Shell saw an uncountable number of bubbles come out of nowhere and fill Soda Boy's head with fizz.

"I take it you want to follow them?" Topher asked. Shell nodded and set the pace for the two of them, making sure not to get too close.

Well out of earshot of the couple ahead of them, Topher asked, "Are you going to call you parents tonight?"

"I should, huh?" Shell had not considered reassuring her family. She did not feel any closer to understanding what happened to her, nor to finding the person from her dream, but knew her family would not let her finish any of this if they found her. "I might send them a text message or something. You?"

"I doubt they're even worried. I'd text them, but they don't have cell phones. If they are worried, they might put my picture on the 'Missing' app and then my face will be all over everyone's Armers, video displays, and refrigerators. That might actually be fun."

"That sounds scary to me. I'll send a text in a bit."

"I'll probably call," he concluded.

Shell kept her gaze focused on Soda Boy. She thought it amazing how she could see something so unexpected. She thought of him as some sort of failed comic book science experiment guinea pig that was left to walk the earth as a bubbling combination of liquid and gas, and wondered how his ability would relate to what he looked like to her.

Maybe he's a swimmer that only floats. Maybe he tastes super sweet. Maybe he can turn water into soda. She wondered if her ability meant that she looked a certain way. She thought she could look like a cloud or a tornado to someone who could see things the way she did. But then she doubted she had any abilities at all, since she couldn't see anything when she gazed at herself.

The couple turned right onto 95th Street toward Columbus Avenue, and walked two long blocks. Soda Boy's hand brushed his date's before he quickly stuffed his hand in his pocket. Still, as Shell watched, she kept seeing the waves around their feet intermingling.

"Don't they seem awkward to you?" Topher stated with a envious tone.

"I don't know. They seem fine."

"It's like he's never been on a date before, or something."

"Oh, and you have? Please do share your infinite wisdom on the guidelines of dating."

"I've… I mean… it's not like everyone doesn't know what to do on a date."

"Okay Mr. Expert. What's he doing wrong?"

"Well, if you want to hold someone's hand, you just do it."

"Like you just reach out and grab someone's hand when they're not looking?"

"Exactly." As the words left his mouth, Topher reached out for Shell's hand and grabbed it. She felt the same rush she experienced in the hospital closet earlier that day, but stronger this time. The feeling rushed through her body like a wave, making her tense up and grip Topher's hand tightly. A moment passed before she realized what had happened and quickly let go of his hand, shoving her own into her pocket. Beads of sweat formed on her brow. Topher reluctantly placed his hand back in his pocket.

The couple ahead of them approached a second busy intersection. Shell noticed Central Park across the street and thought about that nice day earlier in the summer when they set up the picnic for her mom. She reached for her phone, ready to turn it on and send her mother a text message.

"They're turning again," Topher interrupted as the couple took a left on Central Park West.

They walked another block and then entered a descending staircase.

"I think they're going into the subway."

Shell put her phone away as they crept up to the top of the stairs, not sure if they'd wind up in another situation where Soda Boy could spot them. They tiptoed down the steps despite the fact that the noise of the city could drown out a marching band, making an obvious spectacle of themselves. A mother with a baby hanging in a carrier across her chest and two more children holding her hands looked over at Topher and told him to watch his step.

"Do we really need to keep this up? We have no idea where they're headed," Topher complained.

"We can't lose them!"

"Will you just go talk to him already? He's with a girl. He's not some criminal."

"I'm scared, okay? I'm going to feel like an idiot."

"Fine. I'll do the talking." Topher rushed to the subway stairs with Shell following right behind him, pleading for him to not say anything.

They raced down the soot-covered stairs, dodging pedestrians headed in the opposite direction. By the time they got to the bottom of the stairs, they spotted the couple casually passing through the turnstiles.

"I'm out of rides on my metro-app," Shell admitted.

She glanced around the damp station that looked like it still needed to recover from the storm several nights ago. Crevices dripped like sweaty armpits where the ceilings met the walls. Muddy shoe prints coated slippery floors like directions for complicated dances. A "Caution – Wet Floor" sign lay folded on the ground, kicked into a corner. Even the lights on the advertising screens seemed dull.

Shell spotted a yellow kiosk that would let her purchase rides and a man in a booth she could buy rides from. She glanced back and forth between the two, unsure of using her Armer to buy a ticket, then realizing she had used hers for her bus tickets. *I'm terrible at this. If I use my Armer, I could lead people to us. What if they've been tracking my metro-app? The guy in the booth could recognize my face from the 'Missing' app and report us.*

A breeze brushed past her face and flicked her hair into the air. She heard the high-pitched squeal and low rumble of an approaching subway train. The vibrations started at her feet and woke a sense of panic in her spine. *I'm running out of time,* she realized. She wouldn't be able to buy a ticket for her and Topher before the train left the station, and if Soda Boy and his date got onto that train, she wouldn't have any idea where to find them.

Shell heard the train screech to a halt, but she did not see one. She looked past the turnstiles and did not see Soda Boy, but she did notice another staircase headed down, deeper into the subway. She heard the train doors open, and within seconds saw swarms of people walking up that staircase, headed toward them. Others, making their last-second attempts down the stairs to catch the train, fought through the oncoming crowd's surging exodus. Shell considered ducking underneath the turnstiles since she probably couldn't make her way over them. She figured she could go under and Topher could go over the swinging poles. Then she thought that Topher hopping over them would probably get them caught, but maybe they'd make it onto the train before anyone could stop them. All that might blow their cover and Soda Boy would see them.

She grabbed Topher by the hand, felt peculiar rush, and made her way for the turnstiles when a buzzer pierced her concentration. Just next to the turnstiles the emergency exit door opened up. A short woman wearing a black coat and matching hat with black leather gloves, somewhat overdressed for this time of year, struggled to get her two rolling suitcases through the doors. Topher pulled Shell toward the woman.

"Let me help you with that, ma'am," he offered in his politest voice.

"Get your hands off of my things!" The appalled woman let go of her bags to swipe at him. Her eyes nearly popped out of her head.

Shell acknowledged the woman's reaction, but jumped right into the scam. "He means you no harm, ma'am. We just like to help the elderly."

"Elderly?" asked the astonished woman. "You two are the bane of society."

The two of them grabbed the woman's bags despite her best efforts to shoo them away. The older woman sprayed gibberish-like insults at them, but could not dissuade Shell and Topher from using her exit to gain them entrance to the other side of the turnstiles.

Topher headed for the platform without giving the woman another look. Shell waved goodbye and wished her a nice evening and then chased after him.

"Downstairs!" she yelled when she saw Topher rushing in the wrong direction.

Topher turned around, caught up to her, and then passed her going down the steps, jumping past the last few to the 'Downtown' platform.

The train chimed, then a voice over the PA system directed everyone to "stand clear of the closing doors." The platform had emptied and Topher lunged for the subway car door, propping his foot against the sliding door in anticipation of needing to keep it open while Shell caught up.

Shell raced to catch up as the sliding door began to close. Topher pushed harder and the door bounced back, opening momentarily before closing again on his foot. This time, the door did not recoil. Topher used his hands to keep the door pried open. Shell finally squeezed her way through the narrow opening, making it into the train before the doors closed and pinched hard against his hands.

Inside the car, the two of them sighed in relief and dusted themselves off.

"Everyone's looking at us, aren't they?" Shell whispered.

"Yep."

"Soda Boy's in here, too?" she whispered even quieter.

"Yep."

"Did he see us?"

"Yep."

"Well, at least we caught the right train."

They sat down quietly in a corner of the car, hoping that everyone would soon forget about their spectacle. Shell sat with her back to as many people as she could while Topher slouched in his seat and kept his head down. After a while, Shell glanced over to catch the fizzy foot of Soda Boy out of the corner of her eye.

The grinding, clanking wheels echoed in the underground tunnel. Soda Boy and his date sat shoulder-to-shoulder, smiling and giggling throughout the ride. Shell and Topher sat quietly and far less affectionately, occasionally staring at the cute couple until it felt awkward to do so.

"Where do you think they're headed?" Shell asked.

"On a date, silly."

She kicked Topher in the shin. "But where? We can't just follow them all night."

"That's what I've been saying! I'm going over there." Topher stood up to walk over to them and Shell yanked him back down.

"Not yet."

Topher groaned and sat back down. "I'm hungry."

Every time the train stopped, Shell and Topher readied to run off the train at the last second, but Soda Boy and his date sat patiently, with his date staring into his eyes and Soda Boy staring at the floor. Just as they wearied of the repeated expectations of exiting the train, and assumed Soda Boy planned for his date to take place somewhere near the last stop on the train line, the couple finally exited, nearly catching Shell and Topher unawares. They had as much trouble getting off the train as they had getting on. With fewer people around to mask their peculiar behavior, Soda Boy and his date actually looked back at them with trepidation. Shell waved at them in an effort to downplay their ridiculousness.

Topher waited for them to walk away before mentioning, "Our cover is officially blown. Can we just go up to them already?"

"No. I don't want to ruin their night or his life. Maybe it's nothing. Maybe it's just this genetic thing, like if someone has bad gas, they look like a soda."

They walked slowly, letting the couple disappear ahead of them, but staying just close enough to know what direction they headed. By the time they returned to the street surface, they found themselves still across the street from Central Park. The streetlights painted an aura of security around Shell, but she felt nervous in the city without an adult and so close to the park. Everyone knew not to go into Central Park at night, or any park for that matter. *All the scariest stories start in the park, after dark.*

Looking at it from across the street and seeing how it devoured all of the light around it made her feel even more uncertain.

"We should get back to Betty," Shell offered with a slight nervous quiver in her voice.

"Is that them?" Topher asked while pointing just down the street at two kids running across traffic and into the park.

"I would assume so, unless there's more than one person running around looking like a delicious refreshment." Shell's curiosity re-piqued. "What are they doing in there?"

"Let's go find out!" the reinvigorated Topher exclaimed.

"Are you crazy? No one should go in the park at night."

"They did. It can't be that bad."

"Let's just go back to the church."

"Come on. We've been following this kid for hours and now it's finally interesting. You want to give up?"

Shell pouted as she considered his comments.

"This might be what you've been looking for. Maybe he meets up with other people affected by the storm."

"Okay. Fine. But you have to stay right next me. No wandering off. If I wind up by myself in this park and I don't die, I will personally kill you."

"Agreed!" Topher hopped and skipped his way to the crosswalk.

Chapter 27 - Lightning Bugs

Shell and Topher crossed the street a block away from the entrance they saw Soda Boy run through. They crept along the shadow of the low-lying wall that surrounded all of Central Park, still trying to maintain their already failed attempt at anonymity. Once they reached the entrance, they glanced around the corner, but saw no sign of Soda Boy or his date. Topher quickly maneuvered to the opposite side of the wall, inside the park, still clinging to the shadows.

"Follow me," he insisted. "They had to go this way."

"I think I can see them."

Despite the lack of light in the park, what Shell saw of Soda Boy looked as bright at night as it did in the day. They continued on the path, bearing right most of the way, deeper and deeper into the park until the couple made a left.

"This way," Shell whispered, leading him through a wooded area.

They trotted over some grass and up and down some hills before coming to a row of trees.

"Stop," she warned.

"What is it?"

"Shh. Do you hear that?

"It sounds like whispers," Topher answered.

Shell kept an eye on the couple as they rounded a corner.

"Come on."

They slowly approached the group of trees the couple had just rounded when the two of them stopped in their tracks. Though they each saw their own version of what took place before them, the oddity of it left them both temporarily speechless. Neither of them could explain the sea of bouncing, floating, and flashing blue lights. To Topher, it appeared as a swarm of lightning bugs against the dark, but he had never seen blue lightning bugs before. The odds that these unique insects had either survived or evolved in Central Park proved unlikely. And it made less sense to him that Soda Boy and his date sought out these special bugs for a friendly frolic on a Tuesday evening. Shell saw the floating blue lights mixed in with hundreds of people sized tornadoes.

"What is this?" Topher asked.

"You're asking me? I have no idea."

"Can you still see Soda Boy?"

"Nope. Lost him."

"Should we go over there?" Topher's curiosity had turned into excitement. It had become less of a question of whether or not he would wind up in the middle of the fray, but more of a question of whether Shell would follow him.

"I don't know," she replied timidly.

"Let's get a little closer," he suggested.

The two inched their way toward the crowd of lights and finally came to a clearing. Once they moved past the trees, they realized that the lights were not actually blinking, but only appeared to because of the sources' movement beyond the trees and amidst a crowd of silhouettes. Still, they struggled to grasp what they saw. They crouched down in silence, not sure of what to do. They circled the area quietly and picked up the sound of soft chatter and conversation. Finally, the constantly moving silhouettes became visible once their eyes adjusted.

"It's some kind of party," concluded Topher. "I guess this is how they do it in the city."

They continued to circle the crowd like social outcasts at a school dance. Shell's fear had turned to discomfort as she found herself rather out of her element at this invitation-only soiree.

"I can't tell who's who," said Topher.

"I can't find Soda Boy anywhere," replied Shell.

"Over there." He pointed to two tables, one with dozens of small blue lights glowing on it. As they headed over and saw people picking up the blue lights in sets of two, Shell finally figured it out.

"These are Bluetooth headphones," she whispered, but Topher didn't hear her. He had left her side. Shell looked around and could not tell him from the rest of the crowd. "Topher!"

"Over here," Topher mumbled. "I found food!"

Shell could visualize the crumbling cupcakes falling out of his mouth when he spoke and finally spotted him at the table of treats and baked goods next to the headphones.

"Didn't I say if you left my side I'd make you pay for it?"

"I'm right here," said Topher, sounding like a boy trying to get out of trouble.

"It's a Bluetooth party. My mom was talking about this the other night."

"No way! I didn't even think these things happened. This is so cool."

"What's cool about it?"

"It's like a silent party. Everyone hears the same music through the headphones that are connected to the DJ," Topher pointed to a guy standing on a platform with a dozen blue lights shining up to his face, likely from his turntables and a computer. "The only rule is you can't scream or yell. If you want to talk, you have to take off the headphones. They throw these parties in all sorts of places, but the idea is to not get caught. There's no way this should be going down in Central Park. They're illegal. People get arrested all the time. Something about kids being under-age and illegal mind stimulants and trespassing."

Topher grabbed a set of headphones and put them on. His face lit up with excitement. "This is gonna be awesome." He handed a headset to Shell, who hesitated to take them and responded with far less exuberance than him.

"We're here to find that kid, not party," she explained. She handed the headphones back to him.

"So now you're ready to talk to him? He just got here. You'll be able to keep an eye on him better from the dance floor," Topher explained as he handed her the headphones again. "Blending in is the key."

"What happened to sticking together?" she whispered on deaf ears as Topher already had his headphones on.

Shell gave him a disappointed glance, but she doubted he noticed. Topher hopped up and down to the *textra* beat with a big grin. Shell put her headphones on and could not help but to smirk once she heard the distorted, bass enhanced orchestra music, and felt like a kid getting away with mischief. He grabbed Shell's hand and pulled her into the shadowed crowd.

They joined the jubilant fray as if they belonged. Hopping up and down and swaying their bodies to the music, partying seemed to have come to them naturally. Similarly to the hundreds of parties that go on every day and every night around the world, the collective energy from the crowd grew to a spiritual level. Carefree joy emanated from the partygoers as freely as did their sweat. The duo became one with the crowd as the mass moved like kelp in the ocean current. The rhythmic flow of the blue lights amazed Topher, who found himself embracing the mesmerizing imagery.

Shell saw so much more. The little blue lights dancing amongst the clouds made her feel like she had walked into a dream full of fairies playing in the morning mist. The whirlwinds looked like puffs of blue cotton candy. To her the tornadoes intertwined with one another. It looked like mitosis, but in reverse. The tornadoes merged as they danced together. She saw six tornadoes turn into three and then into one large, softly flowing whirlwind of peaceful energy. The more she watched the crowd, the wider the twister grew and the calmer the energy flowed. She reached out for it and could feel it rushing past her fingers like a gentle breeze. Though the ground felt dry, to Shell it looked covered in a clear layer of water. The collective puddles of the gleeful swayed back and forth like currents on a lazy lake and expanded outward, as if growing.

LIGHTNING BUGS

Time passed quickly. Shell looked down at her Armer and realized that nearly two hours had passed. It surprised her that she had not seen any sign of Soda Boy the entire time. Concern started to press upon her chest when she considered that she had no way of finding Topher. His navy blue shoes had been her only way of spotting him out of a crowd and the little blue lights on the headsets would not provide much help.

Shell weaved her way through the crowd like a mother searching for her lost child. Ironically, short little Shell looked to everyone else like a lost child searching for her mother. She could not see past the people in front of her. She began to panic as all of the tornadoes turned into a dense fog surrounding her. She didn't know which way to go, so she chose one direction until she made her way out of the maze of dancers.

After a lot of bumping and dodging, stepping on feet and having her feet stepped on, Shell finally made her way into a clearing. She scanned the perimeter of the crowd, hoping to catch a glimpse of Soda Boy or perhaps find Topher standing outside of the group. She went back to the table of headphones. No such luck. She took off her headphones, surprised by how quiet everything was, despite the moving bodies behind her. As she placed them on the table, she noticed that hers did not have the same sticker on it that some of the others had. The sticker had "HB" written on it in bubble letters and the image of some kind of weasel looking creature wearing a tie-dyed t-shirt lying in a field of flowers. She saw more stickers lying on the table.

"There you are. You're too short to be sneaking off in the dark, Shell," Topher joked a little too loudly as he took off his headphones.

"Where have you been?" she yelled as quietly as she could.

"Livin' the life, my bell."

Shell did not know what to make of his response.

"Are you feeling okay?"

"I feel amazing. We should do this every day."

"We need to find Soda Boy. It's getting late. I can only imagine what our families are going through."

"That's cool," Topher replied lazily.

"Let me see those." She grabbed at his headphones and saw that his had the same sticker on them. She stared closer at him. She still could not see his face, but she did notice his tornado swirled a bit slower. He reached for his headset, but Shell held it behind her back.

"No headsets right now. We need to find Soda Boy, talk to him, and then get out of here."

"You're right. You're right." His languid dialogue made her feel like he'd be more of a liability than a help.

Shell pulled him around the perimeter of the crowd, but she still could not find Soda Boy anywhere. "I knew I shouldn't have taken my eyes off him. This whole day has been a waste. He could be anywhere. Let's just go."

Topher, by this point, had stopped paying attention to anything she said. His eyes fixated on the center of the crowd. His jaw hung slack, amazed at the sight before him. "So mind blowing." The words drooled out of his mouth.

Topher's slurred speech registered with Shell as much as she registered with him. Her eyes remained fixed as well, but facing away from the crowd. She could not explain exactly what she saw, because she did not expect to see a string of whirlwinds around the clearing that she and the other partygoers stood in. She suspected that what she saw belonged to people or a well-organized pack of wolves, but what could circle an entire field? It drew closer, maintaining a tight ring around the whole party. Shell could not tell if the approaching consisted of more partiers or some group looking to break the party up.

"We've got to get out of here. I think something big is about to go down and I don't want to be in the middle of it," Shell said as she gave him a more forceful tug, but he did not budge. She looked back at him, but could not see the expression on his face. She did see that his shoulders were facing toward the partiers. "Come on, we've got to go."

"It's so beautiful."

"What?" Shell asked, sounding panicked and annoyed.

She turned around to see what drew all of his attention and noticed that all of the blue lights had stopped moving. Through Shell's distorted view, she could only tell how still everyone had become.

"What's going on? Why did everyone stop moving? We need to leave. Something's coming. Does this have to do with the headsets?"

Topher let go of Shell's hand, walked behind her, reached over her shoulders with both hands and gently embraced her chin, slowly tilting her chin upward. She finally saw what everyone in the crowd saw, sort of. It confused her at first, but she figured it out at last.

EARLIER THAT EVENING

Soda Boy, who went by the name Pat, escorted his date, out of the train station at 72nd and Central Park West. He had recently fallen victim to an occurrence that plagued men and woman of all cultures. He had fallen for someone who got him to do things he typically would not do. In his case, a young girl he met while volunteering at a fund raising concert named Abby had convinced him of two things; one, to go out on a school night and, two, to hang out in Central Park after dark. Abby pulled Pat up the block from the subway station and across the street to the 72nd Street Central Park entrance. Not the typical risk-taker, Pat followed willingly. He enjoyed the rush he felt from the external influence. Typically shy, already feeling out of his league, and shocked that such a beautiful free spirit like Abby would spend time with him and take him to something she found so spectacular put Pat on a plane of excitement he had never felt before.

It only took a matter of moments for them to find the party. She rushed him to the table with two piles of headphones and only told him, "Don't forget to whisper."

Abby grabbed two sets designed with stickers on them, putting one set on herself, handing the other one to him, and placed an extra sticker on each of their hands before pulling him into the middle of the mob of people dancing silently in the dark. Pat felt awkward. While Abby jumped right into the party scene, he felt exposed. He felt like the only person dancing to his own music in the middle of a subway car during rush hour. Abby took the lead. She started by twirling around him with a big smile. She caressed his arms and ran her fingers through his hair while she hopped around him and raised his hands in the air so she could twirl beneath them.

LIGHTNING BUGS

As the music picked up and everyone started swaying and hopping in a near-choreographed sequence, Pat finally got in rhythm with Abby and the rest of the crowd. The couple remained inseparable after that. He held her tighter and tighter as they danced through the night, embracing her sweat-soaked body. Repeatedly they locked eyes and smiled at one another. Their pupils disappeared in the dark, except for the reflecting blue lights of the headsets, while the whites around them glowed like hollow moons. Abby closed her eyes and, as he closed his, their lips moved closer and closer until they pressed passionately against each other. Pat's entire body felt like it had woken up for the first time.

Something about that kiss told him that he had found his perfect fitting puzzle piece. Together their lips remained for the duration of nearly two straight songs while they danced to their own beat, slower than everyone around them. Abby gently pulled away with a smile so big she could hardly catch her breath. Pat could not decide how to react. Part of him wanted to pull her back in for another two songs. Another part of him wanted to shout and jump up and down, and still another part of him wanted to play it cool and woo her with a mellow, nonchalant gaze.

Abby hugged herself while she slowly swayed back into the rhythm with her eyes peacefully shut. Her smile shone through the darkness and Pat followed her lead again. He, too, closed his eyes and let the music move him in a way he never felt before. He celebrated in silence while the music vibrated through his body.

The music intensified. The crowd around them jumped higher and danced harder as the DJ brought the party to a higher level. Even with his eyes closed, Pat could feel Abby. He felt like a magnet that could hold onto her from anywhere. With his eyes still closed, he raised his hands and chin to the sky, his smile wide, and he spun in circles to the music. Abby continued her sway of satisfaction.

The two of them reveled in their beautiful bond, but neither of them managed to notice its strength. As the two of them danced in their blind bliss, they failed to notice that Abby's feet no longer touched the ground.

Unaware that Soda Boy's demonstration of affection rippled through the crowd as each witness made sure to share the miracle with friends and strangers alike, Abby floated slowly into the air, swaying and spinning to the music like a ballerina free from her music box, just high enough that people could still reach her feet if they wanted to. But no one did. Everyone, even the DJ, just stood and watched. Couples and dates unconsciously reached for one another's hands and bodies and held them tightly. Tears of happiness streamed down the cheeks of many. They may not have understood why the young girl floated in the air as she did, but they could see and feel the happiness she felt. Their emotion spread through the crowd, taking everyone to that place in their hearts where love lived happily ever after.

Abby remained in the air for a moment longer before she began to slowly lower to the ground. The two of them spun around like synchronized swimmers as she floated down into Pat's outstretched arms. He reached for her, catching her under her arms like a father playing with his baby.

Abby stopped spinning and Pat stopped with her. She felt his arms around her, but it felt more real than it had for the past few minutes. They opened their eyes and only saw each other before they noticed that she still had a few more inches to float back down to the ground. Neither fear nor shock interrupted their miracle. Pat gently brought Abby down to the ground, pulled her to his chest, and hugged her until she knew he never wanted to let go.

She kissed him again. Forehead to forehead they stood before they opened their eyes, took a breath, and then saw everyone staring at them. The moonlight revealed hundreds of soft and sympathetic gazes. Abby rested her head on Soda Boy's shoulder, and he rested his head on hers. They closed their eyes, sighed, and swayed to the music. Couples around them did the same.

***

Shell initially only saw small hazy blue lights spinning around in the air. As her eyes adjusted, she saw the calm spinning of a tornado somehow floating above the crowd. She could barely make out the silhouette spinning around and around like a gravity defying top. She joined everyone else in staring at the phenomena before them.

And that was when the lights came on. Bright spotlights aimed directly at the party shone from every direction.

"Everyone, stay where you are!" The voice boomed through a megaphone.

The partygoers came out of their trance and took off their headsets. Most people looked confused by the interruption and the distorted message they failed to catch before they took their headphones off.

"This is the New York Police Department!" the voice boomed.

Chaos ensued. The whole crowd scattered. The once peaceful audience who snuck into the woods and witnessed a miracle of love like no other did not represent the small percentage of the population that one would expect to stick around and explain their cause to the police of such a prohibited activity. Everyone dropped their headsets and scattered like roaches—everyone but Shell, at least.

"Now I really need to talk to him," she told Topher as she grabbed him and headed straight for the middle of the circle and Soda Boy.

The lights filled the entire open area, leaving no place to hide. They had to get to the darker parts of the park. People ran into each other as they fled in every direction. They nearly trampled Shell on multiple occasions as she ran into the fray. Topher voluntarily took the lead. Though he planned on clearing the way for Shell to get to Soda Boy, he did a better job of absorbing all of the run-ins that would have knocked her to the ground.

By the time they made it to where they last saw Soda Boy and Abby standing, they only found themselves closer to the chasing police who had also pinpointed the location of the lovebirds. More concerned with where the couple went and less about the approaching police, Shell quickly looked around the area for the bubbling boy, finally spotting him and his date headed toward the woods, but in the direction of one of the spotlights.

Another couple, also headed for the lights in front of Soda Boy and his date, tripped right in front of them, allowing the police to pounce and zip tie them like rodeo calves. Soda Boy and Abby froze in fear. Shell and Topher used their hesitation to catch up without bothering to look behind them to make sure they weren't being chased. Despite the severity of the situation, to Shell this all felt like a massive game of freeze tag. She always did pretty well, as it served as another opportunity to prove she could hang with the bigger kids. She also knew she had an advantage as a smaller target. Soda Boy and Abby started to take off in another direction when Shell grabbed Soda Boy's hand.

"Come with us," she yelled at them.

The pandemonium of the situation didn't give him much time to consider the request. Nor did Shell have time to acknowledge the energy she felt by touching him.

Topher eyed the scene. "This way," he ordered to the group. Shell followed along without argument, having noticed the water-like waves flowing in the direction Topher led.

He held onto Shell while she held onto Soda Boy, who held onto Abby. The interlocked foursome slithered through the anarchy. Topher pulled them toward the tables where the headphones and treats lay, as less light shone in that direction and a large number of people had already made that their escape route. The route, however, had not worked perfectly for everyone.

The table funneled people in two directions. Based on the number of partiers on the ground or stumbling over one another and writhing in zip ties, it looked like the police repeatedly tripped up people that took those routes. Topher attacked the trap head on.

He pulled the group straight to the tables. They ran hand in hand, dodging the debris of soon-to-be arrestees, until Topher pulled free and leapt on top of the table. He stood tall like a general surveying the battlefield, ordering his comrades to follow his lead. Shell slid underneath the table while Soda Boy and his date hopped on top. They spotted a few officers headed after some of the other partygoers. Topher picked up a cupcake and hurled it at one of the cops, catching him in the face, and buying them some time to get away.

Soda Boy and Abby followed suit and the three of them started a one-sided food fight. Even a few headphones were tossed about. Although the pastries did not ensure everyone's freedom, they did, however, add just enough turmoil to help the foursome get past the trap. The three of them hopped down off the other side and joined Shell on the ground before bolting off into the woods.

The commotion behind them lessened as they ran deeper and deeper into the heart of Central Park. The sound of wind through trees and the stampede of wayward feet soon replaced the moans and screams of frightened teens.

"We've got to get out of here," Abby suggested. "Cops ain't too kind to us intruders. We'll lose them this way." She took off and the rest of them did their best to keep up.

Despite the moon's best efforts to light the way, the trees canopied their path, leaving them in the dark. Abby appeared exhilarated by the circumstances. She sprinted ahead and hurdled overgrown roots like a jungle cat in her natural habitat. Topher and Soda Boy looked a bit more frightened, as they and Shell heard the random faint chirps, hisses, and croaks from the park's litany of occupants. Shell had the burden of seeing many of the noisemakers, but felt relieved that she hadn't seen anything bigger than herself.

"You've dealt with this before?" Shell asked while panting. "The cops, I mean."

"A couple of times. They like to ruin our parties," Abby explained. "They keep you overnight and force your parents to bail you out in the morning."

Shell could not decide if she felt relieved or not. She thought the police had come for her. The group came to an underpass, paused in the shadow of the bridge, and then Shell screamed.

"What is it?" Topher demanded, whirling around to fend off whomever—or whatever—had followed them.

Shell timidly glanced back at what made her jump. What she initially took for a large slithering oily black snake revealed itself as a family of rats crossing the underpass' path. Their individual whirlwinds looked odd in the darkness of the cave-like surroundings. "Just rats, I think," she replied.

"Do you hear that?" Soda Boy asked.

The rapid crunching of sticks and leaves rustled in the distance and grew louder with each step.

"Let's keep movin'," urged Topher.

"We're almost outta here," Abby reassured.

The four of them took off. Soda Boy looked behind them and saw a single person chasing them and said so, but quite a distance back. Shell saw a whirlwind and a cloud approaching, but could only confirm what Soda Boy saw. They finally came to a park exit. Shell and Topher had little idea of where, though.

After creeping silently toward the stone wall that surrounded the park, they quickly peered out to the sidewalk and checked for any police officers patrolling the perimeter. Spotting no one, they quickly exited, and ran across the street. They hustled down a few more blocks, ignored a few crosswalks, and finally raced down the steps of the closest subway station they could find. Soda Boy looked back in the direction they ran from and saw the same single man quite some distance behind them continuing to give chase.

Following Abby's lead, the four kids hopped over and slid under the turnstiles in front of an indifferent booth attendant. They expected a fast getaway, but only Abby realized that trains don't come as frequently late at night in New York, and shared that fact with the group.

"Let's go down to the end of the platform," Shell suggested. "If anyone's after us, we'll see them coming."

"And go where?" Abby inquired. "I doubt you're ready to deal with the rat tracks."

Shell and Topher looked down at the train tracks. It only took a second for them to spot a rat scurrying across the rails. Shell saw the same little twister around its fat body.

"We'll be fine," she stated nervously.

"If they come in here, we'll be trapped," Abby added. "We should stay by the gate so we can hop downstairs for the uptown train if they do come in."

"How do we know anyone's even coming?" Topher chimed in.

"I saw someone chasing us out of the park," Soda Boy confirmed.

"There you go," said Abby. "We wait here and hope the train comes before the guy does."

Everyone's silence confirmed their agreement. Each of them went back and forth from looking at the stairway to looking down the tracks for the approaching train lights.

"Someone's coming," warned Soda Boy after they all heard the tapping of hard-soled shoes sprinting down the steps. They braced for action. When the owner of those shoes rounded the corner and came into view, they saw a young woman dressed in high heels and a skirt, and breathed a sigh of relief as they watched her stumble down the platform to an old wooden bench.

"Who was it you saw coming?" Shell asked Soda Boy.

"I don't know, some guy," he answered.

She and Topher exchanged a fearful glance.

A low rumble and the high-pitched grinding metal echoed down the tunnel. They all peered over the edge of the subway platform to see an approaching train. The soot-filled wind blew through everyone's hair. Shell looked down at the tracks again and saw something she couldn't quite figure out. Hundreds and hundreds of little whirly spinning tornadoes in a collective fog moved in unison over the tracks. It looked like a stream over water-smoothed stones, but she found it odd that it seemed to create its own path diagonal across the tracks and around the columns holding up the subway station. The train slowly screeched to a halt right over them.

The doors opened and the kids rushed in to an empty car and grabbed seats. The doors closed behind them, but with an alarming thud. They all turned around to see the man in the white suit, sweating and out of breath, pounding on the glass. Shell and Topher freaked out.

"I can help you," the man yelled through the glass and metal barrier between him and the kids. His words came through muffled, but Shell heard them. The train took off slowly, leaving the man standing on the platform, watching the kids escape him again.

"Do you know that guy?" Soda Boy asked.

"Not really," remarked Shell as she and Topher exchanged a guilty glance.

"Thanks for getting us out of there," said Soda Boy to the other three.

"Thanks for getting us out of the park," Topher said to Abby.

"What was that?" Soda Boy asked in general.

"That was the party crash of all party crashing," explained Abby. "It's never been that intense. Awesome, right?"

Shell sat in amazement as she stared at Soda Boy. She had followed him all night and had seen how he looked with all of the bubbles rising in the air like an old bottle of pop, and even now that she sat right across from him, she still couldn't help but stare. Topher noticed her rather rude behavior.

"I'm Topher, by the way," he said, as he extended his hand to Soda Boy.

"Nice to meet you, Topher," Soda Boy shook Topher's hand. "I'm Pat and this is Abby." Topher and Abby shook hands.

"I'm Shell," she finally chimed in after Topher gave her a friendly nudge.

"Nice meeting you two," said Pat. "Hey, didn't we see you guys on the train earlier?"

Shell and Topher exchanged a guilty blush.

"Yeah... it's a long story," said Shell. "That whole thing that you did, the floating at the party thing, had you done that before?"

Pat reddened.

"That was awesome," interjected Abby. "Can we do that again?"

A look of relief washed over Pat's face.

"Well, like that, not really," Pat began. "I guess I first noticed it two mornings ago when I woke up and my blankets were hovering above me. They stayed there for a few seconds and then fell down on top of me. Since then, sometimes when I reach for things, they'll float into the air before I can grab them. I don't really know why it's happening or when it will happen."

Topher and Abby stared at him with open-mouthed smiles while Shell sat focused, ready to interrogate.

"Did you get caught in the rain on Sunday night?" asked Shell.

"No. I don't think so. I'm pretty sure I was playing video games. I figured it was my last chance to play before I started getting homework again. Why?"

"Are you sure? You didn't go outside the entire night?"

"No way, that storm was crazy. Why would I go outside?"

"Tell me exactly what you did Sunday night and Monday morning."

Pat looked at Topher and Abby for confirmation that Shell's questions deserved answers. From their curious expressions, he decided to continue.

"Well, I went to bed Sunday night, woke up, took a shower, ate some breakfast, got ready for school, took the garbage out, and then headed off to class. I remember feeling tired all day, so I took a nap when I came home. That's when I had my first weird dream and when I woke up and saw the sheet hanging above me.

"So it must have happened before school."

"What must have happened?" Pat sounded worried.

"It wouldn't make sense, I don't think, for it to happen in the shower, but maybe... When you took out the garbage, did you touch anything wet?

"Yeah, everything was wet. I had to move the trashcans and the garbage bags out to the curb."

"Did you see anything weird..."

Topher chimed in before Shell drove Pat any crazier.

"Here's the thing, Pat. Shell thinks that…"

Shell jabbed Topher in the arm, not wanting him to tell her story.

"Okay. Last question. What was weird about your dreams?"

"I don't know. They just seemed more realistic than usual. I remember something about a boat and woke up feeling really dizzy and sick."

Shell gestured to Topher that now she wanted to share her story.

"All I ask is that you don't tell anyone what I'm about to tell you. Can I trust you?"

Abby agreed enthusiastically, which made Shell nervous. Pat agreed more fearfully.

Shell explained what had happened to her and how she thought Pat fit into everything. He and Abby took the story pretty well. Topher's contributions helped legitimize her accounts.

"So what do we do now?" Pat asked.

"I have no idea," replied Shell. "Like I said, we're just trying to keep Betty away from all the needles and find someone who might have some real answers."

They rode the train a few more stops, relatively at ease and with little concern that they'd wind up in any trouble as a result of their escapades that evening. Shell chuckled a bit to herself when Topher asked Abby for detailed directions on how to get back to the church. Shell made sure to take mental notes on the probable chance that Topher would still have trouble getting them home.

"I think this is your stop," Abby said.

"Well, I'll do some searching, but let me know whatever you find out." Pat handed Topher his network card with more the a dozen different ways to track him down. The four of them exchanged hugs and goodbyes, and then Shell and Topher exited the train.

The duo enjoyed a quiet walk back to the church. They kept a fearful eye out for the man in the white suit that seemed to find them wherever they went, but enjoyed recapping the excitement of the day. When they knocked on the door, a distressed Father Jon opened it.

"Things are not well," he said ominously.

Chapter 28 - Dark Strolls

"What do you mean Betty's not well?" Shell fretted.

"She seems to be suffering from some sort of memory loss. We were catching up on old times when she got quite worked up about not knowing how she got here."

"Her chart at the hospital said she has Alzheimer's. I don't exactly know what that all means, but she tends to forget things. She's forgotten me a couple of times, but it normally kicks back in. Where is she?"

"The dressing room," Father Jon directed, pointing to a door left of the pulpit.

Shell walked to the door apprehensively. *Did Father Jon lock her in there? Could he now see Betty's quilt-like appearance? Is she hiding?* As Shell reached for the door handle, the door opened and Betty stood before her, dressed in full nun attire.

"Hello, my child," Betty greeted with an air of holy sanctity.

"Betty? It's me Shell."

"Greetings to you, young Shell. How may I be of service to you today?"

Shell looked back at Father Jon for comment, but he only shrugged his shoulders.

"Betty, it's me, remember? We just got here today. You're not a nun. Are you?"

"I do not know this Betty you speak of, but I am more than happy to help you find her."

"No. You're Betty. Remember, you were in a hospital this morning. We..." Before Shell could finish, she saw Betty's fabric-like face turn. Her wrinkles doubled over her features and tears began to well in her eyes. "It's okay. We made it out. We're safe now."

"It's... It's my fault." Betty sobbed between sentences. "I just... I just wanted to take them to get pumpkins. I shouldn't have been drivin'. It's all my fault." Betty wailed as she stumbled to the nearest pew.

Shell shared her confused expressions with Topher and Father Jon, pleaded for help with Betty, but only the priest came to her aid while Topher backed away.

"You're here with us Betty," Father Jon began. "We're safe here. We're all fine." Betty sobbed a bit more before opening her eyes.

"Jon, is that you?"

"Yes, it's me," he said relieved.

"It's been so long. Oh, my, decades even." His face grew concerned again.

"Do you remember, Betty? We came earlier today," Shell interjected.

Betty turned to look at Shell. "You're alive!" she cheered. "By the heavens, you're alive. Oh my sweet, dear Annabel—you're alive!"

Not sure of what to say, Shell let Betty wrap her arms around her and rock her side to side. Her gut told her no good could come of this. Even her time as a candy striper did not prepare her for this. If she told Betty she wasn't Annabel, Betty would be devastated. If Betty found out on her own, who knows how she'd react. Shell knew she'd feel embarrassed if it happened to her. So she remained quiet and rocked with Betty.

"Betty. Betty," Father Jon repeated gently. "This is Shell. She brought you here from the hospital. You told me that they were experimenting on you and you ran away and came here."

Betty let go of Shell and looked down at her. She sniffed as she stared down into Shell's eyes. "You know what, you do kinda look like Annabel," Betty commented as she choked back a tear.

"I get that a lot," Shell replied with a grin.

"Oh, my. Have I been cryin?" She let go of Shell and fanned her face to halt the tears. "Goodness me. What time is it? And why am I dressed like a nun?"

"About eleven p.m.," Father Jon answered, sounding relieved again. "And we figured it was a good disguise while you hid in a church."

Betty collected her thoughts for a moment, turned to Shell, and very sternly asked, "Darlin, what are you doing here?"

It dawned on Shell that she had some explaining to do. As she guiltily recapped their afternoon and explained why they could not go home, Father Jon brought out a pTV, a small cube that you aimed at any surface to project streaming media. He turned to the news. Shell sat with her back to it as she told her story, unaware that her story unfolded on the news as she explained it.

"That's where you were," Betty declared while pointing to the image of a girl floating in the air.

Shell confirmed and continued on about their getaway and seeing the man in white again.

"My dear, how do you wind up in these situations? I know things are crazier than usual these days, but you are a magnet. How do you seem to just understand all of this stuff?" Shell stared back blankly. "There's more to this story you're not telling me, young lady," Betty interjected at the conclusion of Shell's story.

Shell looked at Topher for reaffirmation that she could share the truth with Betty. He gave her a nonchalant nod while Father Jon positioned cots in front of the pews. She figured the time had come to lay her cards on the table.

"You know how I told you I'd been having weird dreams since the night of the storm?"

Betty nodded.

"And you said that you were having them too and that you were noticing weird things happening since you got caught in that rain."

Betty gasped for a moment, recalling a recent memory when Jon saw her in the back room holding a metal broom and a chair made of straw. She glanced over at him to see him staring back with confused eyes.

"Well, for me," shell continued, "ever since the storm, I've been seeing things." And so she explained her story yet again.

"Yarn?" Betty's response indicated a significant level of doubt toward Shell's observations. "A quilt?"

"That's what I said," Topher interjected reluctantly, but Betty did not look at all pleased.

"I followed you. I followed you..." Betty's loss for words made Shell feel doubtful again.

Shell continued. "I know. I knew something happened to you and I knew what they would do to you if you stayed in that hospital."

"I just don't know." Betty stood up and paced. She kept repeating that phrase over and over again and didn't stop until she noticed Father Jon reenter the room with a tray of sandwiches and juice. She shot him a troubled glance before walking past him and down the steps into his room. The priest brought Shell and Topher something to eat.

"Sounds like one heck of a day."

They nodded in agreement.

"And you were there? You saw that girl floating in the air?"

"It was incredible, Father," said Topher.

"No strings attached or anything?"

"No way. We talked to the kid who did it. He said he had been making things float by accident for the past few days."

"Will miracles never cease? And young Shell, did I hear that you can sense, somehow, which people are capable of these miracles?"

"Yes, sir."

"Truly inspiring. You have a special gift," the priest told Shell as he patted her head. "We all do," he continued while looking Topher in the eye. "Life is about the decisions you make with the gifts you're given. Continue to do what is in your heart and all will be as it should," he told them with a smile. "You two eat up. I'll talk to Betty."

Shell and Topher barely said a word after the priest left. They ate their dinner and lay down to sleep. Betty came up a short time later to find the kids on their cots. Father Jon managed to calm her down and it pleased her to see the kids were safe. She tiptoed to her cot and fell asleep next to them.

Father Jon left the room, and while Betty fell asleep rather quickly, Shell didn't feel so relaxed.

"Do you think our parents are going to worry?" she whispered to Topher as they both nestled into their cots.

"Do you think they're going to notice?" he responded sarcastically, and they both gave a little chuckle.

"Well, I'm too small, apparently, so maybe they won't notice I'm gone."

Shell pulled the blanket over her shoulders and let out a deep breath. She tried to imagine her family freaking out about her. Part of her wanted to calm them down. The other part of her would be glad to know they cared enough to become so distressed. She didn't feel like her family didn't love her and she didn't consider this running away from home. She just needed to help Betty and maybe figure out what happened to both of them. She didn't want to do this on her own; she just didn't think she could turn to her parents for help after hearing how her parents would treat others like her.

"Mine are probably a few bottles in by now. I'd give them another day or two to notice," Topher admitted with a hint of disappointment in his voice. "I'm glad you're back at school with me again. I missed you last year."

"It sucked being left back. Everyone seems so much older than me. Plus it was pointless. Now I'm the oldest kid in the freshman class," Shell stated.

"Why did you stay back?" asked Topher.

"I overheard my parents talking one night. I think my mom interviewed some expert on how certain kids benefit from repeating a year of school. She said something about getting better grades, how eighth grade is an important year to prepare for high school, and that being shorter than everyone makes it difficult to make friends in high school. A year to boost my social confidence, or whatever. I mean, my grades went up last year because it was my second time doing everything. I don't think it made a difference. Now I feel even more out-of-place. You all are a year ahead of me and I'm stuck in a class where I know even fewer people."

"Everyone sort of mixes together in high school. Plus, you can still graduate with the rest of us if you take extra classes," suggested Topher.

"Do you think I should let my family know I'm okay?" Shell asked.

"What are you going to tell them? That you stole an old lady from a hospital and smuggled her into a church in New York so she can hide because there's a slight chance she was infected by the rain? Plus, they might be able to trace us to here. If they're looking for us."

"She's not infected," Shell retorted before pausing. "I'm going to check my phone."

"Don't do that! Gah. Hand it to me before you have a S.W.A.T. team banging down the door." Shell passed him her Armer. Topher swiped it a few times and tapped a few buttons before handing it back to Shell.

"I'm going to sleep." He yanked his blanket over his head and remained silent for the rest of the night.

"Is it safe for me to use?" Shell asked as she gazed with a puzzled expression toward her Armer.

"Should be. I adjusted your settings so they shouldn't be able to see where you're connecting. But I never understood how any of that really works, so we'll see."

"Seriously, that's your idea of reassurance?"

Topher did not respond and it did not take long before his heavy breathing joined Betty's in echoing through the church.

While resting on her cot, Shell anxiously turned on her Armer. "Updating" flashed across the screen in the cartoon form of hopping puppies. When it finished, the device notified her that she had fifteen unread messages. She scrolled across her touch screen before clicking on an icon labeled BLink. The application opened and Shell found a slew of messages including ones from her mother, one from her brother, and even a couple from Nurse Janie from the hospital. The guilt in Shell's belly rose to her chest. *I am so busted.*

Shell opened the messages from her mother first. They started out asking where she was and why she was missing dinner. Then she read a message saying she needed to come home immediately. Her mother's messages grew more and more frantic. "A man in a suit came by the house," "the hospital called," and she had "called the police, the news stations, and scanned the Internet." On and on the messages streamed. Shell could feel her mother's rollercoaster climb from nervous to scared, twist from angry to sad, then jerk to furious and plunge back to calm. Mrs. Wayburn only referred to

Shell's dad being worried once. Shell pictured him busy experimenting on people.

Shell closed that string and opened the message from her brother. It read, *"UR SO BUSTED."* After reading questions from the nurses about them not getting their dinner and if she knew anything about Betty going missing, Shell decided to reply to her brother.

She thought it a bit late in the evening for her brother to be up, but considered the fact that she had never received a text from him before a good reason to reply. *"You still up?"*

A few seconds later, the LED light started blinking and the Armer started vibrating. Skitch replied, *"ur so gonna get it."*

"Tell me about it," Shell typed back on the keypad on her screen. *"What's going on back home?"*

"whr r u? Mom dsnt thnk ur at a sleepover."

"I'm fine. Can you tell Mom and Dad," but before she finished, she deleted the message and then sent, *"Can you keep a secret?"*

"So u dnt wnt me 2 tell thm?"

"No for now. I'm not at a sleepover. I shouldn't be on my Armer. If they find out that I sent you a message, they'll trace me down."

"u really dnt knw how 2 use tht thing do u?"

"Topher tweaked it, so I should be OK."

"Ur w/ toph?"

"Ignore that. So why doesn't Mom think I'm at a sleepover?"

Skitch responded, *"Its been a crazy nght. 1st, Mom wntd 2 call the police when u mssd dinner, but Dad told hr it ws 2 soon and they wuldnt do anything yet. she calld anyway and Dad was right. I thnk thts whn she txtd u a bunch. She rlly freekd out. Thn sum guy in a white suit came over with a few cops, said u ran*

*out of the hsptl with sum old lady and a boy and tht ur probly
headed to NY. Thn they left and sed they were lukin in2 'ur
friend'."*

"*All I wanted to do was help someone. I'll be back
tomorrow. Thanks, Skitch.*"

Shell ended the conversation with Skitch. She felt
far worse about the whole ordeal, and could not decide
what to tell her mother. *Should I tell her when I plan to go
home or that I will go to school tomorrow?* But then she
wondered how much trouble she would get into if the
police came looking for her. *What about Topher?*

If the police went to his house, too, then Jack
would probably freak out and then the foster care people
would find out and take him away. Shell decided to
discuss it with Topher in the morning. Feeling guiltier
about all of this, she closed her eyes and fell asleep
wondering if she would have another crazy dream again.

Chapter 29 - Elsewhere

Back at Shell's home, the light over the kitchen sink shed a cloudy aura around the decorative lily placed upon the windowsill and shone against the recently wiped granite countertops. Four wooden chairs that surrounded a matching dining table sat pushed under in their nightly retirement positions at their corresponding accenting placemats and chargers. Oven mitts, napkin holders, salt and peppershakers—everything in its precise place. A chandelier of pots, pans, and cooking utensils canopied a picturesque kitchen island and a distraught news anchor.

Still dressed in the white lace-lined black blazer that millions of people saw her wear while she reported on day two of the world-sweeping storm's aftermath, Victoria Wayburn sobbed and felt the heavy weight of each shudder on her shoulders. The heavy tears looked like drops of milk falling from her eyes, reflecting her paling makeup. She took a deep breath, having succumbed to a state of acceptance that no amount of crying would bring her peace or resolution.

She closed her eyes, squeezing out another tear that fell from the jaw line that typically balanced her highly publicized smile. She forced herself to sit upright on the barstool that tucked her legs slightly under the dining side of the kitchen island. She slowed her breathing and fought back the spasms her crying had induced.

Slowly she inhaled, and then exhaled. Her shivering calmed. The tears stopped. Several breaths later, she opened her eyes. "I will find my daughter."

Chapter 30 - ANTithesis

Shell joined her family at the dinner table. Her mother and father passed the serving bowls around while her brother shoved a third forkful of food into his mouth.

"What would you like to drink, my love?" her mother asked.

"Just water," Shell replied.

"That's my girl." Her father beamed. "That other stuff will kill ya," as Skitch gulped down half a glass of soda.

Mrs. Wayburn poured water from a white ceramic pitcher while Shell continued to make her plate. She waited for her mother to put the pitcher down before reaching for her glass to take a sip, but stopped short. She stared at the glass, which glowed a bright blue. Shell looked to the others at the table. No one paid her any attention. She thought it odd that she could finally see their faces but, still, she expected her family to watch the joke play out on her. Everyone just continued to stuff their faces like starved jackals. Shell picked up the glass and took a closer look. Whether someone decided to pull her leg or not, she could not figure out what made the glass of water glow. It radiated a bright blue, like a light beaming from the floor of a swimming pool. Shell brought the glass to her lips, staring past her nose and into the glowing water spilling toward her mouth. Just as she readied for the first sip, she heard a voice call out "*Find me*," and she set the glass down.

The plea echoed in the distance. Shell slid her chair back, making enough noise to warrant at least a passing glance from her family, but they all continued to ignore her. She got up from the table, walked out of the kitchen through a door that led to the back yard, and strode out into the evening.

Again she heard the cry for help, but could not see where it came from. She spun around in circles in search of whoever had called out, but saw no one. She spun and spun, and by her seventh teetering rotation, everything had changed. Instead of trees and house, the yard had grown in every direction into a field of tall reeds flowing in the wind with a tall hill in front of her.

The cry for help sounded like it came from the top of the hill, so she raced up the steep mound, listening, as the shouting grew louder. As she climbed, the grassy hill turned into a pile of sand. Every step took more and more effort as the sand gave way beneath her feet. By the time she approached the zenith, the cry sounded like it came from just feet away. Shell peeked over the top of the hill, but found no one. She climbed to the crest, looked around, and saw only the valley below. She spun around again, taking in the full view, and turned to see the sand at the center of the peak falling into a hole, like that of an hour glass. She took a step back to avoid getting sucked into the sand-devouring crater when from it emitted giant ants. One by one the ants paraded out of the mound and down the hill until they started to cover the entire valley, but after the ants stopped, a yellow cloud spewed from the hole, not taking any form, but continuing to grow until it loomed over Shell. It seemed to bend over, as if to stare at her eye to eye, inches from her face, and then she heard the warning again, "FEAR ME!"

Shell woke up instantly. She sat up in her cot, shivering and taking deep breaths. She looked to her right to see Topher sleeping soundlessly.

Another nightmare? Something about it felt similar to the dreams she had the night of the storm about the cloud and the lake and the little boy at the edge of the waterfall. She glanced around the church, saddened to wake up in a strange place away from her room at home. Shell rested her head back upon her pillow and tried to sleep again.

Chapter 31 - Good Night, Sleep Tight

Everyone rested peacefully that evening, despite the soft symphony of nighttime noises. The cavernous acoustical ceiling reverberated and amplified the unharmonious tones of the moment with perfection. The church itself reflected its age, creaking and whining as the wood complained about its lifelong servitude. A slight hum from the fans the priest set up in the church to keep the air circulating added a droning pitch reminiscent of a chainsaw's groan to Betty's sousaphone-impersonating snoring. Notwithstanding all of that, everyone slept soundly.

They also managed to miss the arrival of a visitor that joined them in the middle of the night. A small, seemingly insignificant little friend sauntered up to the cots where Topher, Betty, and Shell slept and stood amidst the three of them. Had any of them witnessed the arrival of this little friend, they would likely have run, jumped, and fled in fear, or instinctively responded by introducing it to the soles of their shoes. As these unwelcomed visitors habitually elect to attack upon their arrival, people commonly revert to the latter option.

The most uncharacteristic aspect about this creepy-crawler's coming stemmed from its decision to visit a traditionally foodless, trash-less and relatively clean church. Apparently, this guest did not come to feed. As silently as it arrived, it soon left. What came next arrived with far less cunning.

The pitter-patter of little feet that started softly like a spring shower grew to a monsoon. The noise resonated all around the tired trio. It seemed to originate from the beams above them, then across the hall, then below them underneath the floor, and eventually inside the walls.

Topher woke up first. The familiar, unwelcome clicking and tapping woke him from his slumber. He looked around the church hall. His eyes tried to adjust in the darkness as he glanced upwards to the ceilings, to the walls on his left and right, and then at the floor around them. Experience told him to let people sleep rather than deal with the expected screeching from the ladies, so he laid back down and pulled the covers over his head, hoping the little noisemakers would simply pass through.

"What's that noise?" Shell asked as she sat upright on her cot.

Topher grumbled, "You don't want to know." His voice carried a tone of bitterness, as he would now have to keep Shell calm instead of simply enjoying his sleep—and fear, because he had never heard this sort of clamor so loudly before. "Hopefully, Betty's snoring keeps them away."

GOOD NIGHT, SLEEP TIGHT

The clatter grew louder still. Like a catapult, Topher lifted his head with a jolt. What sounded like distant gentle rain on a picnic table was quickly on all sides like a roaring river. He sat up, and like a timid turtle, poked his head out from under his blanket to see Shell glaring at the wall where most of the commotion seemed to concentrate. With only the light of an exit sign to aid them, they strained to see what approached, but saw nothing.

Boom! Everyone jumped and Betty woke with a start. Shell and Topher turned around in time to see a panicked Father Jon holding closed the rectory door he just slammed.

"What's all that bother?" Betty asked.

"Dear Lord, help me!" the priest shrieked as he leapt across the church, frantically lifting his knees high into the air and waving his arms uncontrollably. He raced over to the others, and hopped on a pew by their cots, pulling his feet off the floor and his knees to his chest. The whites of his eyes shook as he scanned the church floor.

"What is it? What's going on?" Shell asked.

"Rats," Topher apprehensively replied while the priest shrieked.

"Bats, you say? I never would have expected those in New York, but this is a church. I wonder why bats like churches?" Betty rambled as she pulled her blanket around her head. "Cover your heads children, bats go for the hair and they get stuck sometimes."

Topher and the priest looked at her with silent bewilderment.

"I think they said *rats*," Shell corrected.

"Oh, rats!" Betty sounded relieved. You could see her smile glint through the darkness. "That makes

227

more sense. This is New York." She kept her blanket wrapped around her head.

Father Jon chimed in with, "I was sleeping and I felt something on my foot, so I kicked at it. I could tell I had hit something, so I turned on my lamp and saw a rat on my bed and an army of them on the floor!"

"Ew, that's gross," added Shell as she flew to the pew next to her cot and stood on it, then looked around, but could not see any rats. She looked up at the beams where she heard scratching and saw a slight semblance of a stream.

To Shell, they looked like the ripples raindrops make in puddles, but the beams on the ceilings blocked most of her view. She couldn't see anything running along the floor, but she and everyone else in the room could hear the clawing and squeaking coming closer and closer.

"I don't see any in here. Are they still in your room?" Topher asked the priest.

"Maybe. Probably. I've been in this church for a long time and seen rats in here before, but not like this. Not so many. They were headed down the hall. Not really up the stairs." Father Jon's voice seemed to quiver more now. "They could be headed to the kitchen. This is terrible."

Topher got up and headed to the priest's quarters on the lower level of the church. Only a moment later, he bolted back up the stairs. His stomping gave reason to panic. Shutting the door behind him he sprinted back to his cot, leaping the last few feet as if the floor had teeth. "Hopefully they won't come up the stairs."

The rushing cacophony dissipated. The four of them sat and stood still, afraid that any sudden movement would bring the swarm of angry rodents back for more. The constant clicking had softened, though it sounded like a few stragglers lagged behind. After a minute or two, when they only heard the hum of the fans again, they relaxed.

"I think we survived," whispered the priest. He walked back to his door slowly, as if he expected a swarm of rats to knock it over. He put his ear to it and, after a solid minute of careful listening, opened it slowly.

"If you don't hear any screaming," he started, and then paused. Had the expression on his face been visible to Shell, she would have seen that the priest was thinking of what to say next. "Actually, I'll just grab a blanket and another cot and sleep up here."

Shell stepped down from the pew and went back to her cot. She wrapped herself tightly in her blanket and laid her head back down. "That was weird, huh? Never heard anything like that."

Topher never responded. Instead, he asked, "Do you hear that?" He abruptly sat upright on his cot.

"Oh, no, not more rats." Shell leapt off of the cot and back onto the pew.

"No, I don't think so." Topher jumped to his feet and stood on his cot.

A rumbling came from the same direction as the rats, but it sounded different. The rats made a heavier, deeper commotion, like a barrel of baseballs and dog toys poured down a bowling alley, squeaking, clicking and droning. This sounded more like metal thumbtacks raining on a chalkboard. They stared at the north wall, behind which the noise seemed to be building.

"All clear downstairs," the priest announced happily as he reentered the church hall. He closed the door behind him before noticing everyone's precarious glances. "What now?" he said with a loud moan. He didn't bother waiting for an answer and placed his blankets on Betty's cot and stepped up onto a pew rather routinely.

The ruckus rolled in like a storm invading an ocean pier.

"What is that?" Shell asked as she peered into the shadows of the unlit wall that levied the rushing wave. Staring directly at the darkened barrier, Shell detected a flow ooze from a crack in the church's dam, pouring to the floorboards, and spreading into the room. From one stream several quickly grew, as one hole turned to tow, to five, to a blistering rash. The holes cracked floor to ceiling while others ripped across the room, letting more and more of the force behind the wall drill its way through.

"Something's coming through the walls," Shell exclaimed as she watched a pulsating puddle build where the floor met the wall and spill toward the group. Dozens of the hazy waves turned to hundreds. Their clicking, chirping, and hissing filled the church with a deafening, horrifying sound. They crawled, hopped, and crept their way toward the group.

"*Roaches!*" Topher screamed.

"Roaches? Oh, no. Roaches will not do." Betty stumbled off of her cot and jumped onto the pew next to the priest.

Topher scrambled to a spot next to Shell, who just stared curiously at the insects. She wondered why she saw these bugs in the same manner she saw people. She wondered why these bugs were not attacking them, but rather passing through, as if they had somewhere specific to go. By the time the bugs reached them, the group realized that they had more than roaches to deal with. Spiders, crickets, centipedes, beetles, and all sorts of flying insects joined the parade. Shell recalled seeing something similar in the train station earlier that night.

"First rats, now bugs. This could be biblical," the priest exclaimed, reaching for a bible out of the back of a pew.

"Oh, hush," remarked Betty. "Eva since 2012, everythang's been biblical."

"But why is this happening? What are they running from? Or why are they chasing the rats?" Topher asked. "Is something chasing them?"

"Maybe it's construction. You know that tends to stir things up a bit," added Father Jon.

They watched the bugs cover the floor with trepidation. When slithering masses started falling from the beams above them, there was only one natural reaction. Shell shrieked first and loud enough to instigate reactions from the others.

"We've gotta get outta here!" Betty exclaimed.

Topher led by example and started hopping over the pews. Bench by bench, he made his way to the church's front door.

"Get outside!" Betty yelled at Shell from a pew across the bug-filled aisle.

Shell could not hear the suggestion over her own screaming, but she eventually saw Topher four pews away and followed him. Betty and Father Jon slowly made their way over their obstacle course of pews, dodging the falling creepy-crawlies like hail in an ice storm. Father Jon kept reaching back for Betty, but she kept swiping his hands away, insistent that she didn't need any help. The four of them hurdled their way to the entrance of the church and finally made it outside.

They took a moment to catch their breath before they noticed a group to their left staring at them with shock and bafflement. No one spoke. Shell punched Topher in the arm.

"Ow! What was that for?" he asked.

"That's for running out of there when I had bugs turning my head into an ant farm," she scolded through gritted teeth.

A moment later, a group of people to their right came screaming out of their home. The trend continued on down the street until every building on the block owned its own petrified expelled crowd.

The police did not take long to arrive. They questioned everyone. Shell, Topher, and Betty hid amongst the crowd, taking advantage of the 3 a.m. darkness. Father Jon got to the police before they reached his group. He answered all of their questions, which kept them from talking to his guests.

The sun had begun to shed its light on that Thursday morning by the time the fumigators, exterminators, and various pest control specialists showed up. Most of them still looked asleep and they took their time inspecting each home. They had more situations to examine than they had staff, which kept everyone waiting much longer than they liked. News vans showed up next. That's when Shell got antsy.

"Can we go back in yet?" she asked.

"We probably need to wait until we get the all clear," Father Jon answered. "The exterminators are inside now."

She looked down the block. She had seen only a few people go back into their homes already. The person handing out the reentry permission slips appeared to go in the order of whom the bugs invaded first. So Shell and company had about five more houses to go. Another news van pulled up. They all recognized it as her mother's station. A news reporter and cameraman hopped out. Fortunately, Mrs. Wayburn assigned another reporter for the on-location story. Either way, Shell feared they might recognize her.

"We've got to get out of here, now," she reiterated.

"We don't have any of our stuff," countered Topher.

"Well, go inside and get it for us."

"I'm not going in there!"

"I'll go," Betty interrupted. "It's only a couple of bugs." The older woman started her way up the stairs, and Shell punched Topher in the arm.

"What was that for?"

"That's for being a chicken again."

"Why don't you all go in?" suggested the priest. "Go hide in my room or the dressing room. I'll keep an eye on things out here."

Shell hesitated and fear consumed her expression.

"Look who's chicken now," Topher jabbed.

"Lead the way, Christopher Columbus," she jabbed back.

Topher slowly worked his way up to Betty, who hadn't been able to build up the courage to go back in yet.

"Hurry up, you guys," the priest whispered up to them. "They're going to see you."

Betty opened the door and stepped in. Shell pushed Topher from behind and nearly knocked Betty over before she closed the door behind her. The three of them stood as close to the other side of the door as possible. After surveying the church, they did not see much out of order. They tiptoed down the center aisle, and each could smell the rancid stench the fumigator's spray. Stepping on the bug carcasses gave them all the shivers. One straggling roach attempted to fly away. The poison from the bug spray suddenly set in and it dropped out of the air, landing on Topher's shoulder. Shell laughed at him when he screamed.

They made it to the front of the church, pulled the cots into the dressing room, moved some storage items out of the way, and defensively huddled their cots.

Chapter 32 - O., I. C.

A knock on the door woke Shell up Thursday morning. Topher didn't budge. Neither Betty, who woke up earlier, nor Shell moved a muscle or made a sound, unsure of who knocked on the door. The knock came again.

"Is anyone awake yet? I've got bagels," Father Jon called through the dressing room door.

Shell raced across the small room, hopping over Topher, while Betty made adjustments to her outfit.

She opened the door to see Father Jon.

"Good morning."

"Good morning," she returned.

"You'll be happy to know that the bugs have left the vicinity and have taken up residence several blocks from here," said Father Jon.

"How weird was that?"

"I take it you two are not going to school today?" he continued.

Dread smacked Shell across the face. So many things she had forgotten crossed her mind. *I never called Mom. I don't know if Skitch ever relayed the message. I can't believe I'm missing all of this school. I'm going to flunk my freshman year. I'll be the oldest kid ever to graduate high school.* She nearly gave herself a headache.

"What time is it?" she finally blurted out.

"It is eight thirty," Father Jon replied calmly.

"A.M., right?" Shell pleaded.

"Yes, my child."

Shell rushed to her Armer. Betty watched and chuckled at her frantic behavior while Shell crouched on the ground, fumbled to turn it on, and then stared at it while it loaded.

"Come on," she scolded. When it finally loaded, she saw that she had missed more than twenty phone calls and had enough text messages from her mom, brother, grandparents, and nurses to keep her busy an entire morning.

She scrolled down to her brother's message. *"ur famous,"* it read.

"Why am I famous?" Shell apprehensively asked out loud.

"It might be the fact that your mother has placed you on the 'Missing' app and mentioned your disappearance on the news this morning," said Father Jon.

Shell's head dropped.

"She also mentioned Betty again, indicating she is still at large and wanted for questioning, but it appears she did not connect you two yet—not publicly, anyway. Assuming that she knows the truth, I presume she would not want to associate you two since there's footage of you leaving the hospital together. She sounded a bit disappointed when she said that Betty's accomplices remained unknown."

"Did you happen to check the 'Missing' app, Father Jon?" mumbled an angry Topher through a blanket and bunched-up pillow.

"Yes, I did," Father Jon replied.

"I'm not on it, am I?"

"No, my son. You are not."

Topher grumbled at the priest's response and rolled over.

"I'm so sorry, my children," Betty shared with the kids. "Perhaps it is time to put this charade to bed."

"And just ignore everything that's going on? There's more to this. Someone out there has the answers. There's someone out there waiting for us to find them. We can't just quit. What would you do? Where would you go?"

"Oh, I don't know, little Shell," said Betty. "Things are crazy out there. Jon says he can get me to a convent upstate next Monday or I can just turn myself in. Either way, you should get back home to your very worried mother."

"I doubt she's that worried," Shell muttered under her breath.

"Well, my fa… my guardians aren't," Topher shared in a mocking tone as he got out of bed. So I'm flexible. We can go to school or we can just see how crazy this all gets. Doesn't really matter to me. Your call, princess."

His sarcasm upset Shell.

"I am always here to help, my children, but if you go outside today you should know that the city's ordered a Check-In."

"Come on!" Shell exploded. "You're kidding me, right?"

Father Jon shook his head glumly. Even Betty gasped.

"There's no way around this?" Shell asked.

"I don't know how they do them in New Jersey, but here, you have to retinal scan in anywhere that uses BLink. If you have it installed on your own device, you just have to scan in and provide your location. They also have several locations set up to scan in, but those lines tend to be ridiculous. Most people, myself included, don't like those types of apps on our phones. You can't access any form of transportation until you're registered. There's security at every subway station and buses and taxicabs won't start unless all passengers verify their registrations. It really does bring the city down to a crawl."

"Why are they doing this today? This can't be because of us."

"Much has happened in the last couple of days. I think a lot of people are scared. Strange things are happening. Things people can't explain. And there's a very concerned mother out there who's reminding everyone that people are starting to go missing."

"So this is my fault?" Shell questioned. "Great! I give up!"

"Sweet. Just as well," Topher commented cynically. "It's been fun, everyone." Topher picked up his bag and marched past Father Jon.

A frustrated Shell raced after him, catching him halfway down the church aisle. She grabbed his arm and asked, "What the heck is all this about?"

"Nothing. It's over, you said so yourself. So go home. Go home to your mommy and daddy who have the whole world looking for you and tell them you're fine. Betty will go to the convent tomorrow and I'll go let Jack relive his glory days by letting my face catch his empty crushed up beer cans!" His shouts bounced off the walls and ceilings like bullets in an industrial kitchen. "Oh, and here!" He shoved his hand into his pocket and pulled out Shell's necklace. "I meant to give this to you yesterday, but things got a little crazy." Rage-filled tears welled up in Topher's eyes as he stormed toward the exit.

Shell's surprise from getting her necklace back injected some momentary joy, which faded quickly as she watched a very upset Topher storm away. She chased him to the door and grabbed his arm again.

"What do you want me to do?"

"Nothing!" he yelled. "There's nothing to do. You heard him. It's Check-In day. If you don't check in by five o'clock, you'll go from the 'Missing' app to the 'Wanted List.' Is that what you want?"

Shell could only stare sadly back at his angry face.

"Wake up! The only thing to do is go home. Do you know what happens when you wind up on the 'Wanted List'?" Topher's condescension escalated, turning Shell's sadness to agony. "They'll issue a worldwide manhunt for you. You'll wind up on every police, bounty hunter, and desperate citizen's radar so they can collect the finder's fee. And the longer it takes to find you, the higher the finder's fee goes. And you know who pays the finder's fee? Your family. Even if they can't afford it, they'll pay for it. Even if your kids have to work it off, your entire family will suffer. So if the wrong person finds you and decides to hold you hostage until the finder's fee is high enough—"

"Will you just shut up?" Shell exploded.

Betty and Father Jon, who had watched from the end of the church, started toward the kids.

Shell's desperation nearly choked off every word she said. "There's gotta be someone we can go to."

"And who's that?" Topher asked.

"Maybe that cop," Shell answered.

"Right. Go to the police; the same police that are looking for us. I'm not going to foster care. Or jail," he snarled.

"So you're just going to hide your whole life?"

"I'm not hiding. I don't hide. I don't run away from my problems. I deal with the infinite level of crap that get's thrown on me. I didn't run away when my parents died because some alcoholic shouldn't have been driving, or when I had to go live with another alcoholic. I face the music."

"But you're running away now. You're running away from me."

"You're running away from reality!" Topher's fury reached an intimidating level. Shell shuttered in fear. "We're fifteen. We can't live like this. We can't live on the run."

"You think I want this? I just want a normal life."

Topher attacked her with patronizing questions. "A normal life? How is that going to happen? Aren't you seeing things all over the place?"

"Topher," she pleaded.

"You can't even see anyone's face anymore?"

"Stop it," Shell begged.

"Didn't you tell me that everywhere you look, all you can see are little tornadoes surrounding everybody? Haven't you been having crazy dreams every night since that storm? Actually, I have an idea, why don't you go find your magical little Soda Boy and have him float you out of the city."

"I hate you!" And with that, she ran out of the church.

Topher's expression barely softened. He turned to catch Betty's disheartened expression.

"What?" he asked with a guilty tone.

"She needs a friend more than anything right now," Betty explained.

"She needs a dose of reality more than anything right now."

"With all that you saw yesterday, how easy do you think it is to grasp reality right now?"

Topher pouted after a moment of silent protest before letting out a disinclined, "Fine…" He made his way out of the church, but he did not see Shell when he went outside. He glanced toward the end of the block in both directions before finally spotting Shell rounding a corner.

"Shell!" he screamed out as he jogged after her. He turned the corner, only to see her one block ahead of him and still running away. Topher broke into a sprint, calling her name as he ran. Block after block they continued on like that. As soon as Topher got a little closer, a crosswalk or stoplight slowed him down. Ready to give up, he turned another corner and nearly ran Shell over.

"Where are you running off to?" Topher stared at her, though she did not return his gaze. She did not reply. Instead, her focus remained on the sight before her.

"Look, I'm sorry about what I said. I…" Topher stumbled through his attempted apology. After finally realizing his conversation fell on deaf ears, he looked up to see what held Shell's attention.

Droves of people filled the skyscraper-enclosed sidewalks and streets, standing in single file lines. It looked like the most boring parade in the history of the world. "Oh."

"I've only seen New York like this on the news," Shell began. "And now it's like this because of me." She started to cry again. "If we get scanned, our parents will find us, we'll get in trouble, you'll wind up in a boy's home, and my mom will ruin my life forever. If we don't get scanned, it will only be a matter of time before we're hunted down and we wind up in more trouble. What should we do?"

Topher could only put his arm around her. Despite the gravity of the situation, his primary thoughts revolved around the fact that he had his arm around Shell, that she allowed him to comfort her. A dozen thoughts on what he should say crossed his mind. He figured the present moment did no present the best opportunity to express his feelings about her, so they stood without saying quietly for a while, watching the lines inch along. Finally, he said, "It sounds like we get in less trouble if we just go home now. Of course, we can't get there without getting scanned. We won't give up Betty. That's what we came here to do, right? To make sure Betty was safe? I think we did that. We just have to wait a little while to get the answers we wanted."

Shell fell into Topher's chest and cried until her eyes hurt. His sweatshirt dampened with all of her tears and frustrations.

"I just wanted to do the right thing. Why does helping people have to be so hard? Why does everything

I do have to seem so impossible? No matter what I do to prove myself, it's never enough."

"You saved Betty's life. Who do you know that tries to do stuff like that? A lot of crazy stuff is going on right now. You're dealing with stuff that no one else ever has. I think you're amazing and brave, but you can't expect saving people to come easily. The world isn't full of heroes."

Shell sniffed back her tears. "Let's just tell Betty goodbye. We'll get scanned and we'll see what happens."

"It'll all work out. You'll see."

They turned around to head back to the church. The line had grown in every direction and wrapped around the corner without them even noticing.

Still, to Shell, she only saw a sea of spinning little gray whirlwinds. The ground seemed to swirl, as if covered in water. Her legs nearly buckled at the wave of nausea that swept over her.

"You all right?" Topher asked while catching her by the arm before she fell to the ground.

"Get me out of here, Toph," she replied.

Shell leaned her elbow into Topher's hand while he draped another arm around her. She felt overwhelmed, as if the world's responsibilities rested on her shoulders. Amidst it all, she felt that familiar rush of being in Topher's embraced. It soothed her. He walked her through the crowd gingerly. She kept her eyes closed most of the way, relying on him to do most of the work. They still had a large chunk of the block to go before they got back to the church, and then Shell spotted something in the rather impatient-looking crowd.

"Wait," she barely whispered.

"What is it?"

"Over there." Shell pointed to someone standing only a dozen or so feet away. "There's someone... different."

"Another Soda Boy?"

"No. Something different. I can see...colors."

Out of the gray abyss of whirlwind-surrounded people forming claustrophobic crowds around her, Shell spotted a spectacular array of light. She grabbed her head in agony.

"Like a rainbow?"

She stepped away from Topher to make sure she could walk under own power. Afraid she had a migraine, she walked with her eyes closed, hoping to put to rest whatever seemed to cause her pain. She nearly tripped, but Topher caught her again. She opened her eyes and saw that the bright light had grown brighter as she approached the source. Now in the presence of the exceptional sight, Shell could tell she had come across a woman.

"Excuse me," Shell said to the woman, interrupting her 'think-link' phone implant-device conversation. "I need to talk to you." The woman could not deny the request of such a deathly ill looking young girl.

The woman, dressed in a tight fitting green one-piece outfit that frilled below her elbows and calves, gazed down at Shell.

"How can I help you?" she asked.

Shell didn't know. She felt weak and overwhelmed. She felt ready to call off her adventure and give herself up to her parents, the police, or whoever else wanted her, but her intrigue about this woman and how different she looked kept her going.

O., I. C.

"I don't really know," Shell responded. "I feel like there's something special about you and I'd like to ask you about it."

"Well, that is a very kind and interesting thing to say. What is your name, young lady?"

"My name is..." Shell hesitated. "I can't really say. I need to know if I can trust you. I feel like I can," she admitted, still wondering if this was whom her dream meant for her to find.

The woman stared at Shell for a moment, appearing somewhat confused. Shell glanced around at all of the dismal whirlwinds standing in line.

"We can take you back to our chu—" Shell fainted, and Topher caught her before she hit the ground, but struggled to hold her up.

"Oh my goodness!" the woman exclaimed.

Topher panicked. His eyes danced from place to place as he backpedaled, confused on where he could take his ailing friend.

"Bring her this way," the woman instructed, motioning to Topher.

Topher scooped Shell up like a bride and gently covered her face with her hood, afraid that people might recognize her. He followed the woman down one block and around a corner, past the growing line of citizens awaiting scanning. They passed a few shops and then opened a framed glass door on the bottom floor of a six-story building squeezed between a dozen other low-rise residential structures. The sign above the door read Chaka's Chakras. Curtains covered the two large display windows on either side of the door.

Topher followed her inside, past several wind chimes, to a find a store cluttered with peculiar things. Tables overflowed with baskets of colored stones and crystals. Stacks upon stacks of books and magazines littered counters. Vials of assorted herbs and minerals decorated shelves adorned with incense. Posters, charts, and maps plastered the walls. Dishes and glass cases displayed a variety of soaps, jewelry, masks, and countless other unrecognizable artifacts. It all came together with a distinct aroma similar to old musty wood and sweet flowers. The only light came from a few rays of sunlight that seeped through the dusty velvet curtains and bounced between the many random shiny objects until they gradually dimmed within the untidy accumulations.

"This way," the woman said as she walked to the back of the store and through a curtain of beads.

"She's getting kinda heavy," Topher noted.

"Just in here. Set her down," the woman replied as she turned on a light in a small, walled-in corner office.

He could tell that he walked along the edge of a more expansive space. The squeak of his rubber soles on a wooden floor echoed in the open room. Inside the small office-like setting next to the soft light, he found three large beanbags. He placed Shell down gently on one of the bed-sized cushions.

"What should I do now?" Topher asked as he stood above his friend. His fear and nervousness glinted as clearly as the sweat on his forehead.

"Where are her parents?" the woman asked.

Topher returned a blank stare, unsure of what good telling the truth or lying might do.

"Are there any adults that can account for either of you?"

He instantly thought of Betty and Father Jon. "Yes. Two."

"Can you bring them here? I don't know what's happened to your friend."

Topher started to make his way out of the small office. "Is she going to be okay?"

"She should be, but it's best to let an adult know," she answered.

Topher left the room and then the store, sprinting back to the church. It did not take him long to lose his way.

Chapter 33 - Elsewhere

Glenn Watkins walked into the police station with his head a little higher than he had the day before. Still dressed in civilian attire two or three trends behind—khaki pants, loafers, a button-up, and a blazer—he enjoyed the acknowledgement from his peers. Though not everyone wanted to pat him on the back, he could not remember a day that had gone by since he became a cop when people didn't make his job a living nightmare.

Years had passed, nearly a decade, since Glenn had joined the force. The nephew of another officer who clawed his way to the top and suffered the ridicule of everyone around him, Glenn slumped his way through the halls of the precinct with a bull's-eye on his back. No one had respect for the cop who barely survived academy training and landed a patrol car gig just for having the right last name. His fellow officers liked him less and less every time he got a promotion for his terrible performance.

"Watkins!" A voice yelled from an office down the hall. "Get in here." Glenn picked up the pace like a puppy eager to please.

"You wanted to see me, Chief?"

"Have a seat, Watkins," the police chief ordered from behind his cluttered desk. As Glenn took a seat, a secretary came in the room and stacked a pile of folders on top of a dozen other folders collecting dust. "You saw the news last night, right? Heard about the park?"

"I, I did," Glenn stuttered, giving away the truth that he had no idea.

The chief sniffed the air. "Had your own good time last night, huh?"

"Oh, uh, some of the squad bought me some drinks."

"Can't argue with that, but you stink, Watkins. You smell like booze and I need you to set an example. You did good last night and now we've got to put you in the limelight. I hope you're ready. New York is going to the dogs and you're the fist that's going to knock some sense back into this city."

Glenn stirred in his chair. This sounded like the first promotion he legitimately earned. He didn't know if he'd actually be able to live up to whatever his chief had in mind for him.

"Check the net. People are floating, Watkins, and that's not all. Crazy stuff is happening all over the city and my men, all of our men, aren't prepared to deal with them. Force isn't cutting it. Some teenager took on six cops last night. We need you to talk some sense into these people. Do whatever it is you do and get these weirdoes under control. You've got carte blanche. Whatever you need to bring them down, it's yours."

"I… I'm honored, sir."

"Don't be honored. Be good. Be lucky. Now clean yourself up. You've got a press conference in five minutes. Tell those weirdoes we mean business. I want 'em all locked up! ASAP!"

Chapter 34 - Oh My

The woman in the green outfit busied herself behind a small chest that sat in the middle of the office. She opened and closed small drawers. She located a metal vile and passed it back and forth under Shell's nose a couple of times before she woke with a start.

Her eyes flared open and she began to sweat. She inhaled and started to cough. The woman rubbed Shell's forehead and handed her a bottle of water. Shell took a few sips before she calmed down.

"There you go, sweetie. Just relax. Everything is fine."

"Where am I?" Shell asked nervously as she scanned the room. "Where's Topher?"

"I assume Topher is your friend who brought you here. Do you remember meeting me in the Check-In lines? You fainted. Topher brought you here and I sent him to go find your parents."

Shell turned pale and nearly passed out again.

"Or guardians or someone. He didn't really specify who he went to go get, but I told him to find some adults who could take care of you."

Shell grew nervous again. "He went by himself?"

"I believe so," the woman replied.

Shell smirked and secretly wished him luck.

"Do you remember meeting me? You said you wanted to ask something of me."

Shell slowly sat up and adjusted herself on the beanbag. She struggled, but finally settled into a relaxed position. "I think so. Did I ask if I could trust you?"

"Well, by now, I hope you can. Perhaps you can tell me a bit about yourself." The woman finally sat down, crossing her legs in a rather flexible looking pose with her back upright. Quietly they sat, staring at each other. The woman closed her eyes, took a deep breath, one long enough for Shell to feel uncomfortable, exhaled, and opened her eyes.

Shell took a sip of water. "My name is Shell."

The woman gestured a greeting with a nod and a smile.

"I came up to you because I'm seeing things. Weird, sometimes scary things." The woman responded with a confused glance. "They're everywhere. I noticed it the first day of school, but I think it started the night of that storm. Ever since then, I've been having crazy dreams, seeing little gray clouds circling everyone, like they're trapped in tornadoes. I'm probably not explaining it well."

Shell thought about telling the woman about what Betty and Pat looked like, but figured it better to avoid jogging her memory in case she recalled any of the recent news reports from the past two days. "But then I saw you. Your tornado doesn't look gray like everyone else. Yours has all of these colors in it. I guess I wondered what was so different about you."

The woman sat, dumbfounded. "You likely did not see the sign on the door when you came in, but my name is Chaka. At least, that's what everyone calls me now. I run this meditation studio. People come to me when they're tired or sick or confused about themselves or the world around them. They come to me when they're looking for an alternative to conventional solutions."

"So you're a doctor?" Shell blurted out.

"Not like you would expect, but in the same way doctors help people, I try to help people."

"Can you help me? Please?" Shell asked.

"My business is helping people, but it is a business. Normally, I would find out what's bothering you and discuss your options."

Shell gave her a disparaging stare. "So how much does that cost?"

Chaka smiled. "Save your money. It looks like you'll need it. Why don't we start with what it is you need help with?" She pondered for a moment, staring at Shell. She pulled out her phone and pressed the screen a few times before a very tranquil melody began to play over the sounds of a gently flowing stream. "Take my hands." Shell shyly reached out as Chaka caught her hands. "Now, close your eyes."

They sat in silence for a moment before Chaka gave instructions. "Focus on your breathing. Breathe in through your nose and out through your nose." She spoke softly. "While you breathe, I want you to concentrate on that little scoop above your top lip and below your nose; that little slope right in the middle. I want you to feel your breath rush down that slope when you exhale and up that slope when you inhale."

The faint whisper of breathing filled the silent air. "I want you to think of your favorite color," Chaka's words flowed slowly and peacefully. "Think of it as a cloud drifting through the sky. Now picture the cloud coming down from the sky toward you. It comes down and hovers right above your head. It floats down a bit further and now the cloud is all around you. As you breathe in, the cloud comes into you with every breath. Feel the cloud enter through your nose. Feel the cloud flow down into your throat. Feel the cloud go down to your lungs and fill up your chest. Keep breathing. Now feel the cloud go up into your mind and down into your feet. The entire cloud is within you. Feel the softness of the cloud. Feel the peaceful energy as it flows through you. Deep breathe in. Deep breathe out. Deep breathe in. Deep breath out."

Chaka repeated this last part over and over, softening her voice with every repetition until Shell breathed in rhythm and without command. Chaka opened her eyes to look at Shell and nearly gasped. A small squeak seeped out of the depths of her throat as she tried to prevent herself from screeching.

Shell opened her eyes. "What happened? What's wrong?"

"You're fine. Everything is fine." Chaka had turned pale. "You said that everyone you saw was surrounded by clouds that funneled around them?"

"Yes, ma'am," she replied with a bit of hesitation.

"And all of the tornadoes are gray?"

Shell found Chaka's line of questioning encouraging.

"Well... Mostly."

"All except mine?"

"Mostly."

"What do you see around me now?"

"Well. Yours is..." Shell found it difficult to put what she saw into words. "Yours is... I see all of these colors. They're like halos. They're all on top of each other like a stack of a hundred hula-hoops, but one is wider than the others. There's a blue one near your neck."

Chaka sniffled.

"Are you okay?"

"I'm just so amazed." Chaka's teary excitement flooded her throat and choked her words. "You have a gift, Shell, a wonderful, wonderful gift. I have never met anyone who was been able to see and so distinctly describe the human chakra system like this."

Chaka couldn't sit still. She adjusted and fidgeted until she wound up sitting on her knees while still on top of the beanbag. Her words rained hurriedly and gleefully. "Our knowledge of it isn't exact, but it's something we've practiced. We've seen it work and we have an idea of its aspects, but I've never read of or met anyone who could see it as clearly as you do. Is that why you came up to me?"

"I guess so." Shell didn't know if she should feel relieved or disappointed. She somehow expected to hear more. She pictured herself disappointing Skitch that her new ability wouldn't allow her to fly or lift cars over her head.

"What else have you seen?"

"I've seen some weird things I can't explain."

"Try, please."

"Well, there's an old lady who looked like a basket of yarn; just this weird combination of threads and stuff."

Chaka gasped silently, not wanting to interrupt Shell.

"Then there was the boy. His name is Pat. He looked like a walking bottle of soda. I called him Soda Boy. I saw him make a girl float into the sky and then back down."

"Oh my!" exclaimed Chaka.

Shell felt such relief sharing with someone. Regardless of Chaka's ability to solve her problems, she enjoyed talking to someone about everything going on.

"Yeah. And you know how on a hot day if you look off into the distance, maybe a hill or something, and you see little clear waves that make everything blurry?"

"Yes," Chaka replied.

"I'm starting to see those around people's feet and around plants and animals and stuff. They're not hot, but it makes everything look wet. Nothing really looks normal any more. I want to keep my eyes closed."

"Absolutely incredible." Chaka could not contain her excitement. "What about your dreams?"

Shell gave Chaka a recap.

"Unbelievable," commented Chaka. "I wonder what they mean. The symbolism, the metaphors, so intriguing."

"So you can help me?"

"Help you how?"

"I don't know. I want to fix it. This can't be normal," Shell explained.

"Why fix it? There's nothing wrong with it, or you. You have something so special that it would be criminal for anyone to take it from you. Embrace this gift."

"But I don't want it. It's weird not seeing anything. And what I *can* see scares me most of the time. It's like I can't do anything without someone's help. I feel handicapped. And if people find out, they're going to hunt me down, just like they're doing to Betty," she explained as her emotions started to get the best of her.

"Who's Betty?"

"The yarn lady."

"Ah. I see."

"And I can't sleep at night with those weird dreams."

"Maybe I can help. Perhaps if I explain what it is I think you're seeing, then maybe you won't be so scared of it."

Shell gave her a desperate, yet doubtful, nod.

"I mentioned before that I think you can see chakras. I think you can see more than that, but I can try to explain the chakra part. I don't know how you're doing it or why."

"What are chakras?" Shell asked.

"Chakras are the energy that flows in and out of everyone and the energy within all things. The largest chakras have colors associated with them. Each chakra is related to the function of a different part of your body to help regulate organ function while it also regulates different emotions. It's complicated, but no more complicated than trying to understand how your brain or eyes work."

"But yours is the only one I've seen with colors."

"Think of it this way; if you had a bunch of different crayons and you colored in the same circle with all of the colors, what color would you wind up with?"

"Brown?"

"Close. Black is the culmination of all colors. The color white is the absence of all colors. If you're seeing grayish tornadoes, it's like the combination of the chakras all mixed together—the black from the mixing of all the colored chakras, and the white from the smaller, colorless chakras."

"So why tornadoes?"

"I would guess it's the energy flow." Chaka reached back into a trunk she had sitting on the floor in front of her and pulled out a chart of a woman with all kinds of arrows and colors around it. "These colors are the main chakras and the arrows show how energy moves in and out of them. Tornadoes do a similar thing. They pull in air and energy through the top of them and through their sides. They suck stuff in and then spit stuff out."

"So why is everyone gray, but you have all of these colors?"

"There's an important life lesson that those of us who believe in chakras follow. The lesson is to 'know thyself.' Very few people pay attention to what they have going on inside of them. I see this frequently when I meet with people who haven't found the help they hoped for from other doctors. Their auras are dark cloudy messes. I sit with them and teach them to meditate, kind of like what we just did. Once they settle down and bring peace and harmony to themselves, it's easier for me to work with them and their auras are a bit clearer. I meditate every day and I focus on all of my chakras, so I guess that's why you can see mine a bit easier."

"You looked at me funny after we did that breathing thing. Did you see my aura? Is it different? Is there something wrong with me?" Shell began to worry.

"Oh, sweetie. No. Nothing is wrong with you. Your aura, it took my breath away. I had never seen anything so beautiful. You know how you saw halos? You see them very easily and you see them always. What you see is far more specific than the auras I see. When I meditate and focus, I can see a colored shadow that outlines people. When you saw my blue halo, you were able to see what I always thought—that my fifth chakra, the one that we associate with the color blue, is my strength, the ability to communicate and heal through words. When I saw your aura, I didn't just see a shadow. I saw a bright purple light shining around you. It was almost blinding. I've never seen anything like it. Whatever happened to you was the most wonderful thing I've ever heard of."

The kind words brought a smile to Shell's face. "Wow, I guess," she replied humbly. "I don't know what I'm supposed to do now."

"I don't know, either," Chaka replied. "There's so much to all of the science around auras and chakras and spirituality. People spend most of their lives just trying to understand it. There are things I can teach you, books I can give you to read, websites for you to visit, people I can put you in touch with; it's really all up to you and how much you want to know. Many people are gifted in many different ways. How you choose to use your gift is your decision."

"Do you know why I am seeing it? Or what it was about that storm that changed me?"

"I honestly do not. I saw the storms, too. I felt that there was something powerful about them, but I don't know how they could have caused what you're experiencing."

"And what about the waves around people's feet and around plants?"

"I'm not sure about that one either. If you're seeing people's energy, maybe it's another form of energy. I think you'll come to understand it. Experiment. Make guesses. You seem like a very smart girl. I think you'll figure it out."

Shell examined the chart Chaka had pulled out. It amazed her that someone had already drawn what she thought only she could see. *Maybe I'm not that special.*

Chaka glanced down at her watch. "So who did your friend go to get?"

"Betty."

"The yarn lady?"

"Yeah." Shell realized that she might have told Chaka too much.

"She's your guardian?" Chaka paused for what Shell considered an endless moment. "This doesn't have anything to do with… You two are the ones who helped that old lady escape the hospital, aren't you?" Chaka asked.

Shell went rigid.

"Relax. It's okay. I won't say anything. You can trust me. I think you two are very brave. That newswoman hasn't stopped talking about your friend. And now her daughter is missing."

Shell blushed.

"No way! You're her daughter and you helped that…Oh, wow."

"Please don't say anything," Shell pleaded. "We were just giving up on the whole thing and were headed home when we saw you in that line."

"I'm so glad you came to me, Shell." Chaka dug through her trunk again and pulled out a paperback book. "Please, take this book and take anything you like from the store out front. The more you learn about your gift, the better off you'll be. And do come by again."

Shell said goodbye and walked out to the store. The eccentric collection of knick-knacks overwhelmed her. She picked through all of the scattered items in the darkened store and, after a couple of minutes, left.

She stood in front of the store and admired her new little trinkets, a bookmark describing chakras and Chaka's business card. She glanced back at the shop and exhaled a deep breath. She felt like she had finally made some progress, maybe not enough to save Betty, or anyone, from a life of poking and prodding, but progress nonetheless. Her dream continued to plague her mind. She wondered if Chaka had turned out to be person she needed to find, but something told her that whomever she needed to find still needed her help, and not the other way around. It also made her worry about who she still had to fear.

Chapter 35 - Connect the Dots

Shell gazed up and down the street, unsure of which direction she came from and which direction she should go. She considered that Topher went to get Betty and they'd come back to her. She thought that if she went to the church, she could either bump into them or miss them completely. The idea of taking a cab crossed her mind. She figured that if she got to them soon enough, then she wouldn't have to worry about them tracking her down. Of course a cab meant using her Armer and that could give away her location. In either case, she felt the need to get away from the store. She felt guilty for taking up Chaka's morning and did not want to burden her further.

Unsure of what direction she chose, Shell eventually headed south. She came upon a larger intersection, but found the streets eerily empty. She could tell now what direction she needed to travel to find her way back to the church, but she wondered why the streets seemed so empty. She realized that Check-In had redirected people to specific parts of the city, but the lack of cars, people, and noise disturbed her. Even the buildings seemed empty. Off in the distance she heard sirens.

Get back to the church, she decided, and made her way there. She started off at a jog, hoping to return to Betty before things got any weirder. She had only gone a block when something caught her eye. The image reminded her of what she saw in the train station the night before when they ran from the park with Soda Boy and in the church earlier that morning. A fog of cloudy whirlwinds amidst pulsating waves rushed toward her like rain toward a sewer drain. After her experience that morning, she had no doubt about what headed toward her now. Within seconds, the flood had surrounded her feet. An army of crawling bugs of all shapes and sizes passed her like a migrating herd. *If they're not following me, where could they be going?*

In the midst of an army of like-minded insects, she dared not take another step. She feared that if she stepped on one, the lot of them would retaliate. The waves engulfed her feet. Shell felt barefoot in a toxic stream. Despite her apprehension about the situation, she found a peculiar beauty about their symbiosis. She was inspired by the way they moved together. The pulsing of the wave they created and its yellowish haze intrigued her. The horde flowed away from her, as if guiding her along a path, beckoning her to its source. She lifted a foot and the bugs parted just enough for Shell to take one step forward.

Step by careful step, Shell followed the mob deeper into the sea of insects. With each stride, she heard the sirens grow louder over the buzzing encircling her. She followed the coursing flow of energy toward several residential buildings. She headed toward a cheap four-story building that looked perfect for this sort of occupant, but the throng instead led her through an adjacent alley, and to the back service door of a far more prominent abode; prominent, it seemed, in comparison.

"Maybe this was the place Father Jon mentioned the bugs taking up residence."

Clicking, chirping, and buzzing vibrated within the abandoned apartment tower, enough to drown out the sirens Shell assumed blared in the front of the building. In droves, the bugs herded along the ground and swarmed through the air. The infestation created such a cloud that when it mixed with Shell's visions, she could no longer see her hand in front of her face. Still, she did not dare inflict any harm and the bugs continued to grant her passage.

Unexpectedly, the swarm took off, blazing past her and out through the back door she had just entered. She did not have time to scream, and the instant thought of having several unrecognizable bugs flying into her mouth kept her from doing so. But had she not crouched down, even little Shell would have fallen over under the force of the massive pack of pests. She did not feel the millions of legs and wings scurry their way over her body and through her hair. Instead, she felt heat, as though a gigantic hair dryer was turned on full blast.

By the time Shell opened her eyes, she found herself crouching amidst a domestic battlefield of death and decay. The blaring sirens just around the corner from the lobby she found herself in flashed red, blue, and yellow lights.

Something big happened here. Shell imagined the bugs had trapped people inside and forced the residents to fight their way out. Shoes, blankets, sheets, towels, tennis rackets, cans of bug repellent, and the scattered scraps of worn out homemade, bug-fighting, gut-covered weapons remained behind. It surprised her that even with the recent departure of all those bugs, Shell still saw that tranquil flow of energy that drew her into the building. She felt compelled to continue her course to the source.

Shell followed the stream like a hiker in the woods. It led her to the stairwell, where she saw the energy trickling down like a splash-less waterfall over carcasses and debris. Three flights into her climb, she looked up the pitiless winding staircase and opted for the elevator. She opened the stairway door leading to a slightly less disheveled third floor hallway, found the elevator and pushed the *up* button. She glanced around the hall while she waited, taking notice of weaker, stagnant, pulsing waves, emanating out from under apartment doors. The elevator *dinged* and the door opened to reveal a carpet of gooey, sloppy, crunchy, oozy remnants of bug juice. She stepped in reluctantly and the door shut.

At the top floor, Shell almost slipped on a viscous puddle of bug carcasses as the elevator door opened and she ran into the hall. *This was a bad idea.* She tried to violently shake clinging spider webs from her hand. "What am I doing here?"

Shell trudged through the musky and murky corridor that once served as a hallway to the penthouse level of this Manhattan tower. The top floor of the high rise felt hollow, like an old basement, with webs draping the walls and ceilings. Nearly void of light, wisps of broken sun dribbled through the dusty hall. Bugs of all varieties crawled along cleared paths on the floors and walls. Fragments of sacrificed insects slumbered in pillow-like cocoons. Their remains crunched and squished beneath her feet, providing theme music for her journey.

The pulsating flows led her to 21C. Shell's hand reached for the doorknob. She imagined Topher pleading with her.

"You don't have to do this," Topher would say. *"Let's just go."*

"I wish you could see this," Shell would reply. *"I wish everyone could see this. Everything. Everything is…,"* she paused as she looked around the hallway. *"Beautiful. It scared me at first. But now I see it. It's like a song. All these things move together and work together and it's perfect. The birds in the sky; the schools of fish in the water; you knew there was something between them, but now I see it. And I feel it, too."* Her enthusiasm rose. *"It's like when you get butterflies in your stomach when you're excited. There's an energy and a connection around everything, and it's wonderful."*

"These are bugs, Shell," Topher would remind her.

"I get it, but something is bringing them together. They're up to something big. And the answer is behind this door."

Shell twisted the doorknob, opened the door, and saw, shockingly enough, a tidy, pristine apartment. She closed the door behind her and took a few steps deeper into the apartment, curious as to how this unit managed to survive the scourge that ransacked the rest of the building.

A window shattered off in distance. Twenty-one floors down to the street, airy thumps sounded with increasing fervor, preceding the crashing glass that sang like wind chimes. She stood motionless and confused. Seconds later, more glass shattered. It sounded closer. Her fear began to consume her. Alone in this odd place and under attack, Shell could do little more than look for cover. The thunderous shattering continued to grow louder and closer until a window in the apartment where she stood exploded. Responsible for the destruction, metal canisters clanked and ricocheted off of the exposed brick walls and the granite counters in the kitchen. They bounced down to the hardwood floors and rolled around before spewing clouds of poisonous smoke.

Leaving the apartment registered as the only course of action for Shell. She turned back to the door she came in from, but in her path stood an intimidating combination of continuously mixing yellow gases and liquids in the peculiar shape of a portly man. At least that's how she saw him.

She hardly noticed the bugs circling around her feet and hovering around her body until a few of them fell dead in front of her. The tall figure bent down toward her, as if to get a closer look. What she assumed to be its head hovered in front of her face until she could see eyes staring back at her amidst the swirling yellows. She stared back. The image brought her back to her nightmare the night before. A phrase came to her lips and as she uttered the words, she heard the same words come from the suspicious cloud before her. Their two voices in unison sounded more like a question than the declaration from her dreams. Fear me.

Gas continued to fill the room. Shell grew weary and fell to the ground. While her vision faded, she watched the person before her take off his shirt and cover his nose and mouth with it. As she passed out into a pile of dead bugs, she wondered whose voice she heard in her dreams.

Chapter 36 - Bug Tussle

Shell woke up from her poison-induced slumber to the faint sound of screaming and gunshots. Flashing red and blue lights painted the ceiling in a frighteningly reassuring way. She struggled to her feet, still coughing somewhat, and walked to a half shattered window. The view from the penthouse level apartment showed the police had someone surrounded in the middle of an intersection. It looked like whomever they had cornered stood alone. She could barely make out a speckled cloud hovering over everyone in the intersection. The scene appeared frantic.

Shell made her way to the elevator and rode the gooey, crunchy shrine of exoskeletons down to the first floor. She heard the ruckus and saw the lights bouncing through the lobby but, despite her curiosity, she thought it best to put this whole charade behind her. If the day had taught her anything, she learned she did not have what it takes to deal with everything going on. She had passed out twice already. *Why go for number three? Anything out there will be way worse than anything I've gone through so far.*

Shell turned to her Armer, wanting to call Topher, but he didn't have a cell phone. She thought about calling Betty, but realized that after all of this time, she never bothered to get her phone number. She no longer worried if anyone traced her signal any more. She reluctantly decided to give her mom a call and flipped open the screen and saw black. She pulled out her phone and saw another black screen. She had run out of battery power. "Awesome."

Thoughts bounced through her collage of concerns. *Where could Topher and Betty have wound up? If they came looking for me at Chaka's place, they would have guessed that I'd gone back to the church. If they didn't see me there, they'd probably assume I got into trouble. If I got into trouble, I'd have either been picked up by the police, ratted out by the Check-In scanners, kidnapped by the man in white or, based on how this week has gone so far, in the midst of the most preposterous of possibilities available.* Shell considered the high probability that the mayhem outside and her recent magnetism for chaos would likely suggest that Betty and Topher came to look for her there and figured it wouldn't hurt to take a quick peek, just in case.

Shell stared through the crowd that had formed around the intersection to get a better view of all of the action. Fire trucks, police cars, blow horns, walky-talkies, news reporters, one large, angry, shirtless man in the middle of an intersection screaming at everyone, and what seemed like a million bugs, made for more chaos then Shell could fathom.

She crept through the flustered crowd, keeping her hood over her head to fend off the flying bugs and any opportunists in case her 'Missing' status became more important than a crazy person wreaking havoc in New York with a bunch of insects. She snuck by another news van from her mom's station and overheard the reporter refer to the large angry man as Carl Matheson, a former tenant in the building she just left evicted for non-payment after losing his finance job and who lived now as a homeless beggar.

The translucent waves Shell saw around the ground still amazed her. She could see waves emanating and rippling from Carl like ocean waves drowning the mere puddles at the feet of the police and bystanders. She scanned the crowd. Everyone looked mostly the same with their gray swirly tornadoes, so she snuck in for a closer look. When she got a clear view, she saw the yellow man with his churning gases and liquids. It initially surprised her to see the negotiator standing right in front of Carl, but then she figured it made sense. *Who else would be able to handle a gifted person than another gifted person?*

Shell watched as Officer Watkins slowly approached Carl with his hands high in the air, signifying his peaceful intent. Carl welcomed him with a barrage of insults and rude gestures. Officer Watkins looked more nervous than he did the other night with the gunmen in Times Square. And like that night, Shell saw his splattering of blue lights start to pulse faster and faster with every step he took toward the angry man.

Carl's legs wobbled a bit and he nearly fell to one knee. It seemed like Officer Watkins' plan would work again. Then Shell saw Carl's true colors. The yellowish gas and liquid bubbled in Carl's round cauldron-like belly, and in a matter of seconds, erupted out of him in the form of a foul yellow gaseous, attracting every bug in the area. The swarm rushed out of the crowd, away from the flailing police officers and pedestrians, and as though by command headed straight to Carl.

With Officer Watkins so close to him, the bugs headed for him as well. Shell could not help but giggle as she watched him run timidly, high stepping and swinging wildly.

The snow globe-like encasement of bugs surrounded Carl. Between the bugs in the air and those along the ground, crawling on top of each other in a terrible game of leapfrog, Carl had amassed an intimidating spectacle. As a twenty-foot high and twenty foot wide dome of stinging, sucking, biting, crawling little creatures loomed above on-lookers, even those who watched from their balconies feared Carl's apparent control.

Shell watched the pulsating wave of energy below Carl's feet repel the isolated waves of the intersection's onlookers who cowered and ran away. It looked like the push version of tug-o-war with Carl winning.

He must have sensed it, because that's when he attacked. Instead of sending his minions off in every direction, he waged a targeted strike, sending his horde after one victim, then another. He turned to Officer Watkins with brutal intent, burying him in a suffocating avalanche. Shell watched him fight for his life as he battled his way into a police car, shut the door, and continue to swing wildly at the hundreds of bugs that entered with him. In a flash, the horde transformed the car into a hostile hive; forcing Officer Watkins to roll out of the car onto a bed of creepy-crawlers before he stumbled his way clear from the intersection.

Once Carl saw his soldiers following Officer Watkins away from the scene, he redirected them back to the police who had him surrounded. The living debris scurried and fluttered and hopped around the intersection. It was such a thick cloud of insects that one dare not open one's mouth for fear of swallowing something live. No order had been given to fire because, frankly, no one had a target. Those armed and ready had to fend off creatures that forced themselves into every eye, nose, and mouth they could find. Groans of fear and agony leapt from failed resistance.

Shell fought her way out of the veil of vermin to a side street where others had retreated. She could finally see clearly. The city intersection looked like the inside of what you would expect if a New York City dumpster had been transformed into an ant farm-beehive hybrid. One wayward centipede crawled its way toward her foot. She laughed at how helpless it looked and considered it brave. Just as she decided to step on it, she noticed the ripples emanating from it completely disappeared. As she lowered her foot to rid Carl of one more minion, the little guy used all of its tiny feet to run away. Compassionately, she decided to leave the creature alone.

At that moment she decided that since she had not seen Betty or Topher, she needed to go back to the church and wait for them there. *Maybe Father Jon knows where they are or how to get in touch with them.* From out of nowhere, Officer Watkins scampered by. He looked like a victim of chicken pox with his face covered with red and pink welts from stings and bites. His soaked and ragged clothes reeked from all the stench of crushed crawlies.

"It didn't work, huh?" Shell said to him nonchalantly.

"Come again?" Officer Watkins retorted.

"Your little trick. That thing you do to get people to fall to the ground. What is that, exactly?"

"Who are you?"

"I'm like you."

The response caught Officer Watkins off guard. "Listen kid, I don't know what you're talking about and I don't have time for games."

"That's fine. Good luck out there. My guess is that the only way to take him down is to get close to him. Maybe some of those beekeeper outfits would help."

"Right," he responded doubtfully. "I'll just whip some of those right up!"

"Great! Have fun!" She returned his sarcasm as she started her way back to the church.

"What do you mean you're like me?" he shouted after her.

Shell turned around and started to blurt out her answer, but noticed the people around her and thought it better to whisper than to shout. "You were out in that big storm the other night, right? You probably had a crazy dream and you woke up with powers, right?"

The officer stared back at her without nodding or shaking his head.

"It's okay. You don't have to pretend. I was in the storm, too. I don't have any cool powers like you. My brother would probably want your autograph."

"Well, what can you do?"

"Nothing, really. I can just see what other people can do." Shell hurried to explain what she saw in him and Carl.

"And the beekeeper outfit was the only idea you could come up with?"

"Sorry. But at least the bugs seem to leave me alone." Shell started to walk away.

A wicked grin crossed the officer's face. "Do they now...?" Shell nodded confidently. "How would

273

you like to be my deputy? I've got an idea and you might be just the person to help me."

A super important adult wants my help? It occurred to her that Officer Watkins might be whom she needed to find while Carl was the one she needed to fear. Her excitement exploded out of her. "Totally!"

They darted around the corner, moving at a quick pace, and slipped behind a fire truck parked at one end of the intersection.

"What's your name, by the way?"

"Shell."

"As in Michelle?"

"No. Just Shell."

"Nice to meet you, Shell. You can call me Glenn." They exchanged a smile.

As they approached the cloud, Shell watched the pulsating wave on the ground expand outward beyond the perimeter of the bugs themselves, washing over the intersection. Shell hid with Glenn and watched the expanding puddle flow around her like an island. Then she looked to Glenn, whose own puddle of energy shrank almost out of existence.

Shell walked around from behind the truck, closed her eyes, and took a bold step into the potpourri of pests. She felt their fury fluttering just in front of her face. She took another step forward and disappeared into the cloud. Only the buzzing of the bugs whirling by filled the air around her. She could feel their energy like heat from the sun, but she could not feel them. She prepared to take another step when someone grabbed her arm and pulled her out of the cloud. Free from the bugs and back behind the fire truck, she opened her eyes to find Betty holding her with Topher standing next to her.

"What do you think you're doing?" Betty shouted over the anarchy.

But before Shell could reply, Glenn grabbed Betty's arm and said, "This is an official police matter. I need you to step away."

Suddenly, wave of overwhelming energy rushed over Shell. She looked over to see Glenn gripping Betty's arm and saw the threads on Betty begin to move. The colors from her hands to her forearms began to change all the way up to Betty's shoulders. One arm turned blue and the other turned purple.

The transformation must not have gone unnoticed because the swarm redirected itself to Shell's location behind the fire truck.

"I can't see anything. What happened?" Glenn panicked. He held on to Betty still, but fretted over his eyes. "Everything's all blurry."

Betty's eyes rolled back into her head. She grinned and blushed.

Shell remained calm and took it all in. No sooner had she watched Betty's arm's turning colors, she turned to Topher who had turned into the poster child for a health class diagram. He looked like the course of a river that started in his brain, went down his spine, and branched off into his arms and legs.

"Everybody stop!" Glenn commanded as he let go of Betty, rubbed his eyes, and abruptly broke the interactive chain.

That's when the bugs engulfed the foursome. As the insects started crawling up their legs again, Betty's expression returned back to normal, and Shell's new visions left her.

"That's better," Glenn regretted uttering as he watched a flock of flies dart for his face.

"No, wait, I figured it out!" Shell drummed on Glenn's shoulders excitedly. "Betty, hold on to both of us again." She complied and all of the feelings came back.

"What's happening? This is terrible," Glenn complained.

"Trust me, Glenn. Open your eyes and lead us to—," she interrupted herself. "Never mind, I got this. No one let go. And, Topher, stay close."

"You got it," Betty replied lazily through her daze.

"Wait, you wanna go in there?" Topher said skeptically.

"I can't keep you safe if you're not near me and it's the only way to stop this guy."

"Let the cops stop this guy Shell. That's what they're here for. This doesn't have to fall on you. You don't have to prove yourself to anyone."

"The world is always going to keep holding me back. I need to prove to myself that I can do what I think is right." Shell took a step into the cloud, this time with her eyes open, and managed to keep the bugs at bay. She looked down at the energy pooling around her feet and realized it had grown. She stepped farther into the cloud, looked back at her group and confirmed that her plan was working. She tugged on Betty's arm, guiding her into the cloud, then reached for Glenn, forming a circle around Topher. Whatever she did to keep the bugs away from her worked for Betty and Glenn, and with Topher safely placed in the middle, he remained safe also.

They carved through the swarm like wind through a cane field until they found Carl. Shell and Glenn spotted his glowing yellow gaseous bloat easily in the darkened cloud. Betty would have also, had she not been limited to her smile and clenched eyes. Carl stood like a conductor orchestrating his anarchy.

"Carl Matheson, you are under arrest!" shouted Glenn.

Carl laughed and directed the full force of his attack, summoning every bug in the intersection, at the human chain confronting him. As wave after wave of the concentrated barrage turned on the foursome, the wake of his destruction was revealed: suffering victims and several lifeless bodies relied on police officers and EMTs to drag them away from the fray.

News reporters continued their coverage while the remaining onlookers watched with hopeless curiosity as Carl pounded the small group with cartoonlike ferocity, with cloud upon cloud of flying bugs, like a fist pounding a square peg into a round hole. Despite Carl's best efforts, however, he had no effect on the girl, the boy, the nun, and the heroic cop who withstood the melee. Their fortitude inspired everyone around the intersection and every intersection onlooker.

In the middle of the intersection, Shell stood close to Betty, Topher, and Glenn as they fended off the onslaught. Between each wave she watched the fiendish smile on Carl's face flicker from exasperation to frustration at each failed attempt.

"Give it up, Carl! Your bugs can't help you now!" Officer Glenn Watkins yelled over the buzzing.

"You are making me out to be the bad guy?" Carl retorted.

"You're not exactly being the nice guy," Shell interjected.

"Why should I be nice? Are you kidding me? What do you know, little girl? I'm the one that gets kicked and stepped on. I'm the one in the shadows and ignored. I played the game by their rules. All it got me was fired. Thrown out on the street like garbage. I didn't ask for this – bugs that follow me everywhere. But they're listening to me! So if the universe wants to finally pay me back and let me take back what I deserve, then why not?"

"I've got to put a stop to this. You and your bugs are creating havoc. I think you've even killed some people here tonight," Glenn replied.

Meanwhile, Shell began to notice the waves around her feet growing, spreading farther away from her and keeping the bugs further away as well.

"Stop this? That's exactly why I'm out here. I ain't got nothing left but my life and the second I give up, you're going to take that away from me, too. I've got no choice. This street right here, this is my courtroom. And it looks like you're my judge." Carl gestured to Glenn. "And the rest of you are a jury of my peers." He chuckled at the ridiculousness of his situation.

"You can control it," Shell commanded. "You have to!"

"Control what? I don't even know how I'm doing it. I just think of something and these bugs do the rest. I ain't acting out or carrying out any plans. What would you do if your thoughts came true?"

"We can sort it all out later but, for now, you've got to stop this," Glenn reiterated.

"Like I said, I don't know how to stop it. They're just thoughts. How much can an idea do?"

Shell saw the element bubbling inside Carl again. She knew he had something up his sleeve when she saw the currents of energy at his feet multiplying and pushing against the currents coming from her. The currents crashed against each other like waves in a stormy ocean.

But she also saw other waves, strong unified waves, rolling toward him from all around.

Carl stood only fifteen feet away when he lowered his shoulder and charged at Shell. The group braced for impact and Glenn pulled out his gun and took aim. Shell saw the nerves in Carl's legs go dull and disappear and knew that he fell victim to Glenn's powers had used his powers against Carl. Carl then summoned a wall of bugs around the foursome, blocking their view from his attack. Seconds later, he barreled into Glenn and wrestled him for the gun.

Betty lost her grip on Glenn and Shell couldn't use Glenn's ability to make Carl go numb. Topher jumped on Carl's back, hoping to pull him off of Glenn, but his small stature had no impact on Carl, who flung him over his shoulder without breaking his hold on Glenn's gun. Eventually overpowering him, Carl jammed a closed fist into Glenn's face, ripped the gun out of his hands, stood up and aimed at Glenn.

The look on Glenn's face told Shell that his ability would not work fast enough for him to stop Carl by himself, so she lunged at Carl.

In the heat of the moment, Shell had no time to take note of everything going on around her. She did not have an exact plan beyond making Carl drop the gun or miss, but she sensed a collective desire to stop him at all costs. That desire empowered her. Though she remained unaware that the currents of energy at her feet began to flow inward to her, she sensed a surge rush through her body. To her it felt like a million voices screaming on a battlefield, rushing the enemy for a full-on assault. With a tidal wave of energy from their collective consciousness focused against Carl, Shell shoved Carl in his chest before he could pull the trigger. She then saw something she did not expect.

The yellow figure stumbled back from the force, spilling over its' feet hobbling for balance. The actual hairy, sweaty, shirtless mass of Carl, however, only faltered one step back. Shell saw both of them for an instant. The yellow figure stood there momentarily, as if to take a final look at Shell. When she looked at the version of Carl everyone else could see, she only saw a man with no tornado, just a man with a scared look on his face. Carl dropped to the ground, closed his eyes, and did not move again.

The bugs scattered as if a massive light had just switched on. They scurried and flew away in every direction. As people watched the bugs flee, they observed the aftermath and gazed upon Carl's lifeless body lying on the ground amidst thousands of dead insects with Shell standing over him. Betty and Topher walked up to her first, mesmerized, and gave her a big hug.

Glenn walked up behind them. "Wow. A nun and two kids. Great work, guys," he said with a deceptive and sarcastic tone.

ZCHERRRRWHIP. ZCHERWHIP.

Officer Glenn Watkins had Shell and Betty's hands zip tied behind their back as he recited their Miranda rights. He had another officer try to arrest Topher, but Topher shook off the cop and ran through the nearby crowd and out of sight.

"Why are you doing this?" Shell asked Officer Watkins.

"After what she did for you, this is how you treat her?" Betty reprimanded.

"You killed a man," Officer Watkins told Shell. "You cannot take the law into your own hands. And you're an accomplice," he said to Betty.

"I didn't. I didn't kill him. I—I—pushed him, but I didn't kill him. I was trying to help... He—he was going to shoot you. He wanted to hurt everyone. All I did was push him."

"You'll have to come with me until we sort everything out. If you didn't kill him, you can go home."

Officer Glenn Watkins placed Betty and Shell in the back of a police car and had them driven to the police station at Times Square.

Shell looked through the crowd as the pulled away. The whirlwinds still surrounded everyone and the waves of energy at everyone's feet flowed much more calmly now. She could not make out Topher's face in the crowd who watched Shell get escorted away from the intersection. She turned to Betty and looked at her intertwined yarn-like companion. "I didn't mean to kill him, Betty. I didn't." Shell wanted to wrap her arms around Betty to give her a hug, but she could not budge with the zip ties fastened to her wrists. She began to cry and just leaned over and put her head in Betty's lap.

"There, there, my sweet. I know you didn't. I know you didn't."

Chapter 37 - Busting at the Seams

Shell and Betty spent a brief period sitting on a bench inside the police station while officers filled out paperwork and casually chatted with a woman in uniform who sat behind a desk.

"I'm sorry I got you into trouble, Betty," she whispered to her friend.

"I'm sorry I got ya'll into trouble, dear. If I hadn't created such a ruckus at the hospital, I wouldn't have drawn so much negative attention. I neva wanted ta put your lives at risk." Betty's emotions started to get the best of her. "I neva wanted anyone ta get hurt. I'm so sorry."

"Don't be sorry Betty. We're fine. I mean... we're alive." Shell turned red with embarrassment. "You took care of us. We wouldn't have made it this far without you. You just saved a whole city from the cockroach king. How did you two know to find me there?"

"Oh, we just looked for the last place we'd wanna find ya, and there you were." They shared a sad chuckle.

"What do you think will happen now?" Shell asked.

"I don't know. I really don't know."

"Do you think that stuff my dad said is true? Do you think that they'll take us somewhere and study us? Do you think they'll use us and the things we can do against our will?"

"I think it depends on who *they* are. But we're with the police. It's not like they can sell us to the highest bidder." Betty paused for a moment. "But they probably could give us up to the government. I don't know what would be worse."

Two officers led the friends through a set of double doors, down several cold hallways, past some rather angry looking uniformed officials, and into another room that smelled like no place either of them ever wanted to visit.

Cinderblock walls lined a room where metal bars portioned out six large jail cells. Faint lighting and a musty odor accompanied a grim ambience set by the angry, bitter, and solemn inhabitants. The officers escorted Shell and Betty to a cell at the far end of the room. They turned right, where a concrete bench wrapped the three interior walls. The first officer typed in a code and the second officer opened the door with a key. The cell door squeaked open and the officers ushered them in, to where a random assortment of relatively unintimidating people sat bewildered.

Shell smiled.

"Why do ya think they put us in this cell? Ya think it's 'cause we're not real criminals? Maybe this is the misdemeanor cell," Betty quipped.

"I've got a guess or two," Shell replied with a grin.

She looked around to the half-dozen people in her new cage and was privy to a lot more diversity than anyone else. Ideas flooded her mind. She recalled a lot of those news reports and web blogs about odd things going on in the city.

A well-dressed woman sat on a bench with her legs crossed, repeatedly cleaning out her nails. Shell saw a spark plug. A man dressed like a janitor sat in a corner. Shell saw what looked like camera flashes to her. Another middle-aged man dressed in a business suit lay on the floor, possibly asleep, but his body flickered from visible to invisible despite its restful state. One woman stood by the bars of the cell, yelling at the guards. Shell thought she looked as metallic as the bars that closed them in. She saw another chubby man who looked relatively normal in her eyes, sitting in the corner, his hands cuffed behind his back with a blindfold over his eyes. It pleased Shell to find herself in similar company, but she felt most concerned about a boy, who looked no older than her brother, rocking back and forth on the floor in a corner with his hands over his ears.

Shell walked over to him, knelt down by his side, and placed a gentle hand on his knee. "Are you okay?"

The boy replied without looking up, "I'm so sleepy."

Shell looked him over with the eyes her ability gave her, and saw slowly sifting sand, like that of an hourglass too full in both ends to ever expire.

"We're getting out of here, Betty," she whispered in her friend's ear.

"Oh, Shell, I think enough is enough," Betty replied.

"We didn't do anything."

"A man died. We have to take responsibility."

"We can get out of here. I know we can. Everything we've done has been to stay out of someone else's cage. We didn't go through all of that just to fail now."

"Did one of y'all say something 'bout getting outta here?" The metallic-looking woman came over to Shell and Betty, which got everyone's attention.

"I can help," said the pudgy Indian fellow with the blindfold on.

The janitor stood up and walked to the huddle forming in the middle of the cell. "Listen, guys," he began, "this isn't a game. We're all in here for a reason."

"You're right," Shell replied. "But do you know what that reason is? Do you know why they put us in this cell together and not any of those cells with the really scary criminals?"

"It doesn't matter," said the janitor. "Anything we do from here is just gonna make things worse."

"It's going to get worse if we stay in here," said the metallic-looking woman. "I say if we can get outta here we ought a."

"You people go ahead," the janitor chimed. "My day's gone bad enough. I don't need it to get any worse."

"You're still not seeing it," said Shell. "We're all in here because we're being blamed for things we didn't mean to happen; or things they can't explain, right?" Most of the group nodded reluctantly.

"He deserved exactly what happened to him," said the well-dressed woman sitting to the side, still focused on her nails.

"Yeah. Speak for yourself, little girl," the janitor added.

Shell persisted. "Do you know what's going to happen if you stay here? You're going to wind up in a lab and people are going to experiment on you to find out how you can do what you do." Everyone in the cell gazed at one another, unaware of what they shared in common. "Don't believe me? Ask her." Shell pointed to Betty who nodded on queue. "That's where she was just two days ago. One day after the storm, they were on to her and we've been surviving ever since. They've been chasing us all over New York and we wouldn't be here if I hadn't offered to help out one of us who turned out to be a back-stabber."

"What are we?" Asked the little boy.

"We're gifted. That's what we are. But we can't make it alone. Trying to figure this out alone got all of us in here. If we're going to get out of here, we're going to have to work together," Shell explained as she looked for an argument out of the janitor and the woman working on her nails.

"It looks like time's up, too," claimed the janitor.

"How's that?" Shell asked.

"The transport's here. People are moving around a lot outside. There's a bus and a bunch of extra security people in it."

"And how do you know that?" the metallic woman asked.

"I can see it," replied the janitor.

"Interesting... How, exactly?" Shell inquired.

"I can see what happens in places I've been to."

Shell grinned. "Okay. Here's the thing: all of us have powers, or gifts, as a lady told me today. Either way, all of us have them. I got mine the night of the storm. My name is Shell. My powers aren't as cool as yours, but I can," she hesitated, still unsure of how to explain her abilities to others, "I can see what makes people special." She started around the room, and went to the woman still fidgeting with her nails. "I'm guessing you can control electricity."

The woman looked up at Shell and then at the people staring at her. Her silence acknowledged her admittance.

"Please, what's your name?"

"Lina," the woman responded.

"And you," Shell continued as she went to the metallic woman, "what's your name?"

"Krissy," said the milky-skinned blonde.

"Krissy, you can do something with metal, right?"

She nodded. "They pulled me in here 'cause I got hit by a cop car and didn't get hurt none. So I was like get off me. Next thing I know, dey was all pointin' guns at me. I tol' 'em to go somewhere and den dey arrested me."

"Can someone help me with these cuffs, or at least take this blindfold off of me?" said the pudgy man.

"What's your name and what do you do?" Betty asked.

"My name is Gautam. I can sort of control people."

"Why are you blindfolded?" Shell asked.

"I can only control people I can see."

"So if we unmask you, will you promise not to control us?"

"I promise."

Shell doubted his sincerity but figured she had to trust him, so she took off his mask and jumped back. His eyes looked clear, but not see-through, like pools of water. Shell looked at the others and no one seemed concerned about him. She gathered her wits and went back to the janitor.

"And what about me?" interrupted the balding forty-year-old pot-bellied man dressed in a torn and wrinkled suit. "What can you see in me? What's my ability? Can you tell me how I wound up in here? I don't really know what happened."

"I've got a couple of guesses, but what do you remember?" Shell asked.

"I wish I knew. I woke up in here. One second I'm in a meeting with three of my bosses, sitting there getting beat like a *piñata*. They blamed me for a deal not closing. I'm ready to send my fist through all of their faces, and the next second I'm in here on assault and battery charges."

"Well, by looking at you, I don't really know what to call it. You know how people sometimes say they have angels sitting on their shoulders? You've got several full-size versions of yourself with angry looks on their faces standing behind you."

"Really?"

"Yeah. They sort of blink on and off, but they're definitely all versions of you. Are you in?" Shell asked.

"The name's Strauss." He joined the huddle.

Shell watched as the pool of energy built around their feet and began to radiate outward.

"And your name, sir?" she directed to the janitor.
"Trent."

"Are you in, Trent? Are you all in?"

"Wait," interrupted the little boy. "My name is Chen. I don't know what I can do. They sent me here because I gave some people nightmares, but I was wondering what you did." He pointed to Betty. The question surprised Betty, who looked at Shell.

"I really don't know," Betty told the little boy.

A smile crossed Shell's face as she recognized Chen's face from her dream about swimming through New York. "She's going to tie this all together in a nice big pretty bow," Shell answered.

"Okay, we're in. What's the plan?" asked Trent. "The transport people are making their way inside."

"This is gonna be fun!" Shell hopped in place. "All right. This will feel a little weird. Just don't freak out and listen to what I say."

They nodded uneasily.

"Trent and Gautam. Am I saying that right? It's like 'got-em'?"

"Works for me," he replied.

"Okay. You two, grab Betty's hands."

They did so, Gautam with his back to her since his hands were still cuffed. Shell saw Trent's eyes go clear and Gautam's body begin flashing like a strobe light. Betty quivered with pleasure as her hands and arms turned red and dark blue.

Shell barked out the commands. She had Trent use his gift to find the security guard. She combined his power to see the guard with Gautam's eyes to control that guard. Gautam forced him to walk all the way up to the jail cell. Trent had seen the code pressed for the last four prisoners the guards dropped off, so he recounted the code to Gautam, who made the guard enter it, open the jail door, un-cuff Gautam, and then handcuff himself to the bars inside the cell.

Krissy started to make her break for it.

"Wait!" Shell yelled at her. "We need to go out together."

Much to her surprise, Krissy came back. The inmates in the other cells started to make a ruckus.

"Lina, get the lights." The lights exploded in the room with the cells. An alarm went off and red security lights came on.

"This is gonna be awkward, but all of you grab on to Betty." Not even Shell knew what could happen, but her goal was to make sure that Krissy's gift would keep them all bulletproof. They all began asking questions about what they saw. Shell explained why everyone could now see everyone else's abilities, but chose not to address the waves on the ground since no one bothered to ask a about. After another moment of shared curiosity about experiencing what each other saw and felt, Shell reminded them they needed to get away. They awkwardly shuffled their feet as they held one another's hands and made their way out of the cell.

"Which way do we go now?" asked Krissy.

"We're going right out the front door."

They maneuvered along like a huddled football team migrating through the halls. Lina shocked everything electric she came across; door locks, lights, and every camera she could find. Most of the things blew up.

"We've got people approaching in the next room," Trent said.

"You're up, Strauss. Keep those guys occupied."

They opened the door to see several armed transport guards in black jumpsuits approaching them. Strauss sent a swarm of his duplicates after them, making them grab the guns from the armed men and buying the group enough time to get to the police station lobby. Two officers, the woman who worked behind the desk and the officer who had escorted Shell and Betty to their cell, stood armed and aiming at the escapees. Gautam "hopped" into the woman and made her aim her gun at her partner, who in turn turned his gun at the woman. With their attention diverted, the group of eight shuffled their way past the last two officers and out of the police station.

"We're going to make our way to the subway once we're outside," Shell called out to everyone.

They went out of the building and into the cool night air. They found themselves on 8th Avenue and less than half a block from 42nd Street. Shell looked up and did a double take. *The police station is inside the Port Authority, too?* The group let go of each other's hands and melded into the unassuming crowd. Shell and Betty lead the way, crossing the street and turning into the first subway station they came to. Two cops chatted casually at the entrance, unnerving Shell, who decided to walk past the entrance to find another one. The escapees followed her lead, but their expressions began to reflect their doubt in her.

The walk down 42nd street seemed to go on forever. Shell's head swiveled from side to side, looking for another subway entrance. Instead, she found entrance after entrance to restaurants, theaters, and retail stores. Her pace quickened, as did the heart rates of the escapees. As they neared the end of the block, they spotted two more subway entrances, one on each side of the street. Shell grabbed Chen's hand and broke out into a slow jog. Betty and the others followed suit. The closer they got the subway, the faster they ran. Less than twenty yards from their sanctuary, police cars with sirens blaring, pulled up in droves, blocking their getaway. The group backpedaled. Within seconds, they found themselves with their backs to a brick wall under construction and surrounded by police.

"Put your hands in the air and drop to your knees!" yelled Officer Glenn Watkins through a megaphone. Shell could feel her legs getting weaker. The others standing by her may not have understood, but she knew that Officer Watkins had made his first move. All of their legs went numb and they couldn't keep themselves standing upright.

"What's happening?" Chen asked.

"Everyone grab Betty," Shell ordered. "Especially you, Krissy."

"I said freeze!" Officer Watkins yelled.

"Grab her now!" she repeated.

The group, nearly down on their knees, crawled their way to Betty, who stood in the middle of the line of eight.

"Fire!" Officer Watkins ordered. His men hesitated, unsure of why an officer would order them to fire into a crowd of unarmed civilians. "Fire, I said!"

They each reached Betty just in time to feel the bullets bounce off of them like heavy drops of rain. Krissy had made them bulletproof, though they remained paralyzed from the hips down.

"We've got to keep that guy in charge occupied!" Shell yelled over the gunfire. "Gautam, can you see him, the guy with the megaphone?"

"I'm on it," Gautam replied. He looked up at the officer and took control of his body. He forced Officer Watkins to swing his megaphone at one of his fellow cops. Shell watched the skirmish between Officer

Watkins and his counterparts. The feeling came back to their legs, and they stood up.

"Hold your fire!" screamed one of the men in the black jumpsuits as he and his team of transport guards arrived and positioned themselves around the escapees. "We need these prisoners alive. Switch to pelts." He signaled to three of the transport guards and pointed to the escapees, "Arm your Tasers and take them down."

All of the armed men eagerly switched out their bullet magazines for pelt magazines, preferring to fire the more humane bruising rubber bullets. Shell heard the commands as well.

"We're going to have to fight them off," Shell began. "Strauss, can you do your thing?"

"I can't fight them," he whined.

"Use Lina's electricity and Krissy's metal to hit them as hard as you can and break their Tasers."

Strauss sent his replicas into the fray. Three versions of the undersized businessman charged after the approaching guards who shot at the replicas. The coils connected, stopping Strauss' duplicates in place, but they did not fall. They each gave an angry glance back at the guards and sent a wave of violent electricity along the coils right back to the source. The Tasers exploded in their hands, shocking the guards and leaving them writhing on the ground.

"Smoke 'em out," ordered the leader of the transport guards.

Pop, pop, pop. Gas canisters whizzed through the air. The huddled escapees looked up at the approaching cans with more fear than hope in their eyes. Just feet from landing amongst them and releasing their poisonous fumes, they changed course, as if someone had picked them up and thrown them back toward the police surrounding them. Shell looked around, wondering how that could have happened. None of them could explain it.

The police ran from their positions as the cans headed for them. Some that held their ground were able to put their gas masks on, but many failed to do so in time. Of those who managed to protect themselves, they began to choke after someone or something ripped their masks off.

"Open fire!" ordered someone in the mob of police.

Nothing in public stayed private, especially in Times Square. From a less-than-safe distance, observers had watched the battle play out. Pedestrians used their cameras and phones to upload pictures, stories, and videos to the Internet. The news showed up soon after and set up cameras on top of their vans to catch every detail. Everyone had their cameras ready when the order came in to open fire.

Rubber bullets hailed on the group, scaring all of them and especially Chen, but Krissy's gift kept them protected. Unfortunately, no one could control where those bullets bounced. Some embedded into the street or nearby cars. Some struck camera equipment and people. Only the bravest kept their cameras rolling.

Shell kept her eye on the energy waves crashing along the ground between her and the police. It occurred to her that the strength of the waves reflected the desires of those with the same wants. Her group wanted to escape and the police wanted to stop them. She wondered if her ability to see the waves somehow gave her the ability to manipulate them, and, if so, maybe that's how she killed Carl; not that she wanted to kill him. She regretted her comment earlier that 'this would be fun.' Shell focused on her group's energy and tried to push their waves against those of the police. She didn't know if it worked, but something inspired Lina to unleash her fury on the entire onslaught.

Lina repositioned herself to the front of the group while still keeping a hand on Betty. She aimed her hand at a massive billboard in the intersection. The lights exploded and the billboard went dark. Then she sent out a storm of electricity toward the police officers, detonating the cop cars they hid behind.

The crowd cheered and Shell's wave grew stronger. Strauss launched his own full attack. He sent more replicates into the fray, flanking the police with a barrage of kicks to the shin, punches to the jaw, and knees to the groin with an extra bit of shock therapy and a heavy metal hand.

Shots rang from all around, but did no damage to Shell and her group. Gautam took over as many bodies as he could and ran them full speed into blunt objects. He looked exhausted from the running around. They all started to get the hang of their combined abilities. Betty seemed the most relaxed out of the bunch. Shell watched her threads change color and weave into patterns based on who borrowed what ability.

Then more backup for the police arrived. Attacks fell on the group from every angle. Shell watched the energy waves of the attacking police surround them like a moat around a fort and collide against the energy waves emanating from her and her group. Still, the longer they held out, the stronger her wave grew. Shell could feel the support for her group like a superstar in a championship game.

Lina redistributed electricity from the nearby billboards, buildings, and cars until the area nearly went dark. Strauss had duplicated himself nearly a dozen times and relished his rampage. One of his duplicates actually picked up a gun and started shooting at the police. It scared Shell, but she kept her focus on motivating her group.

Then they all felt a pain in their chests and their arms go numb. Shell felt like letting go of Betty.

"Don't let go," she encouraged. Her heart fluttered and she figured Officer Watkins had made his next move.

The group started to lose focus under the agonizing burden. Strauss pulled away first. Shell watched his replicas get sucked back into him like fish on a line. She scanned the area, looking for Officer Watkins. She couldn't find him before Trent let go of Betty and dropped to his knees. Then Krissy lost control and let go. The next pelt that came in hit Gautam in the shoulder. He screamed in pain. Chen had stayed close to Betty, hiding in the folds of Betty's robe.

"Psst," whispered someone from amidst the group. Shell looked around quickly but saw no one looking to get her attention.

Another pelt got through and nicked Lina on the leg. Krissy stood up and stood tall, doing her best to ignore the pain in her chest and raised her hands in defiance, enticing the gunmen to fire in her direction. She took pelt after pelt. Each one stung a bit, but Krissy held her ground until her legs started to go numb.

"Please stop!" Shell screamed, but no one heard her over the firing. "Can you see him, Trent? Watkins? That cop in the bad suit?"

"I can't...I can't tell where he is," Trent moaned.

"Cease fire," ordered the leader of the transport guards, but the police paid him no attention.

"Can anyone see him?" Shell frantically looked through the crowd, but she could only see tornadoes and no spotted blue man. She gave another sweep. The police had tightened their circle around the group. They still kept their distance, but she noticed a tornado-less shadow just a few feet from her group. It didn't move quickly but seemed agile nonetheless. She called out to the shadow at the risk of looking crazy, "If you're here to help us, please do so."

"Name's Rick. As far as I can tell, people can only see me in direct sunlight. How can you see me?"

"Nice to meet you, Rick. I'll explain later," Shell replied. "Grab the nun. Everyone, grab Betty so we can get out of this mess. I promise the pain will go away."

"Speak for yourself," uttered Gautam. "I've been shot."

Struggle as they did, they eventually got a hold of Betty and, in an instant, vanished.

"If that Officer Watkins can't see us, he can't hurt us," she explained. Within moments, the numbness dissipated.

The gunshots continued for a moment, but slowed to a halt when the gunmen found no one to fire upon.

Shell and company looked around at the confused men still aiming their guns at them.

"How are we going to get out of here? We can't do this all day," whispered Trent.

Shell could sense their fear growing. She noticed their wave of momentum had shrunk and shifted in favor of the officers.

"Guys, we're fine. They can't see us," Shell clarified.

Just as the commotion quieted, a new roar of sirens came from around the corner. Large vans with *S.W.A.T.* written across the side pulled up alongside the media vans. Tires screeched to a halt and armed men in riot gear poured out of the cargo vehicles. They positioned themselves in a half circle between the officers and the group.

"It's getting thick," said Krissy. "The whole party is here. More cops, more gun, and the news."

Shell strained her neck to get a look without letting go of the group.

"They've got to be close!" yelled Officer Watkins over his megaphone to the other officers. "Move in!"

"We gotta do something, quick," Trent said with a quiver. "They'll be right on top of us in no time."

"Keep your voice down. They can't see us, but they will be able to hear us," Shell responded. "Give me a chance to think."

"We don't have time for that," Trent retorted.

"They're getting closer. The guy with the bullhorn is looking right over here." Chen's voice shook as he spoke, trying to keep his voice to a whisper.

Shell turned to Betty. "What do we do?"

Betty had a calm look on her face. "We did what we could, sweetie. Let's do what we can so no one else gets hurt."

"They're over here!" Officer Watkins shouted to the others.

"Please! Don't shoot!" Shell yelled back at him.

She let go of Betty and instantly became visible. The others sat by in silence, remaining hidden.

"We're sorry. Please don't hurt us."

Officer Watkins steadied his aim at her.

"You are under arrest! Put your hands in the air and get down on your knees! Now!" He stepped toward her.

Shell shook at his orders. "Why are you doing this? Why did you arrest me? You're one of us."

"On the ground, now!" Officer Watkins' voice grew with rage. His face shook with every word.

Shell felt her legs weakening. "I thought you could help us." She closed her eyes and began to lower herself at Officer Watkins' feet when she felt the strength of her legs return.

"Hey! What's going on?"

She stood back up, timidly raising her eyes to Officer Watkins, only to find him levitating into the air. All eyes were on him. Shell saw an instant rush of energy as the waves below her intensified. She could feel the hopes of everyone in her group and everyone watching come flooding back. She turned over her shoulder and whispered to Lina with a grin, "Blow up everything you can, right now, pretty please."

Specs of debris floated to the ground like dying fireflies. Shell stood amidst the madness like an oblivious dandelion, ignoring the storm around her. Fear. Sadness. Jubilance. The myriad of emotions expressed by the people running around her resonated with her, but held no sway. Despite the burning hole in the brick wall behind her and the burning cars around her, the flashing red and blue lights and the *pop, pop, pop* of the pelts whizzing by her, she stood alone.

"Think before you act. Your spontaneity is going to get you in trouble." The echo of her mother's lessons muted

the continuous cacophony of explosions and screams. *"Yes, we all have instincts, but use them to help you decide, not to decide for you."*

Had Mom been right? Probably. But how could she have predicted this? Shell thought. *A jailbreak at fifteen, that's gotta be a record. After the government and police chasing me, school will be a piece of cake.*

Shell took a deep breath, raised her chin to the smoke-filled sky and closed her eyes. She exhaled. *There's no going back to school after this. There's no normal for me after this.*

"Shell! Get over here," Betty screamed from behind a parked car now riddled with bullets.

"Baby!" a familiar voice screamed from behind a flurry of gunshots. *Mom?*

"Shell! Over here! This way!" Topher hollered from a few feet away. He had Pat with him.

Shell began to see through the fog the tornadoes created. She picked up on the difference in their emotions by the combination of colors that spun around them and how the waves flowed around their feet. Some colors glowed brighter than others. The waves at their feet either flowed with Shell, in unison, or against hers, like crashing waves. It looked like a musical chord; several notes all played at the same time to make a unique sound. A little of this color sounded like that note; the flow of a wave felt like a certain emotion. They all came together to form a single hue, a single tune, an overall vibe that indicated to her what others felt and how they felt. It finally made sense to Shell.

Chapter 38 - Foggy Clouds

Aimless days of confusion turned Dr. Hunter into a bit of a nomad, roaming aimlessly through the Spanish city of Cadiz. Still unable to sleep he journeyed from bar to restaurant hoping to satisfy his thirst for memories with alcoholic beverages. He only succeeded in having his credit card canceled. When he called to have it turned back on, he failed to offer enough proper information to access his account.

Wandering alone so far from home, it surprised him how much attention he garnered. Everywhere he looked, eyes followed him. He assumed his drunken stupor played tricks on him and people happened to gaze in his direction, or that the memories he tried to piece together did not actually happen but, for the past day, it occurred to him that people followed him.

He recalled the hotel doorman who stood outside his room when he left for a late dinner after returning from the hospital. That same doorman now stood outside of the coffee shop Dr. Hunter found himself in, staring through the window with shameless aggression. He remembered a mother dressed in yellow pushing a stroller past a construction site, and now that woman sat at a table just a few chairs down from him.

He looked at the faces of the other people in the coffee shop and found their gazes meeting his. Each of them appeared slightly familiar to him. One man even looked like a member of the crew that he took out on his expedition.

What happened out there? He asked himself.

The doctor struggled to stand up. The hours and hours of drinking made him weak and unstable. He sat back down and tried to stare back at the man he took as his crewmember, but could not keep his eyes open. When he opened them again, a woman in a white wool suit with white shoes and a white fedora hat sat down at his table.

"Do I know you?" Dr. Hunter mumbled.

"No, you don't, Dr. Hunter."

The stranger's knowledge of his name confused the doctor. It made his head hurt trying to understand everything happening around him. The noise from the television on the wall overwhelmed his hearing. He turned to see a news report showing a man floating in front of a girl in Times Square amidst some sort of police confrontation and a lot of explosions.

"Who are you?"

"I'm what you call a disciple; a loyal member of an ancient organization focused on the preparation for the return of wonder."

"The return of wonder?"

The strangers eying Dr. Hunter approached him and the woman in white. They stood around their table, stared at the doctor and listened to their conversation.

FOGGY CLOUDS

"Yes. While many truths exist, we know of a single truth. Our founding father, the one you have record of, the elderly blind gentleman washed ashore in his tattered white robes thousands of years ago, witnessed the wonder that made believers out of citizens from ancient civilizations, which in turn spawned the many religions of the world."

"Atlantis?"

"Partially."

"You know what happened?" Dr. Hunter asked with growing excitement. "You knew where it was?"

"No. We are believers, much like you. We believe there is a single truth behind the many beliefs of the world. We believe that the events at Atlantis hold the secrets to what happened to gods of our ancient myths. We believed that this day would come. We have searched the world for answers and continue to do so. Members of my organization have been dispersed around the world in response to the recent events." The woman in white glanced up to the television screen and pointed at the news report of the violence and the girl in Times Square. "One of my associates has been tailing that little girl there with little success," she admits with a disappointed tone.

The crowd around the doctor and the woman in white swelled, filling up the entire coffee shop.

"So you can tell me how all of this happened?" The doctor began. "You can tell me how all of this craziness started and why all these people are staring at me?"

The woman in white looked around at the empty coffee shop before replying, "What people?" He paused before continuing. "Dr. Hunter, we were hoping you could tell us."

303

Chapter 39 - The World Stops for No One

The ash-filled sky retold the story of how the previous night unfolded for everyone who bore witness to the Times Square debacle. Sad, angry, frustrated, dejected, and embarrassed, Mrs. Wayburn, covered in soot and weary from a sleepless night, trudged through the lobby of her office building. Even the security guard made her feel uncomfortable.

What did I do wrong? The question had plagued her since Tuesday. Now Thursday, she had no idea what the day would bring, or any other day. She had no hope that any day would ever answer her question.

She walked in to her dressing room of an office, but left the lights off. The clock on her desk read four thirty-one in the morning. She hadn't seen anyone but the security guard so far, and she felt no rush to see anyone sooner than she had to. She figured if she kept the lights off, people would assume she hadn't come in yet. She sat down on the chair behind her desk. The red light on her phone indicated she had voice messages to listen to, but she did not want to know what people had to say. If they had questions about work, she didn't want to answer them. If they had questions about her life or how her daughter took out a city block, she didn't want to answer them. She didn't even know how much longer she'd have her job.

She sat in the dark and in silence, then took a deep breath. She could still smell the evening's remnants on her skin. The images of the things her daughter did felt so ingrained in her thoughts, she could not help but see them replayed in the dark. She exhaled a troubled, broken sigh and began to cry.

"Don't cry, Mom." The words scared her into a sniffle.

"Shell?" Mrs. Wayburn didn't bother trying to compose herself.

Shell approached her desk out of the shadows of the office. "Yeah. It's me." She stood in front of her mom's desk. "I don't think I've been in this office before."

Mrs. Wayburn burst out of her chair, rushed around her desk, and picked her daughter up, hugging her tighter than she knew she could. She didn't let go for quite some time.

"I love you, too, Mom."

After another few moments, Mrs. Wayburn put Shell back down. She sat on the corner of her desk while her daughter stood.

"Are you okay? Are you hungry?" Mrs. Wayburn's franticness made Shell giggle.

"I'm fine, Mom. I just wanted to say I'm sorry for putting you through all of this and thank you for everything you've done for me."

"Don't be sorry. Don't be sorry at all. I feel like this is my fault. Tell me how I can fix this."

"I really don't think this is your fault at all. Something happened to me. Something happened to a lot of people. I don't think I would have been able to handle it the way I did if you didn't do all the things you did."

"Do you want to talk about it?"

"Are you interviewing me?"

"Of course not."

"I'm just joking, Mom."

No one laughed.

"There's no way I would have predicted that I'd find myself with a group of people like this, fighting our way out of jail, and running from the authorities, looking for a place to hide in a world where privacy is only an idea."

"Did you read that somewhere?" Mrs. Wayburn asked, but Shell didn't reply. "I'm so sorry, my love. I'm sorry I held you back. I'm sorry I didn't get you all those things you wanted growing up. I'm sorry I wasn't home to wake you up for school. I'm sorry I almost... I'm just sorry for all the times I wasn't there for you. I don't think I ever learned how to let you make your own decisions."

"It's okay. I honestly did not know you loved me until this morning. I'm sorry I didn't realize it until now. I just want to say that I love you, too." Shell turned to walk out of the office.

"Where are you going? Are you going home?" Mrs. Wayburn asked desperately.

THE WORLD STOPS FOR NO ONE

She heard the door open and her heart sank. Some light from the hallway bounced off the open door and into the room, where Shell stood halfway between the door and the desk. The light shone on half of her daughter. Mrs. Wayburn noticed how mature she looked covered in dirt, ash, and bruises.

"Eventually, Mom. Eventually."

Shell disappeared in front of her mother's eyes, and then the door closed. Mrs. Wayburn sat in the dark. "Shell? Mi Shell?"